FEARSOME DREAM

EVA CHASE

SHADOWBLOOD SOULS - BOOK 5

ONE

Riva

A borrowed power ripples through my veins. It's as familiar as the men standing around me but exhilaratingly new at the same time.

I test my sense of the energy inside me like a flexing of muscles, looking around the clearing where we're holding this demonstration.

The warm breeze ruffles the fronds on a nearby palm tree and licks under my braid. December in southern Spain feels like spring has in most places I've been to before.

I shift my feet against the thick grass and study the other, bushier trees that surround the clearing. All I need is a single, small branch jutting away from the others.

I'd rather not chop down an entire tree—or even half of one—by accident.

There. One of the shorter trees, barely more than a

sapling, has a long twig with just a sprinkling of leaves poking from its trunk below the thicker boughs.

I gather the roiling power behind my eyes and focus it into heat. Then I slice that heat down through the base of the twig.

It only takes a moment. A whiff of smoke laces the air with a crisp woody scent, and the twig drops to the ground, its severed end charred black.

As I glance at Zian and nudge the tingle of energy from me back into his brawny form, Rollick brings his hands together in a brief round of applause. "Fascinating. Both in how far your skills have developed and how seamlessly you can exchange them."

Our host smiles at us, his dark blue eyes twinkling. In his human guise, the millennia-old demon has the stunning good looks of a movie star—and I find him as difficult to read as if he really was only a mask made of special effects and studio lighting.

The beings like Rollick—who call themselves shadowkind but most humans who know of them call monsters—haven't often been friendly to my guys and me. Many of them don't trust beings like *us*: hybrids with both human and shadowkind characteristics, capable of major supernatural power but lacking the few weaknesses that can hinder other "monsters." Shadowbloods, as our makers named us.

Which is probably fair, because the humans who created us did it specifically so that we could go out and kill shadowkind on their behalf. They weren't counting on us developing strong enough minds of our own to decide *they* were a hell of a lot more monstrous than our supposed enemies.

And Rollick has proven more than once that he doesn't consider us the enemy either. It's thanks to him that we made it away from the worst of our captors just yesterday.

I'm not sure how many other shadowkind might be watching the demonstration he asked for after we told him about our new abilities. One thing they can do and we can't is merge into patches of darkness in their truest shadowy forms.

There could be dozens of beings watching us from beneath the trees without us having a clue.

We've already traded powers a few times while Rollick watches. Without speaking, Andreas looks toward me. He meets my gaze with a softly reassuring smile as I feel the quiver of one of my shadowblood powers coursing out of me.

He turns his head with a jostle of his dark brown curls and fixes his gray eyes on a butterfly fluttering through the clearing. Before my heart can even finish skipping a beat, the insect plummets to the ground.

Rollick is watching more intently now. My most brutal talent, the vicious banshee shriek that can rend bodies apart with its hunger for pain, has always worried the shadowkind the most. And it's developed new dimensions too.

"You didn't make a sound," the demon says to Andreas as Drey passes my power back to me with a little jolt.

Across from me, Jacob's mouth forms a tight smirk. He's always appreciated my powers, as terrifying as they might be. "She can scream just in her head now. Which I guess means any of the rest of us can too."

Beside him, Griffin nods. "We haven't found any power we *can't* borrow from each other."

It's still a little strange seeing the twins side by side after four years of believing Griffin was dead. They're mirror images of each other in so many ways, but time has shaped them a little differently.

The sharp angles of Griffin's face look a little softer than Jacob's harder edges. His golden-blond hair drifts shaggier around his face, while Jacob keeps his shorter strands swept back from his forehead.

I notice those minor details because I know them both so well. A stranger would still mix them up.

Rollick taps a finger against his mouth. If he's disturbed by the progression of my talent, it doesn't show in his languid voice. "This is all very interesting. I can't say in all my centuries that I've ever heard of shadowkind *trading* powers."

Dominic lifts his head where he's standing next to me, his short auburn ponytail swishing across the collar of his long-sleeved tee. His two slim tentacles, a more orange hue than his olive-brown skin, protrude from two notches cut in that collar just below his shoulders.

"We aren't shadowkind," he points out in his usual quietly thoughtful tone. "The guardians made something totally new with us. It's not the only way the six of us are connected."

My hand rises automatically to the top of my chest, where a line of five thumbprint-sized splotches decorate my collarbone like a tattooed necklace. The marks connect me to all of my men, each blooming the first time our shadows merged alongside our bodies.

It was when the last of the guys and I had sex, with the forming of the final mark, that the connections between us opened wide enough that we could exchange powers as well as our simple awareness of each other's presence.

"We're blood," I say. That motto got us through our childhood of imprisonment and torturous experiments. It's kept us going through our escapes that've so far either failed or been far too temporary.

And it's true. We are blood—the only people on the planet quite like us, bound not only by our shared heritage but by all the years we've had only each other to count on.

But we aren't the only shadowbloods in the world. The guardians made more after us, if with weaker talents.

I don't think I could share my powers with anyone other than these five men. There's something a little more that binds the six of us together.

Of course, there's no telling what else might be possible now that our most powerful enemy has started making shadowbloods of his own.

The memory of receiving the news of Balthazar's latest scheme yesterday tugs at my nerves. I've been craving answers since that moment, but Rollick insisted that we put more distance between us and our former captor's last known location before further discussions.

None of our previous jailers—Balthazar or the guardians—should be able to track us here. When the guardians hunted us down before, it was with the help of Griffin's locating skill. The times when he refused, we could evade their notice even without the support of a very powerful demon.

By the time we arrived at Rollick's Spanish estate last night, the six of us were exhausted. And he wanted to have his people question Toni, the woman who turned against her employer in the end to help us, before he listened to any more stories about Balthazar's plans.

I shift my weight from one foot to another, unable to completely tamp down my growing impatience. "You have a pretty good idea of what we can do now. It doesn't really matter *how*, does it? We have to figure out what Balthazar is going to do next—and stop him."

"Patience, little banshee," Rollick says in the droll tone that's sometimes reassuring but I'm currently finding infuriating.

As he opens his mouth to say something else, a shorter figure comes charging through the trees of the country estate's vast grounds.

Zian springs to my side faster than anyone would expect from a man of his bulk, his fingers curling as if to form his wolf-man claws and his muscles tensing defensively beneath his peachy-brown skin. But before he can even growl, he must recognize the bouncing blond curls, like I just have.

"Hey, shadowbloods!" Pearl comes to a stop at the edge of the clearing and beams at all of us. She has a large canvas sack clutched against her curvy body. "Are you done showing off for the boss? I've got new clothes for you."

We've been stuck in the same smoky-smelling clothes

since yesterday. Despite my restlessness, my spirits lift. "Thank you."

The curvy succubus waves her hand toward the house. "Come on. It'll be easier to sort through them on the table on the back lawn. I don't know how well those doofuses followed my instructions… *I* should have gone to collect these."

"*You* have already shown yourself around Balthazar's people," Rollick reminds her, but he strides after her as we do. "When we don't want to give them any hint of where their escapees have gone, caution matters more than fashion."

He's kept his tone light, but I think I catch a hint of tension in his words. Balthazar managed to breach even the demon's defenses—stealing a laptop from his hotel back in Miami while Rollick was distracted with his rescue efforts.

The laptop may have been the key to Balthazar perfecting his process for creating new shadowbloods. But I can't blame Rollick for losing it. I'm the one who told Balthazar where it was, not realizing how big a mistake that would be at the time.

We emerge from the trees and cross the lawn to the broad wrought-iron patio table that's painted white to match the walls of the sprawling mansion beyond it. The building's arched colonnades and clay-tiled roof give it a traditional flair, but its overall vibe is modern enough that it doesn't stir up bad associations with the old Italian villa where Balthazar had us trapped.

Pearl upends the sack over the table, sending a deluge

of fabric across the white surface. The guys and I gather around to paw through the offerings.

I've just dug out a hoodie that's a size too big but otherwise looks appealingly cozy and a pair of jeans that I think should fit when Pearl makes a small, tight noise in her throat. I glance up to see her gazing toward the house.

Three figures have just emerged. Sorsha—the only human-shadowkind hybrid we know of who wasn't created by the guardians, who has the fiery powers of a phoenix—and a roguish shadowkind man named Ruse flank a tall, wiry woman whose sleek black bob is unusually ruffled.

Toni. They're finally letting her come talk to us again.

All thoughts of the new clothes flee my head. I have just enough self-control to walk around the table rather than leaping right over it.

Sorsha and Ruse escort Toni all the way to us. Sorsha tips her head with a swing of her bright red ponytail. "We're confident that she's being honest about her intentions. I think you can trust her."

Rollick folds his arms over his chest. "Let's hear what Balthazar's minion has to say, then."

Toni's lips tighten in a faint grimace at being called a minion, but I don't see any emotion in her dark eyes other than sadness. She reaches into the pocket of her slacks. "Before we get into anything else—when I snuck into Mr. Balthazar's office to turn off your bracelets, I saw this. I think it's yours, Riva?"

She holds out a silver chain dangling a charm of a cat curled around a ball of yarn. My pulse hiccups in surprise and relief.

I dart forward to take it from her. "Thank you. I didn't know what he'd done with it."

The necklace, given to me by Griffin years ago, has been missing since I first woke up in Balthazar's villa.

As I fasten the chain around my neck, Jacob fixes his sky-blue eyes on Toni in an icy stare. "Are you going to tell us why the hell you worked for that psychopath at all?"

Toni ducks her head, her shoulders hunching slightly. "I'll do my best to explain, but I don't expect you to necessarily understand. I know I didn't always make the best decisions. I'm trying to fix that now."

"Go ahead," Griffin says, his peaceful attitude as different from Jacob's as their looks are similar. "We'll listen."

She drags in a breath and lifts her gaze to face us properly. "I've been working for Otto Balthazar for fifteen years now. When I was in college, studying business management, I had an unpleasant encounter with a—with one of the things you call shadowkind—and of course no one believed me when I tried to explain what happened. But Mr. Balthazar heard about it and came to talk to me. He was still working with the Guardianship then."

I raise my eyebrows. "And he decided to hire you?"

Toni gives a small shrug. "I was doing well with my education. He was starting to think about branching out more independently with his… unofficial business. And I can't imagine that it's easy to find people who both know about shadowkind and have the right skillset. It made it easier for him, not having to hide what he was pursuing."

Dominic smooths his hands over a shirt he's picked

out from Pearl's loot, his attention trained on Toni. "What exactly did he ask you to do for him?"

"I managed everything that *wasn't* part of his public business ventures: his work with the Guardianship, his individual efforts against the shadowkind, various things to do with his personal life. Mr. Balthazar had a lot going on. He needed someone to keep everything in order, to delegate what was needed, and to alert him to any problems."

My hands tighten around the hoodie I'm still clutching. "And you did all that for him."

"Yes," Toni says. "For him and his family."

For a moment, as she looks at me, a shimmer comes into her eyes that looks almost like tears. Her jaw works before she goes on.

"I was around a lot. I became close with his wife— Willa—and to some extent with his son. Peter was only seven when I met him, so it wasn't like we had a lot in common, but he was a good kid. Willa accepted me like I'd been there from the start. She had this way about her… She just emanated warmth. I've never met anyone else like her. Mr. Balthazar was steadier back then, but he had moments of frustration, and she could always talk him down."

Griffin is studying her intently. "And you loved her."

The flare of a blush that colors Toni's tan cheeks tells the answer even if she doesn't admit it outright. "She loved her husband. I don't think she was interested in women like that anyway. I just liked getting to be around her. That was enough."

As she pauses to gather herself, I have to stop myself

from gaping. It never occurred to me that this woman's deepest loyalty might not be to her former employer but to his wife.

"She grounded Mr. Balthazar," Toni continues, her voice getting a bit rough. "She and Peter both did. But then—Peter fell in with a rowdy bunch of friends in high school. There was some kind of altercation, and he ended up shot. Mr. Balthazar always claimed a monster was involved, that they were attacking his family now. I'm not sure anymore if that's true."

Zian frowns. "Is that when he got so crazy?"

Toni's mouth twists. "He definitely ramped up his efforts—working more aggressively, branching off more from the Guardianship with plans they didn't know about. But it was really… He launched a major offensive against shadowkind in his home city. Had silver and iron embedded around areas they liked to congregate, places where they'd feed in their various ways. Figured out where a nearby portal was and messed with that too."

Rollick's head comes up. "I heard something about that, a few years ago."

"Yes." Toni sighs. "He must have slipped up somewhere, though. Maybe with the shadowkind contacts he manipulates into giving up intel. A few of the… monsters… realized who was behind the offensive and tracked him down. When they got to his house, he was away, but Willa was there. So they tore her apart. Literally."

Her voice has gone outright ragged with the last few words. I know without any mind-reading ability that she saw the results of that attack. And maybe I can understand a little why she would have found it hard to sympathize with anyone connected to the monsters who destroyed the woman she loved.

"It broke something in him," Toni says. "Losing both of them. Knowing it was his mistake that put Willa in danger. He never admitted it—I heard him rant so many times about how incompetent everyone else was to let the monsters continue to threaten us—but he knew. He left the Guardianship and threw all his time, energy, and money into building up his economic influence and political power."

"So he can take over the world," I fill in, remembering what Balthazar told me. "He wants to convince or force all the major governments into launching assaults on the shadowkind."

Toni inclines her head. "That was why he wanted all of you shadowbloods too. Especially after he found out the six of you had escaped and it'd taken the Guardianship so long to recapture you. He didn't trust them to use you properly."

Jacob takes a step toward her, his stance menacing. "You stood with him through all of that—through everything he did to us. After you *knew* how badly it went before."

"I thought he was right," Toni protests. "I hadn't seen anything from the shadowkind except violence. It seemed like the lesser of two evils. And Willa always asked me to look after him for her when she couldn't be there... She wouldn't have wanted me to abandon him after he'd already lost so much."

She stops and shakes her head. "At least, that's what I

thought for the last three years. But I didn't know just how cruel he could be. I didn't know how much *she* didn't even matter to him anymore."

Andreas knits his brow. "What do you mean?"

Toni looks at me rather than him. "You're his daughter —but you're *hers* too. The last piece of her still alive. And he was willing to torture you for not immediately doing everything his way. He put you through so much…"

The pieces click together in my head. Toni was there when Balthazar revealed my full genetic heritage to me. I'd thought she seemed shaken, but I hadn't realized why.

I'd been too busy reeling from my own feelings on the subject.

It was soon after that meeting when she approached us and said she'd try to help us escape. Her loyalties didn't really change, though. She just realized that the woman whose values she'd attempted to uphold would have been on our side rather than her employer's.

On my side.

A wild giggle bubbles at the base of my throat. I spent all that time horrified and frightened of my connection to Balthazar, but the same connection was what won us our freedom in the end.

"I'm sorry," Toni says. "It shouldn't have taken that long for me to see the truth. It shouldn't have taken that much. I didn't *like* a lot of what I saw him doing, and I knew he'd gotten dangerously obsessed with his quest, but after Willa died, I kind of shut off a lot of my mind. I went on autopilot, being who I thought I was supposed to be."

When her voice peters out, the guys remain silent. I

feel their attention shift to me, as if my response is the one that matters most.

Maybe it does. It's because of me that she's here.

I sort through the whirling emotions inside me and settle on one true thing I can say. "I'm glad you came to us. Even if it took a long time, it's better now than never."

A hesitant smile crosses Toni's lips. "I'd like to think so."

She glances around at all of us again. "But whatever we're going to do to interfere with Mr. Balthazar's plans, we can't take our time with it. Now that he's confirmed his method for creating new adult shadowbloods, I don't know how much havoc he's going to wreak—but he'll be working fast. And he won't let anyone stand in his way."

Two

As the group Rollick has called together takes seats around the long table in his Spanish mansion's vast dining room, I can't suppress a prickle of apprehension.

It's not our surroundings that unnerve me. The house's interior is reassuringly different from our previous digs, the walls the same stark white as the outer ones and the furniture sleekly modern.

My concern is more about the company we're keeping. All of the shadowkind joining us were vetted by our demonic host… but beings working under him have attacked us before.

Some of the faces are familiar. Sorsha sits partway down the table with two of her regular companions at her sides: Thorn, .the massive, crystal-knuckled man who can sprout dark angelic wings, and a tall, slim man with brilliant green eyes and golden curls, whose shadowkind powers I'm not sure of. He keeps one hand resting on Sorsha's arm where it leans against the table as if he thinks *she* needs protection.

I'm pretty sure she could burn down the entire estate in a matter of seconds if she wanted to. Having seen what she did to Balthazar's villa, I'm not totally surprised that most of the shadowkind are wary of hybrids.

Pearl has joined us too, perched in the chair next to Rollick with an air of delighted triumph at having earned that choice spot. The succubus was instrumental in Rollick's scheme to rescue us, using her seductive skills to cajole the secrets of the hill's hidden passage out of one of Balthazar's staff.

Her friend Billy the faun isn't around anywhere I can see, and neither is Ruse, who also tends to stick close to Sorsha. I'm guessing they're watching from the shadows. There simply aren't that many chairs around the table, especially with us shadowbloods and Toni taking up seven.

Rollick's newer companions make me the most uneasy. There's the guy whose jumble of wild curls falls across his glinting violet eyes, who's smirking to himself as he carves lines into the tabletop with his terrifying three-inch claws.

My cat claws, barely a quarter as long, make me feel like a kitten in comparison. Those must be the one monstrous feature he can't will away even in human guise, like all shadowkind have.

Somehow I don't think he gets invited to many parties.

Beside him sits the bulky, stubble-haired man with a square stone jaw, which I know reflects his shadowkind nature. He can shift into a totally stony gargoyle, bat-like wings and all.

Then there's a woman who looks totally human except for the deep blue hue of her cascading hair—and the ominous atmosphere that seems to hover around her, giving me the sense of an impending thunderstorm. And a squat but muscular man with shiny metallic scales dappling his forehead.

And finally, definitely not getting invited to parties, is the burly dude with a scruffy brown pelt on his head and a pair of incisors so thick they jut against his lips. Appropriately, I heard Rollick call him "Fang."

I'm not sure what abilities the bunch of them bring to the table, both metaphorically and literally, but I doubt their powers have anything to do with sunshine and roses.

From the whiffs of uneasy pheromones my guys are giving off, I don't think I'm alone in my wariness. My fingers curl around my newly restored cat-and-yarn charm, but I resist the urge to give in to my nervous habit of clicking it open and shut.

We're here together. Completely united in ways we hadn't even imagined.

We'll get through this like we have so much else.

As one more shadowkind flickers into being in the last of the chairs, Rollick lifts his chin where he's poised at the head of the table. "All right. Let's get down to business."

The blue-haired woman drums her fingers on the tabletop. Her voice comes out both melodic and low with displeasure. "There are *more* of these shadowbloods being made? It seems to me that's the big problem."

The demon's gaze flicks to her. "Let's keep a respectful tone when it comes to our guests, Shanty."

I feel like there are a few things we current shadowbloods should make clear right away.

I draw up my slight frame as tall as I can manage. "No, we agree that it's a problem. We already are the way we are, and we can't do anything about that. But we wouldn't have chosen this. Balthazar needs to be stopped as soon as possible, before he warps more people than he already has."

Sorsha shifts her gaze to Toni. "You're the one who worked with this man. What exactly do you know about his plans from here forward? Where is he finding people to transform? What is he going to ask them to do?"

Toni looks as if she's suppressing a wince. "Mr. Balthazar has enough sway that he's been able to arrange access to incarcerated criminals from various prisons. People who don't have families checking up on them so they won't be missed."

Around me, my guys' faces have darkened. "People who won't have reservations about throwing their powers around, no matter who gets hurt?" Dominic suggests.

Toni dips her head, her expression turning even more pained. "And who would be grateful to him for giving them their freedom. He'll ensure their obedience to him the same way he did with you, with the metal bracelets that can knock them out or kill them if need be."

"Criminals," the stout guy with the scaly forehead mutters. "On top of their wild powers. Just great."

I swallow thickly and raise my voice again. "Those aren't the only shadowbloods he has. He's also been holding a bunch of the kids the guardians brought up—like us, but none of them are older than seventeen, and their powers are a lot weaker. We have to find and rescue them too."

Lord only knows what the younger shadowbloods are going through now. When I remember how downcast even neon-loving Nadia became in the last few days before Balthazar wrenched them all away from us, my heart sinks.

We don't even know for sure if all of the others are still alive. At the villa, our former captor murdered two of the kids before our eyes, just to make a point.

"I don't know where they're being held," Toni says. "He split them up across several different properties and kept that information to himself. But I do know where a lot of his properties across North America and Europe *are*, so that could be a start in our search."

At Sorsha's side, Thorn lets out a deep rumble of a grunt. "It sounds as though we should end this villain's life first and worry about rescue attempts afterward. Once he's gone, he won't be able to harm them further."

As anxious as I am to get my friends and the other kids out of Balthazar's clutches, I can't deny that the hulking angel has a point.

Jacob thumps his fist on the table. "We destroy him and any of the criminals working with him. Sounds good to me."

Fang turns his unnerving face toward Rollick. "How hard could it be to kill one mortal man? He *is* mortal, isn't he?"

"Mr. Balthazar had no interest in becoming at all like the shadowkind himself," Toni confirms.

Rollick grimaces. "He has proven to be particularly adept at evading our attacks, though. He doesn't skimp on his silver and iron protections, and he leaves himself plenty of escape routes while preventing even his captives from getting within close enough range to unleash their talents on him. I don't think we can count on the battle being easy, especially with an unknown number of shadowbloods in the mix."

"We've got to find him first," Andreas points out, and motions to Toni. "Where would he want to go next? You haven't said what the next steps in his plans were going to be."

She exhales raggedly. "I don't know the specifics. I didn't even know he and Matteo had finalized the procedure for transforming people into shadowbloods until that last night. But... the first stage he always talked about, when he had the manpower to move forward, was giving the world motivation to go on the attack against shadowkind."

Zian frowns. "And how was he going to do that? No one believes monsters really exist."

Toni meets his gaze, her dark eyes solemn. "He was going to prove it. By having his new shadowbloods rain down destruction with their powers, and then claiming *they're* the monsters that need to be stamped out."

A chill floods me from the inside out. "They're going to go around attacking people."

"Something like that. But I don't know where he'll start. Or when. I can't imagine he'll wait long, though. He's been desperate to get started."

My hands ball into fists, my claws tingling at my fingertips with the urge to strike out. But the man I want to tackle is nowhere within reach.

"We have to find him. Fast." I look down at my arms and rub the skin of my wrist, the bruising there nearly faded already thanks to our swift shadowkind healing. "I wish we had a manacle on *him* so we could track him down. He could be anywhere in the world!"

There's a momentary silence. Then Dominic clears his throat and glances across the table. "Griffin tracked us all across the continent back when we were on the run—without needing any tracking devices."

Every pair of eyes around the table jerks to the subdued guy who's simply been sitting with us taking in the conversation—and the emotions we're all giving off.

Only the briefest flicker of surprise passes through Griffin's light blue eyes. Then he nods. "I did. But only because of the history between us. I've never even *seen* Balthazar in person. I don't have a strong enough sense of him that I could home in on his location."

Zian lets out a growl of frustration. I slump in my seat, the momentary sense of hope deflating.

Jacob turns toward his twin. "You could *try*."

Griffin pauses. "No. I can already tell it wouldn't work. But…"

His gaze slides to me, intent and a little sad. Enough that I tense up before he even starts to speak.

"Riva, you share his DNA. You've seen him, using Zian's power. If you borrowed that talent of mine, you might be able to find him."

THREE

Griffin

Rollick lays out the world map on the pale floorboards of one of his mansion's common rooms. The paper surface is big, a good six feet across and four high, so he's pushed the furniture to the sides of the room to make space. But even so, the imagery printed across the surface only offers a little detail, working on that scale.

The demon tsks his tongue. "You're lucky I could dig up actual physical maps this quickly. Everyone's all about the digital versions these days."

Next to me, Riva rubs her arms and then forces her hands to her sides. Tense anticipation wavers off her into my awareness.

"So I start with the whole world and then narrow it down once we see what I come up with?" she says.

I nod. "After you get down to a smaller area like a city, we can switch to screens for that. But I always found it much easier to get a clear impression when I had a larger concrete map for the initial seeking."

The other guys and a handful of shadowkind have been watching from a loose ring around us. Jacob steps forward to tap my arm. "Are you *sure* you can't do this? I mean, since you have the experience with how to work the power effectively. The procedures Balthazar had that asshole Matteo put us through expanded all of our talents."

I shoot my brother a tight smile. "Not all of ours. At least, not in any way we figured out. Matteo pushed me to locate strangers using names and photographs—even inanimate objects—but none of that ever worked."

Riva glances at me in surprise. "Wait—the procedures didn't affect your powers even a little?"

I can understand why she'd be startled. Jacob's right that the rest of them saw major boosts to their abilities. It was only the younger shadowbloods, whose talents were much smaller to begin with, who didn't show any effects.

Well, them and me.

I give a casual shrug that I hope conveys that I'm not bothered by it. "I wondered if the guardians' conditioning and the way that affected my own emotions might have interfered with any progress I'd have made."

Part of me thinks that's a good thing. I'm not sure I'd want to know what horrifying new dimensions I could have discovered to my powers if Balthazar had gotten his way. My friends haven't exactly been thrilled with every new development they've experienced.

But on the other hand, as I wait for Riva to borrow this one power of mine, a prickle of frustration runs through my chest. Followed by a different sort of jab as my conditioning clicks in, sending pain after the emotion.

I breathe slowly and deeply, not letting the discomfort show. I can't tell whether the lingering effects of the guardians' manipulations are fading or I'm simply getting better at enduring them, but I suppose it doesn't make a lot of difference either way.

I wish I could take this task on instead of heaping one more responsibility on Riva's shoulders. I wish I'd gotten a clearer sense of Balthazar during the weeks we spent confined to his villa.

All I have is a vague, jumbled impression of the tumultuous feelings I picked up on from a distance. I can't even say for sure that every one of those impressions was definitely from him and not a nearby employee.

The best I can do is guide Riva. "You'll want to focus on your memories of him, bringing them as vividly as you can to the front of your mind. And then push the image toward the map, like your memories are a magnet and you're searching for a surface they'll attach to. If it works, your finger will be drawn right to the spot where he currently is."

Riva nods and squares her shoulders. We don't need to touch to exchange powers, but she rests her fingers on my wrist for a moment as she tugs the ability out of me with a light jitter of my nerves.

She closes her eyes, her face tensing with concentration. As much as I hate that I'm leaving her to do the real work here, I can't help admiring the determination she brings to this task like every other, etched across her beautiful features.

This is my woman. The woman I'd follow to the farthest, deadliest corners of the earth, as long as she wants me with her.

I'm never letting myself lose sight of what really matters again.

Quivers of skepticism niggle me from the watching shadowkind, most of whom have never seen us trade powers before. If Riva has any sense that part of her audience isn't sure what to make of her, she doesn't let it distract her. She steps toward the edge of the map and holds out her hand.

Her fingers hover in the air for several seconds. Then they twitch to the right.

As she drops to her knees to follow the pull, a surge of exhilaration wafts out of her. She's excited that she's pulling this off.

A softer smile curls my lips. Even if I'd rather be working my own power than passing it on to her, I do love seeing her take charge. Watching her put all the strength she sometimes doubts to good use.

She's been through more than any of us, had to grapple with knowledge we can barely imagine, but she's still just as committed as she's always been.

Her hand drops, and her eyes pop open. She peers down at the map.

"He's in… Tunisia? Around the middle of the country."

Toni, who's stood back near the doorway, stirs with a frown. "As far as I know, Mr. Balthazar doesn't own property in that country. But it could be a newer acquisition he didn't tell me about."

Rollick hums to himself and shuffles through the paper maps he set on a side table. "It's not too far a jump from Italy, where he was last holed up. I don't think I have anything specifically of Tunisia here… Ah, this'll give us a closer view of the western Mediterranean. We can at least narrow down the governorate, maybe even a specific city."

One of the shadowkind, the squat man with metallic scales on his forehead who Rollick has called "Steel," lets out a brief scoffing sound. "And then we've got to hunt down maps of the entire terrain of that country?"

"Once it's narrowed down that much, I think a digital map should work all right," I say.

A slim shadowkind woman with bark-like patches on her forearms shifts her weight restlessly. "How sure are we that this process is accurate? Even his lackey doesn't think so."

Riva lifts her head before I need to speak. "He's there. I can *feel* him." She grimaces. "It's not a good feeling. I wouldn't be imagining it out of nothing."

The traces of doubt I'm picking up on don't vanish, but in the face of Riva's certainty, the shadowkind don't argue.

Rollick folds up the world map and spreads out his Mediterranean one. As Riva steps to its edge, I let my gaze drift from her over the spectators.

A few of the shadowkind are totally on board with our presence. Pearl watches Riva work with genuine eagerness, and her friend Billy stands nearby, wide-eyed with curiosity. Sorsha the phoenix looks more concerned about keeping an eye on her fellow shadowkind than worrying about what us shadowbloods are doing.

I suspect Rollick has told her about how his people treated my friends in the past, just as my friends have told me. I wasn't there when a bunch of his allies abandoned them and later tried to kill them, but I can taste hints of animosity among the others gathered in the room with us.

There's no outright aggression in their moods—or what I can read of their stances. They're more uncertain than hostile. But most of them still appear to see us as a potential threat, something to monitor.

They don't trust us. They just trust their boss enough to tolerate his involvement in our lives.

And maybe it's also that they realize they're better off bringing the rest of the shadowbloods over to their side than letting Balthazar run wild with his new creations.

I could nudge them toward feeling happier about our presence. Send waves of calm or friendliness through their minds. But I've only worked my powers on a shadowkind being once before, and then I didn't have time to be subtle about it. I don't know what my limitations might be, how big a push would be necessary and when it'd be going too far.

Or how easily they might notice my interference. They definitely won't trust us if they realize one of us has attempted to manipulate their emotions.

I suppress a grimace of my own. That's really all I'm good for in this war we've found ourselves in: intruding on people's minds, bending their perceptions of their desires and fears.

I've helped in other ways. I've used my talent to remind Riva of her convictions, to reassure Jacob of the love they share.

But when the people I care about are emotionally healthy, I can't contribute anything other than messing up that carefully won balance. Almost every time I *have* used my powers on them, it was to serve people I should have realized were our enemies.

The pang of guilt comes with another jolt of conditioned pain. I gird myself as Riva points to a specific spot on the map. "Right here. In or near Kairouan."

Rollick is already bringing up a city map on the tablet he had ready. He adjusts it so it includes some of the surrounding area and then glances at me. "We can simply keep zooming in as we go, I assume?"

I shake off my pensive thoughts. "Yes. If you follow her directions quickly enough, she won't even need to refocus, just kind of chase after her sense of him deeper into the map."

Riva's eyes have brightened with renewed confidence after her first two successes. She taps on the northern part of the city, and then in the middle of the zoomed-in area Rollick offers.

There, she hesitates, a frown crossing her face. "It feels like… he's moving. Like when I try to narrow in on his location, it shifts before I can totally lock on."

Dominic comes up beside her to study the map. "Every inch on that screen is still about a mile. Even a car wouldn't be moving that fast."

I have to speak up, even though the reason I know this makes me even more ashamed. "An aircraft would. A plane… or a helicopter."

I once tracked my friends as they approached one of the facilities by helicopter, hoping to sneak up on the guardians by coming from multiple directions. It only took a few minutes for me to see how the two flight paths were converging.

Riva mutters a curse. "He's in the middle of going someplace else, then. We don't even know for sure if he started that flight in Tunisia."

"Which direction is he headed in now?" Rollick asks.

She refocuses on the map and moves her finger in a slow, halting line. "Northeast, it seems like."

Toni approaches to consider the larger map, her expression still tight. "He does have holdings in Egypt and in South Africa. Egypt would have been closer, but…" She shrugs to indicate she has no definite information on where Balthazar would have gone when he fled.

"All right." Rollick turns off the tablet and tucks it under his arm. "I can send a few of my companions to chat with the local shadowkind near the portals in Tunisia and see if any of them have noticed unusual activity. And we'll check on your would-be world conqueror's location again in a few hours."

Zian rolls his shoulders with an impatient air. "What should we do until then?"

Riva's head comes back up with a flash of hope across her face. "I knew a few of the younger shadowbloods pretty well. Maybe I can track *their* locations. We'll want to know where they are so we can get them out—and that'll give us some idea which of Balthazar's properties he's using to hold people like us."

"That seems worth a shot." Rollick goes to retrieve the large world map so they can start over from scratch. "You seem confident enough now—and I hope my colleagues have all indulged their curiosity in this process."

The demon shoots a pointed look at the gathered shadowkind, a few of whom duck their heads and waver back into the shadows. Then he gestures to Toni. "You should stay, since you're familiar with your former employer's haunts. Maybe the rest of our shadowbloods can make themselves useful too. Sorsha, why don't you take them to the atrium and start sorting out potential strategies once we've figured out where to hit this megalomaniac."

The red-haired woman chuckles and motions for everyone else to follow her. I pause to give Riva's arm a quick squeeze. "You've got this, Moonbeam."

The smile she aims at me in return is almost enough to make up for the fact that there isn't anything else I can offer her. I drift after the other guys reluctantly.

The atrium is a square of garden inside the mansion's sprawling walls, open to the outside with no roof overhead. Sweet fragrances drift off the flowering bushes along one wall.

More shadowkind pop into being as Sorsha turns to face us with a decisive clap of her hands. "All right. First things first—what can each of you contribute in a fight?"

My smile turns tight again, but I only have one answer to give. "I can confuse their emotions. Send them into a panic or lull them complacent. Whatever works best for the plan."

Steel turns his cool gaze on me. "You could do that to shadowkind too, huh, shadowblood boy?"

I give him the most reassuring look I'm capable of. "I wouldn't, though. Not when we're helping each other."

I pretend I don't notice the flicker of uneasiness that stirs in him at my words. And then Toni bursts into the atrium with a ragged breath.

"It's started," she says. "Mr. Balthazar's shadowblood army—they've launched an attack."

Four

Riva

As our helicopter thrums through the air, I flick at the screen of the tablet Rollick lent us, careening from scene to scene of destruction. With each, my stomach knots tighter.

Some of it is amateur footage, shaky cell phone camera recordings punctuated by the startled yelps and breathless exclamations of the locals who witnessed the initial onslaught. The official news crews arrived on the scene later, after Balthazar's new shadowbloods had already fled the scene.

I only catch glimpses of the figures in the amateur footage. No one who survived to post their videos online got close enough to the carnage to capture identifying details.

But the impact is clear enough.

In one recording, a distant form slams his fist into the side of a four-story building—and it crumples to the ground in a hail of rubble. In another, screams ring out as streaks of sizzling blue energy whip through the air to cut down the panicked locals who *were* too close.

It wasn't just Moscow, the first place one of Rollick's shadowkind allies saw a news report on and alerted us about. Balthazar has already built up enough of an army that he was able to send at least a few shadowbloods to five key cities around the world.

I'm seeing broken buildings and bodies from London, New York, Tokyo, and Buenos Aires as well. He's spreading his message across the continents and both hemispheres, looking to get as many eyes on it as possible at once.

And it is a message, quite literally. His shadowblood thugs left words seared into the sides of buildings they left standing or painted them with the blood of their victims.

The monsters are coming for you!
You can't fight our power!
Humanity is doomed!

On and on like that, just as Toni suggested Balthazar's strategy would be. He wants the whole world to realize that the shadowkind exist. To believe that the monsters are rising up against mortals so that people will accept his solutions for getting rid of them.

I don't know if his extermination plan will actually work, considering how resilient the shadowkind appear to be. But I'd rather not watch and see how many get slaughtered in the fallout, even if I haven't had the best experiences with some of them.

Rollick doesn't deserve to be hunted down and

murdered. Neither do Pearl or Billy or Sorsha's men who've stood with us.

And let's be real: Balthazar doesn't like the shadowkind essence inside us shadowbloods either.

I'll bet the second he thinks the full "monsters" are gone and he doesn't need his hybrids to do his dirty work anymore, he'll consign us to the slaughter next.

I lift my gaze from the tablet's screen to the helicopter window, taking in the clouds streaking past below us. "How much longer until we get to London?"

Rollick gives me a baleful look from his seat at the front of the aircraft. "About ten more minutes. This is as fast as the chopper can go, little banshee. And I'm still not sure making the trip was the wisest idea in the first place."

I was the one who first insisted that we had to help somehow, but Jacob speaks up before I need to. "Shadowbloods trashed the city. Now shadowbloods will pick up the pieces. Someone has to tell the real story."

The demon shrugs. "The mortals may not listen to you."

"We have to try," I say, hugging myself. "And maybe if we see firsthand what Balthazar's new shadowbloods did, we'll get a better idea of what they're capable of, their tactics—how to fight back when we go after them directly."

Rollick nods. I think *that* point is the only reason he agreed to escort us to London at all.

My search for Balthazar's current location didn't prove all that useful. If he's going to be moving around all the time, how can we plan an attack properly?

We need more information, more of an edge… And I

can't stand the thought of abandoning all the people he's hurt and terrorized when we're more equipped to step in than anyone else could be.

Griffin has taken the seat next to me. He grasps my hand and strokes his thumb over the back of my knuckles. "We'll do everything we can."

Zian's face is taut with bottled anger. "We can't let that psycho get away with this."

As far as I can tell, it's just us six shadowbloods and Rollick in the chopper, although for all I know a few more shadowkind tagged along in the darkness. After the news came in, Rollick ordered the rest of his people to investigate the more distant incidents that they can reach quickly via their portals to and from the shadow realm—and continue devising strategies for our theoretical counterattack.

"Here we go," the demon murmurs. The helicopter lurches a bit on a gust of wind as it begins its descent. "Brace yourselves."

I don't think he's talking only about the drop to the ground. As the vehicle rushes down toward the sprawl of the city below us, I peer through the window at the chaos of darting figures and flashing lights.

We came by chopper specifically so that we could land right at the scene. A jet might have made the trip faster, but we'd have had to trek through the city from the outskirts after we arrived.

In this aircraft, we're able to touch down on a broad stretch of pavement next to a jumble of pale, cracked stone that has enough glass and carved edges mixed in to make it obvious it used to be a building. Never having seen

London except as a backdrop to an occasional movie, I have no idea *which* building until Rollick shuts off the engine and glances over the scene with a pained slant to his mouth. "So long, Westminster Abbey."

The second we pour out of the helicopter's door, several of the figures picking their way across the rubble and pacing around it turn our way. "Hey, what do you think you're doing?" someone in a bright orange vest shouts.

Griffin steps to the front of our group, his fingers curling toward his palms. With our newly deepened connection, I can feel the quiver of energy that ripples off him as he extends his talent over the scattered rescue crews.

The faces that had twisted with confusion or aggression relax. Everyone goes back to the work they were already doing: hustling uncovered bodies into waiting ambulances, searching the wreckage for more.

I spot a couple of lingering news crews farther away, looking like they're interviewing one of the rescue workers and a couple of passersby. One of the reporters glances toward us, but Griffin sends an extra waft of disinterest her way.

When he speaks, the slight edge to his voice reveals how much of a strain it's taking to impose this calm over all those people at once. "I'll keep my attention on keeping *their* attention off us. I'll give you as long as I can, but I don't know how long that'll be."

The rest of us don't need any further prompting to spring into action. Leaving Rollick in the cab of the chopper, ready in case we need to beat a hasty retreat, we scramble into the ruins of the old church.

I only have a vague impression in my memory of what it might have looked like before, but I can tell it was fucking *huge*. There's a full city block of broken stone strewn around us like low, shattered hills.

I have no idea how many bystanders might have been buried when the criminal shadowbloods attacked. I drag in a deep breath, tasting the air for panicked pheromones, but there are too many lacing the breeze from the people all around us for me to narrow down anyone injured.

Zian's head jerks around. "I can hear a groan—faint, but it's definitely someone down there. Come on!"

We hustle after him until he stops near one of the larger heaps of rubble. Dominic takes a quick glance around. He points to a row of shrubs that just escaped the devastation. "I'm going to grab a couple of those so I have energy for healing."

Jacob is already motioning at the chunks of stone with his hand, his telekinetic powers heaving one and then another slab farther away. As I dive in to heft up one boulder with my supernatural strength, Andreas swallows audibly.

"I'm not sure there's any way I can really help with rescuing people," he says. "I—I'll do a circuit of the scene, peek into people's memories. Maybe I can find someone who witnessed the attack and can give me a clearer look at the new shadowbloods."

I shoot him a quick smile. "Good idea." Then I bend down over the next hunk of rock.

Zian lends both his strength and the cutting edge of

his X-ray vision, wrenching one jagged block out of the way with his bulging arms while he cracks another into pebbles with his eyes. Between the three of us shifting debris out of the way, I've only just started to break a sweat when I spot the green fabric of a sleeve through a gap.

"There!" I pry up the next chunk more carefully, not wanting to send any others crashing down on the victim.

We've uncovered all but the woman's lower legs when Dominic hurries back to us, dragging a bush he's uprooted. His tentacles unwind from beneath the thin jacket he hastily threw on over his tee before we left.

When I catch his gaze, he offers a tight smile. "Anyone who notices might as well see that *some* monsters aren't out to hurt them."

He kneels down by the woman, one tentacle twining with the shrub's branches and the other looping around her arm. She gazes up at him with glazed eyes, blood dappling her cheeks and her sweater.

Dominic aims a softer smile at her, his voice equally gentle. "I'm going to patch you up. It'll be okay."

Before our eyes, the bruising on her forehead fades. The hitch leaves her breath.

Jacob casts his gaze around. "There are probably more buried survivors. We should keep searching."

There isn't anything more the three of us can do for this woman now that Zian has lifted the last rock from her feet. We prowl off over the unstable terrain, our ears pricked and eyes scanning.

Zian lets out an urgent sound and directs us to another spot where he caught a sound of distress. We dig into the rubble again without hesitation. Despite the chilly winter air, beads of perspiration roll down my back beneath my own hastily grabbed jacket.

"It's only a small part of the city they destroyed," Jacob remarks in a momentary pause between shifting boulders.

I think of the footage I watched. "They wanted to be quick, in and out before anyone could pay much attention to what exactly was happening. Before there'd be much evidence for *us* to see and use to track them. The main point was the message."

I pause, adjusting my grip on the rough edge of another stone slab. This one is sculpted with lines I can tell were once elegant.

My throat tightens. "And this was a place that meant a lot to people. Centuries of history. They went for size of emotional impact rather than hitting a whole bunch of buildings."

The fact that I can understand Balthazar's reasoning makes me a little queasy, even though I don't agree with what he's doing. There's a method to his madness.

Toni's words from this morning echo through my head. *Willa was there. So they tore her apart. Literally.*

And now Balthazar is going to tear apart everything the rest of the world cares about until they agree to strike back against the creatures he blames for his wife's death. Never mind that only a few of them—maybe only one—actually carried out the murder.

Never mind that they would have seen it as self-defense after he attacked them first.

I unearth a shoe without a foot in it—one so small it has to belong to a child. My gut lurches in the second before Jacob's eager exclamation. "I see him!"

But just as Zian disintegrates the chunk pinning down the little boy's chest, the boom of a loudspeaker splits the air. "You three near the trees, move off the wreckage now."

Our heads swing toward the projected voice.

I haven't been paying attention to the rumbles of vehicles coming and going. A military-style truck has parked near the edge of the ruin, and three men with rifles are standing around it, one of them holding the loudspeaker. Several more figures in police uniforms have appeared, easing onto the rubble toward us.

I glance at Griffin over by the helicopter. His lips are pursed tight, his eyes wide. As if sensing my look, he gives a slight shake of his head.

He can't push enough emotion on everyone here to stop their interruption. If it wasn't this group, someone else would be coming after us.

All they see are a bunch of unauthorized strangers, poking around where a bunch of *other* strangers just caused this whole mess.

"We're just trying to help!" I call out. "There's a little boy stuck here. He—"

"Back away from any injured parties," the loudspeaker interrupts. "Walk to clear ground and wait for questioning."

Shit. My gaze darts to Jacob, whose hands have clenched into fists, but we aren't here to cause more damage ourselves.

"We have to leave," I say quietly. "No fighting."

He exhales in a rush, but his shoulders come down from their tensed position. Zian nods with a grimace.

Rather than walking to the nearest edge of the rubble,

we head back to the helicopter. Dominic has already moved that way, and I spot Andreas weaving through the people on the fringes to join us there.

Several of the police officers jog over to intercept us. Rollick shoots me a glance through the helicopter's windshield that feels like an *I told you so.*

"Stop right there!" one of them hollers.

A growl comes into Zian's voice. "We're leaving like you wanted us to."

The cop's attention slides to Dominic, with a twitch of his eyes as he takes in the dangling tentacles. "Bloody hell. What *are* you?"

The guys hop into the helicopter. I brace myself to spring after them and fix the cop with my firmest gaze. "That doesn't matter. All you need to know is that the person who destroyed everything here was Otto Balthazar."

Five

Zian

Riva slumps back in her chair and rubs her forehead. "I hate this map. No, I hate *all* maps."

She's been sitting at the elegant white desk for the better part of half an hour, moving between a printed atlas Rollick dug up and a tablet. The late-morning sunshine and warmth stream through the row of tall windows that give a view of the atrium garden, but Riva doesn't look as if she's been able to appreciate either.

I set down the glass of lemonade I brought her, hesitate, and set my hand carefully on her shoulder. We've come a long way from the days when I was afraid of any physical contact with her at all, but I still don't totally trust my instinctive reactions.

When no jolt of panic shoots through me at the touch, I let myself increase the pressure, rubbing my thumb into the tendons of her shoulder in a slow massage.

"You could take a break. You've already figured out where some of the kids are at—he hasn't moved them, right?"

The sigh Riva lets out as she relaxes against my hand sends all kinds of emotions racing through my nerves—a little nervousness, sure, but mostly joy and relief… and enough desire to form an ache in my groin.

I thought it was hard wanting her when I didn't believe I could have her. Wanting her now that I know that I *can* is a challenge on a totally different level.

I don't think she's in a mood for me to sweep her out of the chair and charge off to whatever of the guest bedrooms in Rollick's mansion is closest, even if I was comfortable doing that. So I settle for moving behind her where I can rub both of her shoulders at once.

Riva's eyes drift shut. "The younger shadowbloods are still where I found them before. I wish they weren't scattered across different hideouts, but we figured they would be. It's Balthazar who keeps moving around."

Rollick materializes out of the shadows next to us, already in one of his casually confident stances as if he's been standing there all along. "You could leave him be and check back later," he says. "He'll have to pause somewhere eventually."

"He always does," I agree.

Riva grimaces at us and reaches for the glass of lemonade. "He's heading back toward that spot where he seems to have set up a fortress in the Carpathians in Romania. We decided if he stops there a third time that we should focus on it for our first strike. If I'm right, I should know in another twenty minutes or so. And I'd rather know as soon as possible. With all the reports coming in… who knows what they'll destroy next?"

According to the news we've seen on TV and the internet, Balthazar's shadowbloods hit four more cities last night. Major landmarks destroyed, dozens of people dead. My muscles tighten at the memory of the brutal images.

The demon nods. "I think at this point we can assume that mountain base is his main hub of operations, at least for the moment. I've gotten a couple more reports back from local scouts of his activities there."

"I don't want to assume anything when it comes to Balthazar." Riva takes a gulp of lemonade and leans back over the tablet. "If you want to go on with planning the attack, I've already given my opinion before. And you know what I can do. I'll join the discussion again when I've confirmed his destination."

My chest tightens with the futile urge to take this weight off her shoulders. She's the only one who's gotten close enough to Balthazar that she can do this—and I know she hates it.

Both the fact that she has that kind of tie to him and the constant reaching out toward his presence, becoming more familiar with it every time.

I give her shoulder one last squeeze. "We're going to take him down. It won't be too much longer."

Riva shoots me a smile that looks too weary to really be reassuring, but I don't know what else I can do except follow Rollick to the dining room that's become our command center.

The other guys are sitting around the table—well, other than Jacob, who's pacing with typical agitation.

Toni, several of our shadowkind allies, and the other hybrid, Sorsha, have gathered there too.

Billy stands in one corner with his pipes, playing a softly lilting tune. If it's meant to both soothe and bolster our spirits, I can feel it working a little. I dip my head to the faun with a smile as I sit down.

One of the shadowkind men who seems particularly close to Sorsha, the guy named Thorn who's so massive he makes even me feel a bit small, is pointing to something on a topographical map of the mountain region. He speaks firmly but with a gloomy expression as if he'd rather not be here planning a war, even if he's the best guy for the job.

"We shadowkind will need to focus mainly on deterring reinforcements from coming to Balthazar's aid. The protections he has embedded in the rocks around his fortress would weaken even the strongest of us to a concerning point if we ventured beyond them."

I frown, peering at the map even though I don't have the slightest idea how to decipher the markings. The guardians expected to send us to attack shadowkind in or around areas where lots of people lived—preparing us for vast mountain ranges wasn't high on their list of priorities.

But I know my strengths. The one good thing that came out of Balthazar's manipulations was that I can help in more ways than I could before.

"My X-ray vision can cut through rock now," I say. "Maybe I could carve out some of the protections to give you a way through."

Rollick rubs his chin. "They're deeply embedded and there are a lot of them. And chunks of rock crumbling away would draw attention rather quickly when we're hoping to keep some element of surprise. I'm not sure that'll be the best use of your talents."

I glance at Jacob, who's paused to listen to our exchange. "Maybe if Jake and I worked together, we could do it quickly. He's shaken up mountains before. And Dominic could feed us extra power to help too."

Sorsha taps part of the map. "It does seem like the lower face holds a lot of the toxic metals. If they could chop away that whole section, the more powerful shadowkind could probably tolerate the effects of the other surrounding protections."

Toni leans forward with her hands clasped in front of her. "I don't know how deeply the layers of protective metal go. Balthazar has always been very careful about warding his territories."

The broad, scaled shadowkind named Steel lets out a grunt. "This is mainly the shadowbloods' battle anyway. Are they so worried about handling the brunt of it?"

My hackles rise automatically, but I will down my temper. "It's not that we don't want to fight. We'll be right in there. But we're a lot more likely to get rid of Balthazar the more of us can attack at once."

"Which is good for all of you too, considering he wants to exterminate you," Andreas puts in, keeping his tone lighter than I managed to. He wets his lips. "Maybe if any of the shadowkind are good with illusions, they could keep up the appearance that everything's fine down below until we're all ready to barge in."

Rollick hums to himself. "I have a couple of potential

allies I could put out feelers to. But let's not count on that aspect."

Then he claps his hands with a definitive air. "You've all been straining your heads over this for a while. Take a breather, get refreshments if you need them, and we'll reconvene in half an hour—at which point we should have final confirmation that this is definitely the location we'll focus our first attack on."

A few grumbles pass through the gathered shadowkind as they drift off—either visibly or vanishing into the shadows. My friends head out of the room too, but I take the opportunity to move closer to the table so I can study the map up close.

Even if Balthazar is arriving at this mountain base now, he's never stayed there for very long the other two times Riva traced his presence there. But he seems to stop by once every couple of days.

When we have a solid plan, we'll stake out the place and simply wait for him to return. If we're really lucky, Sorsha will be able to blast him away with her phoenix fire before he even touches down—if he's arriving by something as obvious as a helicopter.

But somehow, knowing Balthazar—and knowing that he's seen the kind of firepower our new friends are capable of—I doubt it'll be that easy.

A figure pops out of the shadows next to me with a wisp of a crisp floral scent, like roses that've been singed. Pearl clucks her tongue as she takes in the map. "This maniac really likes his mountains, huh?"

I automatically take a step to the side to give myself a little more room. But the succubus has a decent sense of personal space despite her methods of feeding—she doesn't show any sign of offense about the distance I've added between us.

With her bouncy curls and bubbly personality, it's hard to think of her as part of the same crew as Rollick's other shadowkind allies. I do my best to keep my tone neutral. "Are you going to be joining in the attack too?"

She shrugs carelessly and grins at me. "I'll see what I can do. I've already been prowling around the towns closest to the mountain to see if I can find any employees to seduce some secrets out of, but no luck so far."

As she looks at me, a sly gleam comes into her eyes. "So, you finally sorted out your issues with Riva, huh?"

My face flushes so hot my cheeks must be blazing scarlet. "I, um— We're getting there."

Are we that obvious? But then, this is a being whose life revolves around sex—I guess it makes sense that she'd pick up on a shift in that part of our dynamic pretty easily.

Pearl's smile is all eager approval. "That's great. I know that the physical part of human relationships isn't *quite* as essential as it is for me, but most people do seem happier when it's working out. And you all deserve to be happy." The gleam turns even slyer. "If you need any tips for continuing to 'get there,' feel free to hit me up. You guys should be treating Riva right."

At her offer, I think my face might burn right off. My gaze darts around the room, which to my relief appears to be empty. Hopefully we don't have a whole audience of hidden shadowkind listening in.

As I grapple with my embarrassment, it occurs to me that there is one thing maybe I should ask Pearl about. If anyone would have a clue what the hell was going on with my anatomy during the act, it's a shadowkind with her level of experience.

I stare down at the map, feeling too awkward to meet her eyes. "There was one thing that was kind of confusing when we... actually got together."

The succubus props herself against the side of the table and cocks her head. "Tell me about it, and I'll see if I can shed some light."

I've gotten started on this path now—might as well dive all the way in. "When I was... finishing, I partly shifted, and my, um..." I motion hastily toward my groin. "It got this bulge right at the base of the shaft. For a minute or two it was like I was stuck inside."

I brace myself in case I keel over from the horror of saying that out loud, but I seem to have survived the admission.

Pearl taps her finger against her lips. "Hmm. I have heard of that sort of thing before. You've got a wolfish thing going on when you shift, right?"

I grimace. "Yeah. Not like an actual wolf, more like a wolf-man in a movie. I've still got the human body, but my face gets all wolfish with the muzzle and fangs and stuff, and I sprout fur there and on my neck and arms."

Pearl nods with a knowing air. "That's probably it. There's this canine thing—comes with the territory for werewolves and so on. Happens with actual dogs too, I think. You get that knot there so that you stay in place for a good long while. To increase chances of the mating being successful."

I'm puzzled enough that I manage to look at her again,

blinking. "Successful?" Getting intimate with Riva felt like a pretty huge success even before that happened.

Pearl's current smile is definitely more of a smirk. "For making babies. At least, when it comes to the actual animals. Shadowkind can't have kids anyway." Her forehead furrows slightly. "I guess we don't know about shadow*bloods* yet."

I open and close my mouth a few times before I recover my voice. "Um, we definitely weren't trying—that wasn't something—"

Thankfully, my heightened hearing still works even in my flustered state. I pick up on the footsteps heading our way in time to clamp my jaw shut, moments before Riva steps into the room.

She takes in me, Pearl, and the otherwise empty room. "Where did everyone go?"

Pearl pushes off the table to amble over to Riva. "Rollick called for a refreshment break. They'll be back in a few minutes. Your wolf-man and I were just having a little strategy chat."

The succubus shoots me a wink over her shoulder and slips out the door.

Riva raises her eyebrows at me. "Are you okay? She always seems to mean well, even if she can be a bit over-the-top about it."

"Yeah. Yeah." I run my hand through my hair, hoping I don't look half as unbalanced as I feel. "It was fine."

With Riva right in front of me after the conversation I just had, I can't help thinking back to that evening when we hooked up. All those thrilling sensations now paired with the idea that some part of my body was trying to get her—

I can't even think it. Fucking hell, I only just managed to get that close with her at all—one time, with Dominic there in case my instincts went haywire.

Whether it's possible for us to have kids, whether it's something we'd want to try for down the road, is so far outside my ability to imagine that it just about short-circuits my brain.

But Riva knows me well enough not to push. She just sidles over, gratifyingly near but not enough to make my nerves jump, and gingerly tucks her hand around mine, reminding me of why I love her so much.

Whatever futures we could dream of, she's always been willing to wait for me.

Twining her fingers with mine, she traces her other hand over the ridges marked on the map. "He came back again. If we're going to take him down anywhere, it'll be here."

Six

Riva

By the time we've finished one final extended planning session around the dining table, a dull ache has formed behind my forehead. It's only late afternoon, the sunlight turning amber beyond the windows, but I feel as if I've been up for days.

Rollick stands first with a brisk swipe of his hands. "We'll see if that last associate of mine can make it here to smooth along our plans overnight. Either way, we head over to stake out the fortress first thing in the morning. Get plenty of sleep, those of you who need it."

I push back my chair and pull out the phone he gave me. I haven't used it for much so far other than checking the news, which is what I pull up now.

At the headlines that appear on the screen, my pulse stutters. Dominic catches my expression and leans close. "What's wrong?"

I swallow thickly. "Three more attacks. Paris, Toronto,

and Singapore. At least a dozen dead and tons more injured from all of them."

Andreas sidles over, slipping his hand around my elbow. "Has anyone looked into Balthazar yet?"

I tap in a search and bite my lip as I scan the results. "It doesn't look like it. Maybe the guy I gave his name to didn't hear me properly. Or maybe he didn't even listen, he was so sure we were part of the problem."

Jacob joins our huddle, his mouth twisting with a scowl. "We should tell them again. Email all the news stations what we know."

"I don't think they'd believe it." I flick through more articles. "They're still talking as if there aren't real 'monsters,' only some terrorist group that's using it as a moniker with special effects to make them seem supernatural."

One of the shadowkind women has picked up on our conversation. Her head jerks toward us, and she rubs the bark-like skin on her forearms. "We want it to stay that way. You can't tell them about shadowkind. It's bad enough when any mortals get it into their head to come after us."

"I don't think we need to worry about that," Rollick says smoothly, inserting himself into our midst. "I've learned to never underestimate the human capacity for pretending away things they'd rather not accept."

He fixes his gaze on me. "I have a little more work for you to do before you get your rest for the night."

Even though I groan at the thought, I straighten my posture, wanting to put on a good front for the watching shadowkind. I know plenty of them are still skeptical about accepting *us* into their community.

We've got to show we're pulling our own weight, fighting our own battles.

"What's that?" I ask.

The demon motions for me to follow him. "Better done in private. But your three boyfriends here can come along too. They'll make a good selection." He pauses, glancing at Dominic. "And we may need that healing power. I've got a room with a few potted plants."

Dominic gives him a tight smile. "That's all I need."

The guys and I tramp after Rollick through the gleaming halls of his mansion and into a small sitting room. Well, small by the mansion's standards—it's still several times bigger than the cell I was confined in back in the guardians' facility.

The room holds a loveseat and a couple of chairs, a secretary desk, and a small patio-style table. It feels like the kind of space where people might come to eat breakfast or sip tea while gazing out at the view over the grounds outside. There are, as Rollick promised, a few large, leafy plants rising from pots along the wall.

There are also two shadowkind men standing by the loveseat—men I know are among Rollick's closest associates but haven't had much of a chance to talk to outside of our strategizing sessions.

The slimmer, younger-looking man grins at us, his expression as energetic as the wild tumble of his black curls. If I remember right, his name is Lance. It suits him, considering that his most distinguishing feature are those long, vicious-looking claws that protrude from his fingertips.

His companion looks equally intimidating with the square, stony jaw that juts from his face even more strikingly than the rest of his burly physique. It's not hard to see the gargoyle in Crag even when he's in human-like form.

Lance bobs on his feet as if he's getting psyched up for a sports game. "Are we going to start right away?"

I turn to Rollick, my stomach making a seasick sort of lurch. "Start what? What's this about?"

If it requires help from Mr. Claws and Gargoyle Guy, it must be more intense than I assumed.

Rollick drops into one of the armchairs and leans back to take us all in. His speculative expression only increases my apprehension.

The demon clasps his hands together on his lap and offers me a small smile. "Your talents are a major keystone in our plans to take on this genocidal maniac. How often have you used your banshee scream on shadowkind or your fellow shadowbloods?"

My skin goes cold. "I— There was that time when Kudzu and Cinder attacked us, and I stopped them…" And nearly mangled Billy beyond repair when he rushed in trying to help us. Just remembering that moment makes me twice as queasy.

Rollick nods. "And your friends?"

"Never." I almost did, once, when Jacob's early cruelties pushed me close to the breaking point. Instead, I ran away from the possibility of hurting them and got myself hit by a train.

A fact Jake also recalls all too well, I suspect. He steps forward as if he thinks he needs to shield me. "What are you getting at? Of course Riva doesn't attack people who don't deserve it."

The demon gives him a measured look. "All of you will be up against fellow shadowbloods when we go for Balthazar. Potentially a shadowkind or two as well, since we've determined that he's coerced at least a few into working for him."

His gaze slides back to me. "Have you used your banshee skill at all in the past several days? The regular shriek or the new silent version?"

I shake my head slowly, hating the direction of this conversation more with each word that's spoken.

"Well, then," Rollick says. "You should test your limits. See how much pressure you need to apply when it comes to beings with some supernatural defenses—how quickly you can affect them—that sort of thing."

I can't restrain a shudder. "What? I'm not going to hurt—"

He holds up his hand to stop my protest. "I'm not asking you to maim them. Freeze them in place. Feel out where the edge of your ability is, where you'd be able to hurt them. Give them a papercut—you've got your healer standing by. I'm sure they'll recover just fine. And then you'll be properly prepared when it really counts."

My throat constricts. That's why he wanted Jacob and Andreas to come along too—why Lance and Crag are here. Rollick expects me to aim my torturous shriek at them.

Every particle in my body balks at the idea. But I balk against refusing too.

I argued with the demon about testing my powers back when we were first traveling with him. My shaky control is part of the reason I wasn't able to pull back from wrenching Billy apart in time to save him from those injuries.

Dominic won't be able to heal the shadowkind men if I hurt them that badly. He helped Billy a little, but the shadowy essence that makes up their inner workings limited what his talents can do.

I can't let that stop me. Shying away from the brutality inside me has never worked in my favor in the long run.

Do I want to rush into Balthazar's fortress and watch the guys beside me cut down because I didn't realize how forcefully I needed to project my power?

For all I know, I won't be able to tackle fellow shadowbloods with my silent scream at all. It would be useful to know if I should go straight to using my voice. And at lower levels of power, I can simply lock people in place, before I get to the point of maiming them.

It's not as if I can't control it enough to make sure I don't outright *kill* anyone.

My teeth have gritted. I force them apart. "Fine. How do you think we should start?"

Rollick tips his head toward his shadowkind companions. "Why don't you begin with these louts? Full shadowkind should be trickier than hybrids, and they'll heal faster. You'll have a better idea how to moderate yourself with your men afterward."

A flicker of doubt crosses Lance's face. "The scream—

it doesn't make people *do* things under your control, does it?"

"No," I say quickly. "If it works, it'll lock you in place so you can't move, and I might do a little damage accidentally, but I can't force you to walk or talk or anything."

His momentary tension vanishes behind another grin. "All right, then."

Crag squares his bulky shoulders, his voice a low rumble. "I'm ready."

I wish I was. I inhale deeply and reach down to the vibration of energy that's always inside me, if faint when I'm not angry.

It doesn't take much to stir up the hunger for pain. I prod it with memories of the destruction I've seen on the news, of the murders Balthazar committed before my eyes and the ones he threatened.

The vicious, starving thing resonates up from my chest to the back of my mouth. But I'm not going to let it out that way, not if I don't have to.

I hold myself rigidly under control, aware of my targets while I train my focus, and hone my thoughts into the thinnest possible shriek that I aim at the figures in front of me.

With mortals—humans or animals—I think it'd be enough to freeze them in place. The two shadowkind men only twitch at my efforts. Lance tilts his head, proving he's not frozen yet.

So Rollick was right. It is going to take more oomph for my powers to affect shadowkind.

I don't know if we'll encounter any at Balthazar's fortress, but I need to be ready either way.

My muscles tensing, I push my silent scream harder and louder inside my head. Ramping it up by careful degrees, hoping I won't accidentally make too large a leap.

Nothing happens.

My eyes snap shut of my own accord. I *feel* the shadowkind across the room from me, two solid presences, and shriek with an extra jolt of might.

Finally, the scream connects. My mind floods with the awareness of their bodies, every bit of bone and flesh I could break to deal out the agony my monstrous side craves. Just a sip—

It happens so fast I can't catch it in time. The knuckle of a little finger cracks.

I wrench my attention away and yank my eyelids open to see Lance holding up his hand, eyeing it with an air of curiosity even though his jaw has tightened. His smallest finger juts at an unnatural angle.

Even as my stomach flips over, Dominic hurries to the shadowkind's side. "Here," he says, reaching for Lance's hand. "I don't even need the plants to mend this small an injury."

Lance lets out a dry chuckle and looks past Dom to where I'm standing. "That's some tricksy talent you've got there. I'm glad we're on your side."

"Me too," I mumble. "I'm sorry."

Rollick waves off my concern. "It's fine. You did well. He can endure a lot worse than a broken finger. Now let's see if you can inflict your power without any wounds this time."

Again? A shiver runs down my spine, but I swallow my protests.

I have to get this right. I have to prove that I won't make a mistake like I did with Billy—to our reluctant allies and to myself.

My second silent scream works faster, because I know approximately how much more force I need to put into it, but I keep an even tighter rein. It wraps around the shadowkind men, but I manage to resist the temptation of their tender points.

The headache that started earlier is expanding across my skull. On my third try, I test how it works when I let out a whisper of sound instead of keeping my mouth shut.

A cut opens between Crag's thumb and forefinger. I clamp down on the urge to drink in more pain, flattening the shriek so it's barely audible at all and then cutting it off when I'm sure I'm controlling it.

Dominic motions to the gargoyle, but Crag lifts his arm toward me first, sending a tiny wisp of his smoky essence into the air. Shadowkind don't bleed at all, at least not anything resembling mortal blood.

"Nothing but a scratch," he says.

I swipe my sweaty palms against my pants, dreading the next step but knowing I have to get there eventually, and meet Rollick's gaze. "I think I have a pretty good sense of what it's like with shadowkind now."

He inclines his head. "Then we should move on to shadowbloods."

Jacob marches into the middle of the room in front of me with no further prompting. He stations himself with his arms crossed over his chest and his chin firm. "You need this, Wildcat. Making sure you'll be at the top of your game is worth a little pain."

Andreas gets into position beside him, his posture relaxed but his gray eyes dark. "Don't worry about us," he tells me. "We can handle it."

They shouldn't have to. But it's almost definite that I'll be fighting other shadowbloods at some point. I need as clear an idea as possible of how to handle them if I'm going to take them out quickly—and avoid breaking my own men in the process.

I start with the silent shriek again, tentative at first. My sense of the guys' bodies sharpens immediately, but I can't tell if that's only because of the innate connection we share.

It isn't enough to trap them. Jacob adjusts his weight on his feet as if to show that he's still mobile.

My fingers curl into my palms, my claws itching at the tips. I ramp up my mental scream a little farther, and a little farther again, and—

Jacob and Andreas jerk and stiffen. Even as I reel back the force of the shriek, a waft of pain hits me, the hunger inside me absorbing it with sickening eagerness.

Drey's foot. When I release them, he stumbles—but Dominic is there to catch him.

Andreas can't contain a hiss as he sinks onto the loveseat. A burn forms behind my eyes as I watch Dom seal the bones and sinews I fractured.

Even with the men I love, some part of me is *happy* to hurt them.

Rollick clears his throat. "How did that compare to the shadowkind?"

I blink, willing back the tears, and do my best to even out my voice. "Easier than with them, but still harder than regular people. I'll probably want to use my voice if I need to hit hard and fast and I don't need to be totally stealthy about it."

The demon hums to himself. "That makes sense. It seems wise to attempt a few more trial runs, don't you think?"

Jacob nods, holding my gaze steadily.

Andreas is already pushing back to his feet. "I'm good; I'm good. No sweat."

It takes me a moment to clear the blur of moisture from my eyes. I'm doing this for them, I remind myself. So that when it's actually life or death, I'll deal out death where it belongs.

"Okay," I say with a rasp. "From the top."

If we do this right, as soon as tomorrow there could be no more need for carnage.

SEVEN

Riva

The breeze cools with the falling darkness. I pull my hoodie tighter around me and finally turn back toward the mansion.

I'd hoped the fresh air and solitude would settle my nerves. I slipped away after our hasty dinner, shaking my head at Griffin when he shot me a questioning glance and counting on him to stop the other guys from following.

He must have been able to tell I needed the time to myself, because I remained undisturbed while I wandered among the trees that surround Rollick's mansion.

The crisp smells of the greenery and the murmur of the breeze through the leaves do set a peaceful atmosphere. That atmosphere hasn't quite penetrated the tension twisted up inside me, though.

I'm not sure anything would.

When I enter the house, a hush fills the halls. I think most of the shadowkind have retreated into the darkness for the night rather than keep their physical forms. But on my way to the guest bedrooms, I catch female voices filtering from a doorway.

It's the kitchen. I pause a couple of steps from the threshold, keeping my silence as I take in the puzzling scene.

Toni stands by the stove, her back to me, stirring something in a pot that wafts a creamy, sweet scent. Pearl has hopped up on the island kitty-corner to her, watching with an avid expression.

"You learned how to make this stuff in India?" she says.

Toni nods. "It's better with saffron and cardamom, but it doesn't look like your boss keeps that wide a variety of spices."

Pearl laughs. "I don't think he does much cooking. A benefit of not needing to eat food: you can wait until there's something really worth tasting. Did you usually learn stuff from the local people wherever *your* boss took you?"

Toni hesitates before she answers. "Not exactly. I didn't really have time. But Willa—his wife—always made a point of mingling with the locals and picking up customs from them. She had a knack for knowing which ones I'd be interested in hearing about too."

Her voice has softened with that last sentence. Pearl's expression softens too. She leans closer as if drawn by the audible emotion. "She meant a lot to you. Tell me about her?"

Toni's head jerks toward the succubus in apparent

surprise, giving me a view of her face in profile. Of the surprise fading into something both sad and grateful.

Has she been able to talk about the woman she loved with *anyone* since Willa's death? It isn't as if she could have commiserated with Balthazar in his grief and admitted she'd carried a torch for his wife.

She gives Pearl a small smile and turns back to the pot. "Her favorite of Mr. Balthazar's regular haunts was his place in Croatia. She always said…"

I walk on as she continues, my skin itching with the sense that I'm intruding on a private moment. I hadn't realized Pearl had taken any particular interest in the full human in our midst, but maybe it only just happened because of whatever Toni's cooking.

Even Toni, adrift from her career and everyone she knew before she met us shadowbloods, has someone to spill her feelings to. A starker uneasiness rolls over me, an impression of being far more alone than I've ever wanted.

I'm not really on my own, of course. I'm aware of all five of my guys through our connection, as they must be of me.

Zian and Andreas have gone to their respective bedrooms. Jacob, Griffin, and Dominic are farther away, gathered in one of the common rooms.

I waver in momentary indecision, and my gut tugs me toward the room that's currently Zian's.

He'll know it's me before I even knock on the door. His "Come in" carries through before the rap of my knuckles against the wood has faded.

I ease inside and find him sitting in the armchair next to

the bed, just turning off the small TV mounted over the dresser. My gaze sticks to the screen for a second as I wonder what new horrific scenes might have been playing out there, but I don't think witnessing them will do me any good.

Zian gets up and comes over to me with the strange mix of eagerness and hesitation that's become the norm since we finally hooked up. He stops a couple of feet away but reaches out to touch my arm. "Is everything all right?"

I grimace. "In theory. I'm just—I'm worried about tomorrow."

Zian's eyebrows lift slightly. "And you came to me to talk about it? I mean—not that I'm complaining…" He trails off awkwardly.

I guess it might seem like it'd make more sense for me to seek out Andreas's easy-going reassurance or Dominic's thoughtful consideration, or even Griffin's calming powers. But it was Zian who helped me the most when I was grappling with the kind of situation I'm stressing about now.

I ease closer, taking his other hand and gazing up into his dark eyes. "You know more than anyone else what it's like to have something monstrous in you that takes over if you lose control of your emotions. To be afraid of how you'll react if you're pushed too far."

Zee frowns, stroking his thumb over my elbow. "Is someone pushing you?"

"I don't know. It's just—after Rollick had me practice my shriek on Jake and Drey this afternoon—" I exhale in a ragged rush. "I keep remembering how angry I got when Balthazar had us trapped. I don't know how I'm going to feel when we find him, thinking of all the awful things he's done since."

"We've been in a lot of intense fights before," Zian points out. "You've never hurt any of us accidentally."

"It's not just you guys, though. We know that at least Nadia and Devon are being held in the Romanian base, and there'll be other shadowbloods there. Even if they were criminals, we don't know what crimes they committed or why. *We've* done illegal things trying to survive. Balthazar could be forcing them—they don't necessarily deserve to die like he does."

Zee is silent for a moment as if thinking over what I've said. "You're afraid that you'll be so angry when we're confronting him that you might take too much of it out on them?"

I sigh and tip my head against his chest—tentatively, giving him time to back away if it's too much physical closeness. "Something like that. I just have no idea how it's going to be."

Zian tenses for only an instant before he slides his brawny arm right around me, holding me against his huge frame. "You don't seem angry like you did before, when it was really bad. Back then, we didn't have anything to hope for. We're free now, and we've got strong allies and a good plan. I don't think you'd feel that 'pushed' again."

I relax a little into his embrace as I absorb his words. "That's true. It's not the same situation."

"And anyway, the whole plan is about getting to Balthazar before he knows he needs to defend himself. If his new shadowbloods attack us after he's dead, then that's their choice, nothing he's making them do. We've all agreed that if we have to fight any of them beforehand, we'll knock them out rather than killing them unless we absolutely have to."

"It's hard to believe it'll be that easy."

"Yeah." Zian lets out a rough chuckle and pulls back just enough to look down at me. "But the most important thing is stopping Balthazar, right? Stopping him and the new shadowbloods from hurting more people. That's got to be the right thing to do. And the shadowbloods he made—they're not really the same as us. They haven't been through all the stuff we and the kids have."

I know what he means, but something inside me resists accepting it. We might not have the same history as the criminals Balthazar has forced into his army, but we're the only people who can understand what they are, that unnerving mix of human and monster.

Talking to him has smoothed out the sharpest edges of my worries, though.

I give him a slight smile and realize I don't really want to leave. I want to stay right here with the comfort of his solid warmth.

Zee and I haven't had much time to enjoy his deepening recovery from *his* traumatic past. Even the one time we had sex, we weren't alone. He wanted Dominic there to intervene if one of his violent panics came over him.

I roll the question around on my tongue before allowing myself to speak. "Could I sleep here tonight?"

Zian stiffens, but the flash of emotion that crosses his face is more elation than anything else. The pheromones of desire lace the air. "You—you'd really want to? I might still react badly, especially when I'm not really conscious…"

I squeeze his hand in mine. "I'm not worried. I can get out of the way if you lash out, but I don't think that's going to happen. You don't have any bad associations with *beds*, right?"

A hopeful smile curls the corner of his lips. "No, I don't." As he holds my gaze, a deeper smolder comes into his eyes, the scent of his eagerness thickening. "Did you only want to *sleep*?"

When he says it like that, with a soft growl of hunger in his voice, my whole body wakes up with my own desire. A quiver of anticipation shoots through my nerves.

I smile back at him. "I can think of lots of other things we can do in bed that I'm sure I'd enjoy."

With a rough noise in his throat, Zian cups my jaw and lifts my face to meet his kiss.

The press of his mouth against mine isn't as tentative as our first explorations with intimacy. He's still gentle, but his lips coax mine apart with a sear of his breath. As he deepens the kiss, he tugs me even closer.

It's a greater thrill than I can express to be able to loop my arms around his neck and give myself over to the moment, knowing he's shaken off the pain of the past enough that he welcomes my touch.

Without warning, Zian slips his arm down my side and hefts me into the air like I weigh nothing at all. His mouth still melded with mine, he walks me over to the bed and lays me out on the covers.

As he looms over me, he eases back from the kiss. His lips brand my cheek, my neck.

"There are so many things I've imagined doing with you. So many things I want to try."

I beam up at him, tracing the ridges of his impressive chest through the thin fabric of his tee. "We can do all of them—tonight or later. I'm looking forward to everything."

He pauses and catches my gaze. "Did you like everything we did last time? Everything that happened… even at the end?"

A flush deepens the ruddiness of his peachy-brown cheeks. I think I know what he's talking about—the sudden, intense fullness that stretched my pussy right as he came.

It was one of the headiest sensations I've ever experienced. I grin up at him. "Absolutely."

His eyes gleam with relief and renewed hunger. "I— you still have the birth control implant the guardians put in, right?"

I break into a laugh. "I'd be having a lot less fun with all of you if I didn't."

Zian grins back at me and skims his fingers to the hem of my shirt so he can tug it upward. I raise my arms to let him peel it off, but once he's flung it aside, he hesitates again and simply gazes down at my partly bared body.

I caress his face, so much love filling my chest that it condenses into the sweetest of aches. "You don't have to hold back with me. You know that, right? I might be a shrimp, but this body is just as strong as yours."

A hint of amusement sparks in Zee's dark gaze. "The strongest of all of us."

"Well, I don't know about that. But it could be

interesting to see just how well-matched we are." My grin comes back. "You were always my favorite sparring partner."

Zian sputters a laugh that has another growl mixed in and bows his head to claim my mouth.

Between kisses, I yank off his shirt too. When I arch up so he can unclasp my bra, he steals the opportunity to bring his mouth to my breasts. We might not have had much chance to practice this particular act yet, but the lap of his eager tongue and the scrape of his teeth have me gasping in an instant.

My fingers clutch at his smooth hair. Zian groans and sucks my other nipple into his mouth.

My hand traces down his chest toward the bulge behind his jeans. I can't quite reach it, but when I lift my knee to stroke against it, my wolfish lover mumbles a heated curse against my skin.

"I don't want to wait," he rasps, groping for the fly of my cargo pants. "We took it so slow before. Now I just need to be inside you."

At the graze of his fingertips over my dampened panties, a pulse of pleasure radiates from my core. I whimper my agreement.

Zee pulls my pants off, and I wriggle out of my panties. He lowers his head over my cunt with a sound that's almost a snarl. "But first…"

He swipes his tongue over my slit. Bliss rushes up from my clit, and a cry quavers from my lips.

Zian hums his approval at my response, the vibration only heightening the sensations he's provoking. He devours my pussy whole, like it's a meal he's waited all his life to enjoy, and I can't do anything but buck against his mouth and swallow the moans that would ring through the entire mansion.

Plenty of urgent noises leak from my lips anyway. I shudder and clutch at Zian, riding out wave after wave of delight.

He lifts his head with a gush of ragged breath and licks his lips. Fanged points glint within his mouth.

His question comes out haltingly. "When we— Will it always be like the first time? With our powers coming out?"

Memories swim up of my more recent interludes with the other guys. "No. It's just the first time that's particularly intense." I pause, and a smile I suspect looks a little wicked crosses my face. "But you can let out the wolf-man as much as you want. I liked it."

A rumble thrums from Zian's chest. His expression turns speculative, and then he wraps his arm around me to flip me onto my hands and knees.

My breath gusts out of me. He dapples my back with scorching kisses as he sheds his jeans, and then he delves his hand between my legs.

"You think you can take all of it?" he murmurs.

A giddy shiver passes through my body. Zian is big *everywhere*.

But I wasn't lying when I said I loved sparring with him during our old training sessions in the facility. Pitting my compact strength against his brawn was always a thrill.

I don't see why this should be any different.

"Everything you can give me," I reply.

His choked sound of need spills across my spine with a

huff of breath. Then he's nudging the head of his cock between my thighs.

Fuck, it's good. I couldn't be more wet for him, and the stretch of accommodating his girth has me panting for more. Pleasure zings through every nerve.

I can't restrain a keening that's close to a whine. My fingers dig into the pillow they're braced against. "Go as hard and fast as feels good. I'll be right here with you."

Zian lets out a hiss that might contain a curse and thrusts deeper into me. I moan and spread my legs wider to give him access.

As he grasps my hip, he starts building a rhythm. He pounds into me with increasing force, each thrust a little faster than the one before.

The impact radiates through my muscles with a blissful burn. I sway back to meet him—and jolt forward with each smack of our bodies colliding.

My forehead nearly bangs against the headboard. I lift myself against it, folding my arms over the curved wooden edge and holding on as if for dear life.

Zee groans and reaches around me to palm one breast. The wolfish claws he's partly extended nick my skin with pinpricks of the sharpest bliss.

"Love this feeling," he mutters against my back. "Love *you*. My Riva."

I let out an inarticulate noise of agreement. "Love you too. Feels so good, Zee."

He groans and slams into me even harder. My body rocks to meet him, absorbing the force and the rising bliss that comes with it.

As the pleasure swells inside me, the headboard shakes

in my grip. I clutch it tighter and push myself back into Zian's thrusts, hungry for even more.

His hand on my hip tucks around to stroke my clit, and more delight sweeps through me. At my breathless cry, he flicks a claw right over that sensitive spot just as he drives home yet again.

My vision shatters with a blaze of white. Ecstasy whirls through me like a hurricane.

I'm soaring on the high of pleasure, vaguely aware of Zian's muscles bulging larger above me, a snarled groan on his lips, a sense of something monstrous but still him following me over the edge. Then my pussy throbs with a deeper strength as the base of his cock expands inside me.

Like it did that first time.

The thickened bulge presses against the ring of muscle around my opening with the same heady burn as before and sends me spiraling into a fresh rush of bliss. If that's part of his wolf-man shift, then I'll welcome it every time.

As our movements slow, Zian keeps holding me, swaying with me. He stays buried deep inside me as if locked in place by that thickened ring.

I relax into the sensations, letting them flow through me in giddy ripples. When Zee dips his head to kiss my shoulder, I hum happily.

"No one else fills me quite like you do," I murmur, glancing over at him.

The wolfish cast that came over his face is fading. A flush that's more than just the exertion creeps up his neck at my remark.

Then he hugs me against his chest. "It means you're literally stuck with me, at least for a little while."

A giggle tumbles from my lips. "I have no problem with that at all."

The surface beneath my hands wobbles. I raise my head, releasing the headboard with one hand to swipe at the sweaty strands of hair clinging to my forehead.

The top section of the wooden slab topples over onto the pillow in front of me. I freeze, my jaw dropping open.

"Um… I think I broke your bed." It's split with a crack that formed along the grain of the wood. A crack I'm pretty sure didn't exist before I grabbed hold of the thing.

Zian peers at it alongside me. Then a deep chuckle resounds from his chest. "Don't know your own strength, huh." He nuzzles the back of my neck. "I'll take part of the blame. But somehow I don't think Rollick will be that upset about it."

Knowing the demon, he'll probably find it amusing. I nudge the broken piece up against the remaining headboard and sag into the covers. "When we have our own house, we'll have to get stronger beds."

If only all our problems came with such a simple solution.

EIGHT

Silence cloaks the craggy slopes of the mountains along with the thickening dusk. I draw up my legs on the rock ledge where I'm perched and hug my knees.

Sorsha has used her fiery powers to warm the area of our camp against the cold of the season and the altitude, but gusts of biting wind penetrate it here at the edge. I curl my fingers in my wool gloves and tune out the discomfort.

Inside, I'm focused on my sense of Balthazar's presence using the talent I've once again borrowed from Griffin. A small laminated map of this stretch of the Carpathian range sits on the gritty rock beside me. I don't even look at it as my finger taps a slow path toward our location.

The six of us shadowbloods, Sorsha, and a handful of shadowkind including Rollick arrived in the mountains yesterday. We made a slow, careful trek to the campsite

Rollick's people had picked out as they investigated the area, following a route they also picked out to avoid any of Balthazar's more distant security measures.

We're right at the edge of his sphere of detection now. The mountainside base lies about a hundred feet below me, invisible at this distance other than a narrow stone lip Crag pointed out to me that he said is the top of the entrance.

While we've been staked out here waiting for our enemy's arrival, the other shadowkind working alongside us have spread out in a wide ring around the base. They'll report back to Rollick if they notice anything that could interfere with our plans—and interfere themselves if more manpower arrives from outside the base.

If we're really lucky, one of those powerful beings will spot the maniac himself and end his life before the rest of us need to move one inch farther. But I'm becoming increasingly sure there's no chance of that.

Andreas comes up beside me and sinks down onto the ledge. "Still getting closer?" he murmurs under his breath.

I nod. I first charted Balthazar's movements toward the base around the middle of the afternoon, from someplace in northern Russia where Toni confirmed he has property. We became increasingly sure he was coming specifically here and not some other place to the south as the hours went on.

Now he's only a few miles away. And he's slowed down as if he's making a final approach. But Rollick's people haven't reported any sign of him back to us.

"He's almost here," I say, matching Drey's soft tone. "But he's got to have some secret way of arriving through the mountains, or one of the shadowkind would have seen him."

Andreas glances around over the steep mountain slopes. Up here, there's barely any vegetation other than patches of coarse grass and an occasional withered shrub.

He motions to the landscape with a flick of his coppery-brown hand. "There are a lot of nooks and crannies across the mountains. Areas it's hard to see unless you're right on top of them. We'd need thousands of beings to keep an eye on every entry point."

And Balthazar is still moving fast enough that my ability to pinpoint his location doesn't do us much good. By the time I'm sure of one exact location, he's already left it behind.

All I know for sure is that he's on his way, and he'll be arriving within minutes.

I lean forward a few inches to peer down the slope through the hazy twilight. "Obviously he wasn't coming by helicopter. At least not using the helipad we know about."

There's a smooth stretch of rock about a hundred feet below and to the left of the base's most obvious entrance, with scuff marks indicating it's been landed on before. Back when Balthazar didn't have to worry about his former shadowblood captives coming after him, I guess.

I turn my attention inward again and let my finger fall to the map. The side of the tip brushes the bump I marked to indicate the base.

My pulse hitches. "He's practically inside."

Andreas raises his head. "Time to move out, Tink?"

"Let me just... Let me just make sure he's staying

there." I wouldn't put it past the psychopath to suspect we were tracking him and fly by overhead just to confuse us.

We can't make any mistakes with this plan. And our time to pull it off properly will be so limited.

It all comes down to the six of us and Sorsha, really. After further examination, the shadowkind decided it was too risky to try to carve a path through the protective metals embedded in the rock around the base. Especially when the associate Rollick was hoping would contribute never turned up.

I hope that's not a bad omen. Rollick assured me that he never explained exactly what he needed the shadowkind he reached out to for, that there's no way he could have betrayed our intentions to anyone, but the reminder that even his connections are fallible leaves a queasy sensation in my gut.

In the end, it all comes down to surprise. Balthazar can't know we're coming. And ripping up the mountainside is the kind of thing that's awfully hard to hide.

We've got plenty of power of our own—partly thanks to our former captor. I smile grimly to myself.

I'm looking forward to demonstrating the results of his efforts on the man himself.

The next fall of my finger lands directly on the bump. I wait a minute, counting out the seconds in my head, and reach my mind toward my sense of Balthazar again.

Still right on the base. He isn't going any farther—at least not immediately.

I push to my feet, my pulse drumming behind my sternum. "All right. Let's do this."

We tramp up the slope to the small plateau where we set up our inconspicuous camp. At the sight of me, my other guys hurry over to join us. No one says a word, but anticipation laces the cool air.

Rollick and Sorsha come over as well. The demon studies my expression. "I take it that it's time."

I swallow past the nervous lump in my throat, my hand rising instinctively to where my cat-and-yarn charm is tucked behind my coat. "Yeah."

"Well, you know the plan. We'll be here to lend whatever help we can."

Andreas looks us over. "Does everyone have what they need? We'll want to get moving as soon as I'm finished."

The guys incline their heads all around our loose circle. Drey reaches for Dominic first.

Thanks to the procedures Balthazar put us through, Andreas can turn other people invisible as well as himself. But the effect only lasts so long—and he's stretching his strength to the limit working his power on all seven of us.

When we tried it out back at the Spanish mansion, the invisibility held for less than an hour. We hoped that swapping the power between us so we could each work it on ourselves might make it more potent, but we quickly discovered that as soon as Andreas passed it on to anyone else, his own invisibility faded.

So we're stuck with a time limit on our concealment. And we worked out who Drey should erase first based on who can most easily fall back without screwing up the plan.

He works quickly through our group, moving to me

and Sorsha last. She's got the most firepower—literally—out of all of us, and I'm the swiftest and fastest killer.

I've returned Griffin's locating skill to him because I don't have any map of the base to use it on. But he has his own methods of finding Balthazar now that the man is close.

His soft voice carries from the seemingly empty space where he's standing. "I can feel him down there—the same kind of impressions I got from him in the villa. He's tense but pleased about something… in an unnerving way."

"Probably plotting how many people he's going to send his army to murder next," I mutter as my body fades from view.

Andreas gives my arm a quick caress as he lets go of me, and we set off.

The six of us shadowbloods can keep track of each other through our awareness of our powers. Sorsha follows along with a faint tendril of warmth she wraps around my invisible wrist.

We clamber quietly down the slope past the ledge where I tracked Balthazar's movements. Past a surveillance camera that's got nothing to see and motion sensors reliant on visuals.

But those aren't the only security measures Balthazar has taken against beings who aren't affected by silver and iron. Closer to the base entrance lies a ring of pressure sensors.

Zian lets out a quiet hiss to draw us to a halt. There's a faint glimmer of ruddy light as he uses his vision to sever some of the wires.

Sorsha will be melting others with her phoenix fire,

but she doesn't give any visible sign of that. Only a brief waft of heat gives any indication that she's done her work.

She clicks her tongue to indicate that she's finished. We can't talk at all now, not when we aren't sure how closely Balthazar might be monitoring audio around his hideout.

Two men stand guard in the arch of the entrance carved into the mountainside. The heavy hooded parkas they wear against the mountain chill work in our favor.

As Dominic saps the life out of them from a short distance, the ruff of their hoods hides the slackening of their faces. Jacob uses his telekinesis to "walk" them back against the stone walls. He snaps off shards of rock that he jabs through their coats from behind to hold them steady.

To any watching cameras, it'll look as if they're simply leaning at their posts.

A quiver passes through the air as Zian accepts Jacob's power. Getting the door open without setting off any alarms depends on him.

With Rollick's connections, the demon was able to dig up various purchase and construction agreements and determine what sort of locks Balthazar favors. Zian spent the better part of the last two days studying their inner workings.

I can only stand there, nerves twanging, while he peers through the steel slab of the door with his X-ray sight and brings Jacob's telekinesis to bear on the intricate pieces.

For a minute, there's nothing but the howl of the wind beyond the doorway and a deepening chill that Sorsha can't risk warming away when we're this close. Then, after a muffled exhalation of relief, the door whirs open.

We hurry past it and send it sliding shut in our wake.

The hall on the other side provokes an uncomfortable twinge of familiarity. The carved stone surfaces look an awful lot like the passages that wound through the mountain at the island facility where we were held by a different former captive.

Clancy wasn't quite as insane as Balthazar is, but he was just as eager to use us for his purposes. I can't say any of my memories of him are remotely happy.

Griffin takes the lead, with tiny nudges of our emotions that give us a sense of where to follow him. At his mental touch, the side doors strike me as dull, the hall ahead of us more enticing.

I stride forward, tuning out the memories of being trapped—both physically and emotionally—as well as I can. Even the mineral scent in the air stirs up more recollections of our former island prison.

Another man comes striding along the hallway toward us, and we flatten ourselves against the wall to let him pass. There's no point in causing more of a commotion than we need to if we can avoid notice completely.

We turn a corner and come to a stairwell. As quickly as possible, we slip past the door and follow Griffin's eager signals down, two floors lower.

My mouth has gone dry. I wet my lips and try to estimate how much time has already passed. Fifteen minutes? Twenty?

How much longer do we have until our disguise falters? Andreas's powers aren't an exact science.

If only I had a watch… Of course, I wouldn't be able to see it.

The thought brings a brief spark of amusement that's quickly swallowed up by my nervousness. We dart out into the hallway Griffin indicates and trail after him to the left.

The stone-walled hallway down here is narrower than the one above, the ceiling lower. My chest constricts with the growing sense of them closing in. An image of the windowless room Clancy kept me trapped in between training sessions floats in the back of my mind.

I broke free of that place, and we'll break out any shadowbloods trapped here too. After we've dealt with our most psychotic captor for the last time.

Griffin's progress ahead of us slows. My body tenses in anticipation.

Then he stops completely, right by a plain white door that looks just like the other doors dotting the hallway. But his certainty that our target waits on the other side flows into me with his power.

Now it's up to the rest of us to see the final part of the plan through.

Mostly, it comes down to me.

I think of Balthazar's uncaring expression while fourteen-year-old Lindsay bled out on his villa floor. Of the plastic case that enclosed Dominic while he left my tentacled guy in a coma for weeks.

Of the rocks falling on our heads in a passage even narrower than this one, one last attempt at caging us in and preventing our escape from his beautiful prison.

A brutal vibration grips the base of my throat. I focus my mind on it and reach out to touch Jacob where I can sense him standing near me—my signal that I'm ready.

He steps toward the door. I don't know whether it's even locked, but if it is, he makes quick work of the deadbolt.

He shoves the door wide with an invisible burst of energy, and I spring over the threshold.

If Balthazar's desk had been set right across from the door, I think I'd have killed him that instant. But all I see in my first glimpse of the room are a pair of matching bookcases—which Sorsha promptly sends up in flames.

As I spin around, catching sight of the desk next to the door and the burly man behind it at the edge of my vision, Balthazar jerks to his feet. He slams his broad hand down on some control I don't have time to scrutinize.

Before I can process any more than that, a piercing shriek that has nothing to do with me splits through the air. It rattles my eardrums and scatters my thoughts, smashing straight through my focus.

I lose my grip on my power. My hands clamp instinctively over my ears as pain spikes through my skull.

In that first moment, I can't see the others, only feel their own agony radiating through our bond. Then the air wavers around me.

Our invisibility is faltering. I catch sight of Dominic's grimacing face, Sorsha plugging her ears with her fingers and whipping around with a sway of her feet—

As we pop into sight, Balthazar is disappearing. His head is just ducking under an opening where he kicked aside a rug beyond his desk.

Bursts of fire shoot up from the desk and the rug, but the deafening siren has obviously shattered Sorsha's concentration too. She staggers and then aims a hostile look at the device sitting on the corner of the desk.

Another rush of flames shoots up there, and the sound squeals out.

"Come on!" Jacob says in a ragged voice, and lurches toward the trap door Balthazar vanished through.

Sorsha leaps after him and swears. I understand why when I jump after them a moment later.

We've ended up in a thin tunnel carved into the mountain. A tunnel where water is spraying from fixtures on the walls and ceiling, like a fire sprinkler system gone haywire. The pale lights spaced several feet apart along the passage glint off the droplets.

Sorsha sputters and swipes her wet hair back from her face. "I can't send a blast of fire after him through this. Now I *really* don't like this jerk."

I push past her and Jacob. "I'll try to get to him."

My pulse racing, I dash across the slick stone floor. My supernaturally powered muscles can propel me forward faster than anyone other than Zian, and the water can't interfere with my banshee scream if I project it with my mind.

As I hurtle onward, my soaked clothes dragging at my limbs, my irritation grows. It fuels the new shriek building in my lungs.

Balthazar can't get away with this. He can't *get away*. I have to stop him.

We're so fucking close.

I shove myself off the tight walls and around a corner —into a widening of the tunnel that's almost a room. And six figures step out in a line, blocking my way through.

I jerk to a halt, staring through the continued spray at the determined faces forming a barrier between me and Balthazar, however far ahead of us he's gotten.

There's Nadia, her thick black pixie cut slicked to her skull with the water. And Tegan, the little twelve-year-old whose perpetually wide eyes gleam with a hardness that makes my stomach clench.

Devon stands with them too, and three other teens I vaguely recognize from the island facility but whose names I never learned. Fellow shadowbloods.

Why are they looking at me like *I'm* the enemy?

"Move!" I gasp out. "I've got to catch up with him."

"We have to do this," Nadia replies tightly. A familiar silver manacle gleams around her wrist—around all of their wrists. "We can't let you go after him."

Sorsha and Zian hurtle into the room behind me. I can sense the other guys not far behind.

With a jolt of panic, I fling out my arms. "Don't hurt them! They're the ones we're here to save."

Except the shadowblood kids seem to have the exact opposite idea.

Nadia's eyes flash with an unsettling light. "Go back! Get out of here!"

"I can't," I retort, tensing to push between her and the others. "I have to—"

I move to spring in mid-sentence—but the young shadowbloods beat me to the punch.

It feels like a punch: the blaze of light that rushes at us with the thrust of Nadia's arms. My vision blurs to gray, and a blast of air sends me crashing into Zian.

A rumble sounds behind us. Dominic's voice calls out,

taut and frantic. "There's more water coming—enough to flood the tunnel!"

Hasty footsteps pound away from us. I stagger, blinking hard and seeing nothing but drifting blotches. A gush of water gathers around my feet.

Jacob swears and stumbles past me. "Zee—how close are we to the surface? Can we break through the wall?"

Zian must be as blind as I am, but apparently his X-ray vision still works well enough for him to judge. "Not far. Hit it hard!"

I fling myself after them, lending my own strength to the task. Jacob slams out his telekinetic talent and Zian batters the stone surface with both his arms and his searing eyes.

The rumble rises. The wall cracks and crumbles.

Just as the roar of the wave reaches the room, we burst out into the cold night air. I snatch at my sense of Andreas's presence and Griffin's. Dominic latches on to us with his tentacles.

The water rams into us from behind, sending us tumbling partway down the rocky slope in a jumble of limbs. My butt jars against a boulder.

I rub my eyes, fragmented vision returning. As I shove myself to my feet, I spin toward Griffin.

The look on his face as he pushes the drenched strands of his hair away from his eyes makes my heart sink. He turns his head toward the mountainside.

"Balthazar's gone. He's already too far away for me to clearly track him."

NINE

Riva

Fang smacks his hands against the dining room table, his exhalation hissing around his protruding canines. "Let me get this straight. You had him right there in front of you, and you still didn't manage to kill this one mortal?"

I grimace at his tone even as my own frustration sweeps through me all over again. "He was prepared—he had this device that totally shattered our concentration. We can't use our talents if we can't even *think*."

Shanty tosses her dark blue waves over her shoulder and purses her lips. Her voice stays melodic even when criticizing us, which makes more sense now that I know she's a siren. "None of you could manage to attack him at all?"

Sorsha pipes up before I have to go on defending myself. "I was there too—whatever he used, he designed it very effectively. I couldn't focus enough to aim my fire.

And after I burned down his villa in Italy, he knew to take specific precautions against my powers. This guy thinks of everything."

I glance down the table toward Rollick, but the demon has been unusually solemn since we returned to his mansion in Spain. I'm hoping he's just thinking over everything we told him and processing our failure rather than debating continuing to help us at all.

Even the shadowkind who supported us whole-heartedly before have faltered in their confidence.

Thorn rubs his mouth and casts a concerned look at Sorsha. "It does seem odd that he had so many measures in place. Is there some way he could have known we'd strike there?"

Lance's unnerving violet eyes flash toward the shadowblood end of the table. "Maybe he has some tricksy way of tracking this bunch that we haven't figured out."

Toni, who's been downcast since we arrived and filled her in on our futile efforts, lifts her head. "No. I saw the monitoring system he had set up. He trusted the bracelets would be more than enough."

"I've checked us over for any kind of internal device," Zian puts in, flexing his shoulders as if daring anyone to challenge his thoroughness.

Jacob braces his hands against the tabletop. "Why do you think we need your help at all? This guy is a maniac, and a fucking smart one. We barely got away from him alive, and we only did because you were helping us then too. We almost died *this* time."

A shudder runs down my back at the memory of the rush of water. The chill that gripped me in my drenched clothes as we staggered across the mountain, all of us too busy blasting through the outer guards to worry about comfort.

Once we made it across the border of protective metals, the shadowkind closed in around us like our own personal guard and Sorsha wrapped us in fiery heat.

But there's still a chunk of ice in the pit of my stomach, thinking of the opportunity we lost. Of the people we left behind.

"We weren't totally prepared ourselves," Griffin says softly, presumably picking up on my feelings. "We thought the shadowblood kids in the base were prisoners, hostages. But it seems that he's managed to enhance their powers after all, maybe using the same process that's transforming regular humans into new shadowbloods."

We hadn't mentioned that part to the larger group yet. At Sorsha's side, the youthful-looking man with the blond curls, who I now know as Snap, knits his brow. "He's made the younger ones like you who were at the same facilities stronger? They stopped your attack?"

"Yes," I say with a heavy heart. "They got in our way when we were running after Balthazar. They definitely acted different—and one of them... Before, she could only give off a glow from her skin, nothing all that extreme. Last night, she blinded us with the light, it blazed so bright."

Dominic nods. "One of the others had some kind of control over the air or weather. They sent a blast of wind into us. None of the shadowblood kids I met before could have pulled off an effect that strong."

The squat, metallic-scaled demon named Steel aims a

scowl at us. "Then they're part of the problem too. We get rid of all of them."

My stomach lurches. The protest bursts out of me automatically. "No. They *are* just kids. We know them. They wouldn't have wanted to hurt us—he must have forced them to step in. They had the manacles like we used to."

They didn't attack us right away. It's possible they could have killed us if they'd taken us by surprise, hit us as hard as they could while we were reeling from seeing them at all.

But they didn't. Nadia told us to leave. They only brought out their heightened abilities when I tried to shove past them.

My mind slides back to the last few conversations I had with Nadia. Her whole personality used to be bright, but she'd deflated in the villa, where Balthazar made it clear he saw her as totally expendable. But she still lit up a little when I got her talking about the kind of life she wished she could have.

Now he's dragged her even farther away from that sort of normal. Made her more of a monster.

Although I can't say I'm completely sure she'd see it that way. The younger shadowbloods expressed disappointment that Balthazar's early procedures didn't affect them like they did us—didn't bring out new dimensions to their powers.

Nadia did tell me once that she wished she could really blaze instead of just the gentle glow she was capable of back then.

Willow, the nymph poised near Rollick, gives a soft

huff and rubs at the bark embedded in her forearms. "It all amounts to the same thing. If they're fighting for him, then you've got to fight against them."

Her use of "you" rather than "we" pricks at my nerves. Is she already pulling back from this war?

"None of the younger shadowbloods have done anything wrong," I insist. "They've been tortured and experimented on for years just like we were. They deserve their freedom. We have to get them out."

Two chairs down from me, Andreas draws himself up a little straighter. "We're in this to save all of you from Balthazar's plans—and the people he's already hurting—but we always meant to save them too. If he's pushing them into the battle, then they need our help *more*, not less."

Fang's lips curl in a silent snarl. "I don't see—"

"You wouldn't," Sorsha says tartly, cutting him off. "You all know a lot from your long lives as shadowkind, but one thing you should remember you know nothing about is growing up. About being a kid, with all the helplessness and uncertainty that comes with it. I agree with the shadowbloods. The ones that aren't even grown up yet—they aren't our enemies."

With a rasp of his chair legs, Rollick stands up. My heart skips a beat before he inclines his head toward me.

"The shadowblood children haven't had a real choice in whether they want to be against us," he says in his light but measured voice. "I'd say they're victims in this scenario. We'll keep them safe if we can."

Crag leans forward, his stony face darkening. "How

are we going to do that if they're going to attack us, whether they want to or not?"

My hands clasp together under the table. I don't have a real answer to that question.

I grip my entwined fingers to steady myself. "It's going to be difficult. But we've pulled off lots of difficult things before. First… First I guess I need to see if I can predict another base Balthazar is likely to return to. We'll be more ready for his protections this time—we can use earplugs, do more scouting to find his entry and exit points—"

I'm interrupted by a faint pop and the sudden materializing of a slim form. Billy gazes around at us, his faun eyes nearly round. "I—I'm sorry to burst in. I thought you'd want to know. There's been another attack, and it's a little… different."

Uneasy silence grips us. We all push to our feet and hustle to the room that holds Rollick's huge flat screen TV, which I knew a few of the shadowkind had been monitoring. Some of the beings vanish to dart through the shadows and stay there, but I can't shake my awareness of their presence.

The TV is on, a news reporter talking in typical clipped tones as a scene of destruction that's unnervingly familiar plays out on the screen. I barely pay attention to her voice, focusing on the distant figures ducking in and out of view. The walls of a massive building are crumbling —some fancy skyscraper in what looks like a downtown core.

Most of the fleeing locals have dark hair and light brown skin, but I can't get a close enough look at them to determine their ethnicity beyond that. And then something appears on the screen that makes my body go rigid.

Next to me, Zian sucks in a sharp breath. Jacob's fingers tighten where he's gripped the top of the sofa.

Soldiers. Soldiers have marched into view at the side of the screen.

That wouldn't be so surprising. We saw military figures at the scene in London when we tried to help with the rescue efforts.

No, what's startling is the woven metal vests draped over their typical uniforms. Glinting pale gray… like silver and iron.

Like the protections the guardians wore in the facilities, that they hoped would ward off our shadowy powers. That didn't work on us, but it *would* deflect full shadowkind.

More metal flashes in their hands. They're holding long, pointed guns like silvery bayonets.

My arms rise to hug myself instinctively. Somehow I'm going to bet that both the brutal stabbing protrusions and the bullets loaded into those things are customized to do maximum damage to beings like the ones around me.

"Fuck," Andreas mutters. "He actually convinced someone to go along with his crazy instructions."

Dominic lets out a strained chuckle. "They probably don't sound so crazy when people with impossible abilities keep bashing up cities all over the world."

Billy bobs nervously on his feet, his gaze skittering between us. "It doesn't really make sense, though, does it? I thought those metals didn't have any effect on shadowbloods. And it's shadowbloods carrying out the attacks."

Rollick's lips have flattened into a tight line. "It isn't what the soldiers do there that matters. It's what they do later, now that they're on board."

"Exactly." I hug myself tighter. "Balthazar doesn't want the other armies fighting his army of shadowbloods. He's prepping them so that they'll be totally equipped when he talks their governments into hunting down actual shadowkind."

And if he's managed to start convincing the world's leaders to take this much of his advice in just one week… how much longer do we have before he's directing squads of shadowkind-killers all across the planet?

TEN

Andreas

The room looks as if it's empty. You'd assume it is… as long as you don't try to walk too far into it, anyway.

I've turned every piece of furniture, every decoration and knickknack, in the guest bedroom totally invisible. But I can still stub my toe on the base of the dresser, like I did just a second ago.

I fumble my way over to the invisible bed and sink my also-invisible body down onto the covers. After a brief rub, the sting radiating through my big toe fades.

There's no particular reason that the contents of my room need to be hidden from the eye right now. I'm just doing my best to recreate the conditions I might face when we go into battle—when I might have to hide a bunch of the people around me, like I did when we invaded Balthazar's mountain base.

Inanimate objects don't take quite the same surge of

energy that living beings do. To get the same effect, I don't have to wear myself out as much. So I poured way more of my power into each of the room's furnishings than I did into my friends yesterday.

It was either that or try to vanish the entire mansion, and I don't think anyone else living here would appreciate the latter.

I need to push myself farther than I did yesterday. Farther than I've dared with my fellow shadowbloods in all the time since I discovered I could use my talent for invisibility beyond my own body.

Maybe if I'd given my efforts yesterday my all instead of holding back just a little, Balthazar's gambit with his ear-splitting device wouldn't have shaken us out of concealment. Maybe we'd have stayed invisible to chase after him in the tunnels, and the younger shadowbloods wouldn't have been able to confront us.

I swallow thickly and flex my fingers against the rumples of the blanket beneath me, checking for any unusual sensations.

Unfortunately, the other maybes involved could have dire consequences in the opposite direction. Which is why I'm conducting this experiment only on myself, not on any of the people who matter so much to me.

Our former captor seems determined to wreak havoc through the entire world. The next time we go up against him, we might not all survive.

But I'll be damned if I lose anyone because *I* fucked up.

The experiment is awfully boring, though. I should

have set my phone to a playlist of podcasts before I concealed it along with everything else.

I can't see the screen now to select anything on it. Can't see the TV mounted on the wall. The view beyond the window remains, since I didn't mess with the walls themselves, but all I've got there is the incredibly dull "Palm trees casting shadows on the lawn" show.

I don't even know exactly how long I've been running the experiment for, although I did have the foresight to set my phone to sound an alert every hour. The first one went off what might have been twenty minutes or forty ago, for all I can tell.

So far, I feel fine. That's a good sign. I've never held myself invisible for this long before.

Of course, we already knew that the procedures Balthazar had Matteo carry out on us expanded our abilities. That doesn't mean there isn't a limit, only that it's farther out than I'm used to.

I catch myself starting to worry at my lip and push to my feet. I've got to do something to distract myself.

Why not practice my stealth skills while I'm in see-through mode? I don't really like the idea of spying on anyone in Rollick's home, but it'd be good practice to simply move through the house quickly and quietly, making sure I don't disturb anyone I pass.

I go through the motions of pretending I'm on an actual mission with enemies around every corner. My hand stays braced on the doorknob until I'm sure there's no sound in the hall outside. Then I slip out as deftly and swiftly as possible.

Riva's outside, somewhere not far to the north of the

house. I can sense her presence distinctly, like I have ever since we first slept together and our matching marks bound our essence together.

My friends, I only have a vaguer impression of—a faint tickle of energy that comes from their powers. If I concentrate, I can tell who's who based on what those powers are and what direction they're in, but not how far away.

And I'm pretty sure that awareness only works when they're not far at all. I'd know how to find Riva no matter where in the world she went, but my awareness of the guys dwindles with distance.

The other beings hanging out around this place, I have no sense of at all. I slink past the dining room, where a couple of the shadowkind Rollick is particularly friendly with are having a conversation about the steaks one of them apparently fried, and pass Billy plinking away at a piano in the mansion's music room, but that's it.

From what I've seen, most of the shadowkind prefer sticking to their shadows unless there's a specific reason they need to take physical form. I kind of wish that wasn't the case, because if I wanted to spy on anyone, it'd be the less friendly allies whose allegiances to us are shakier.

But if they're having conversations about how far to follow us into this war, it's someplace as invisible to me as I am to them—and inaudible as well.

I'm just coming up on the front foyer with its massive looming skylight when the first creeping of discomfort ripples over my skin.

The unnerving sensation squirms through my nerves

from my fingertips to my elbows. I jerk to a halt with a hitch of breath.

When I splay and clench my hands, the feeling eases. My heart keeps thumping on at its sped-up pace.

Should I pull myself out now? If that sign is anything like before, it's only the start.

I don't know if it'll be like before, though. Maybe there won't be any progression, only that mild irritation.

That's why I'm experimenting, isn't it? To find my limits.

To figure out exactly how far I can go with my abilities before I doom myself… and anyone I've worked them on.

I take a few slow breaths to steady my nerves and think back through the many memories I've viewed in people's heads over the years to the avid surfer who chased thrills around the world. His vivid recollections of riding the waves, water roaring beneath him and wind flicking cool spray across his face, were exhilarating, but my favorite moment was a snippet of a conversation I came across.

Don't you ever get scared? one of his friends asked him, and he simply laughed.

As long as I've got my board under my feet or my hand, I know I'm okay, he said. *I'll get through it.*

I'm still here. I've got the floor beneath me and the walls around me, all perfectly tangible. While I have that, I should be able to pull out of my invisibility and be all right, even if it's hard.

I don't actually know if that's true, but focusing on the thought settles my nerves. I walk on out of the house.

It's harder to stay completely unnoticeable in the

outdoors. My body hasn't lost its gravity; my feet press indents into the grass and the gritty soil.

No one's close enough to see those signs of my passing right now, but in a real mission, it could be a problem.

The best solution that offers itself is to stick to solid materials. I leap across some decorative tiles set in one span of the lawn and teeter along the edge of a broad wooden planter filled with drooping flowers.

The minor acrobatics take my mind off my worries until another prickling ripple washes over my skin.

This one wriggles up from my feet as well as along my arms, converging on my chest. My balance wobbles, and I stumble off the planter.

The soft thud of my feet on the grass brings other footsteps from around the side of the house. Toni comes into view and frowns at the apparently vacant garden before her. "Is someone there?"

The prickles are racing right between my ribs now, making my breath catch. Fear spikes alongside the physical distress.

Is my balance still wobbling—my sense of the ground itself wavering?

I jerk myself back toward visibility with a shove of my power. My body reforms, the sunlight glancing off my face and bringing out the vibrant red of my shirt.

And then I seem to dissolve. For a second, the breeze passes right through my chest.

My hands clutch at the air as if I'll find something to hold on to there. My thoughts whirl. When I glance down at myself, my arms look hazy, the grass showing through them.

My feet. Where are my feet? I can't even feel them—it's like my legs end at my knees, and—

"Hey!"

A hand closes around my shoulder. Firm, present, bringing my physical presence back into sharper focus.

My head snaps up. Toni is standing next to me, her eyes wide and her hair windblown as if she ran over.

I'm here. I'm still here.

An eerie tingling sensation keeps jittering through my nerves, like my entire body has fallen asleep and is now writhing with pins and needles. Clenching my jaw, I pull and pull at my sense of myself, dragging every bit of me back into full reality.

By the time I'm totally confident that I'm solid again, sweat is trickling down my back despite the cool winter air. My breath rasps in my throat.

"Fuck," I mutter, hopelessness knotting my gut. The two-hour alert hadn't even gone off yet.

I'm not going to be able to give the others much more of an advantage—not without risking their entire existence.

The hand drops from my shoulder, and I'm abruptly aware of Toni still standing there next to me. "Are you all right?"

I manage to aim a tight smile at her. "Yeah. Now. Sorry if I startled you—and thank you."

Toni blinks at me as if she's still having trouble seeing me. "What happened there?"

I shrug. "What's always happened if I try to hold on to the invisibility for too long. I wasn't sure... I haven't let myself give it my all since the procedures and everything."

Toni gives me a grimace that feels almost like a disapproving teacher, as much as I have any idea what that feels like. "You *shouldn't* take it that far. It doesn't help anyone if you can't come back. Are you totally okay now? Should I get Rollick or your friends or—?"

I wave off her concerned questions. "It's over. I'm good now." Other than the sense of failure and the pit of existential dread that's reappeared in the bottom of my stomach.

My smile loosens and turns crooked at the same time. "I'm just trying to figure out how I *can* help as much as possible. I'm not much good for forcing open locks or cutting down super villains."

Something shifts in Toni's expression. Her mouth tenses, almost as if she's upset, but her voice comes out softer. "I know a little something about being most valued when you're unseen. But I also know you can erase yourself too much and regret it."

A lump rises in my throat. I hadn't expected to find myself sympathizing with Balthazar's star employee, but there's no denying how much she means those words.

I don't think I'd ever want to take another peek inside her head to find out how much she forced herself to tolerate over the years.

Toni eases back a step as if she suspects I'd prefer more space. Then her head cocks. "The invisibility isn't your only power. Your main focus is memory, isn't it?"

I swipe my hand over my face as if to reassure myself that all of my features are still there. "Yeah. But it isn't much help in tackling psychopaths. I can distract people by projecting memories, but that doesn't get us very far."

"And you can erase memories as well." Toni's gaze turns pensive. "If you could do that to Balthazar—simply wipe out all the experiences that made him want to carry out his crusade against the shadowkind—"

I let out a shaky chuckle. "I wish it could be that easy. I'd have to be near him to wipe his mind, and completely blanking a person takes some time. If we want to be sure of stopping him, we're better off getting any of the other shadowbloods in there—except Griffin, I guess. Riva, Jacob, Zian, and maybe even Dom could end him in a second or two."

I say the words without thinking and then pause, remembering that even if she's thrown her lot in with us, this woman was dedicated for more than a decade to the man I'm talking so casually about killing.

"Unless you're hoping we can end this without him dead," I add. "I didn't mean—after everything he put us through and everything he's doing now, that's where my mind automatically goes."

Toni nods without an indication of offense taken. "I can understand that. With everything I've seen, I can't say you're wrong to think that way either. Consider my suggestion just some brainstorming. With all his plans and resources, who knows what tricks we might need to turn to if we're going to stop him?"

I laugh with a little actual humor this time. "Fair point. If it comes down to me and I get the chance, I'll definitely give him a case of amnesia. That just doesn't seem like a great opening gambit."

We drift back toward the house, silence falling

between us. There isn't a whole lot to say to each other after that.

Or possibly there is, because a few steps from the door, Toni glances over at me. "I'm sorry. For—for every way I contributed to what he did to you. I shouldn't have let myself become just a tool for him, putting aside all my own opinions."

The apology means more than I'd have expected after she's already said as much to us as a group. I dip my head to her in acknowledgment. "He did a number on you too. At least you found your way back."

The corner of her mouth curves upward in a sad-looking smile. "Do your best to make sure you always do too, all right?"

I don't answer her, even though I'm touched by her concern. Because the truth is, as terrified as my experience in the garden makes me, I wouldn't let that terror get in my way.

I'd never risk another person's life with my talent, but if keeping myself concealed for a few more minutes made the difference between saving my friends and the woman I love or not? I'd accept my doom in an instant.

I can't even say whether I'm more worried that it'll come to that... or that I'll never get the chance to make that much of a difference.

ELEVEN

I sit up straighter and roll my shoulders. The lines of the map that's spread on the floor in front of me swim before my eyes even when I close them.

I rub at my eyelids and blink, and the afterimage starts to fade. My uneasiness doesn't.

Balthazar hasn't returned to his base in the Carpathians, which isn't really a surprise. He doesn't know how much we figured out about his security systems there, but he's not taking any chances.

Instead, every time I check his location, he seems to be moving between places. I'm not sure he's stayed at any of his properties for more than an hour or two.

He must be conducting most of his business by private jets and helicopters. Placing calls, making plans, even sleeping while in motion.

Which means we can't pin him down. I never know

where he is for long enough that we could get there before he's someplace else.

He's had the younger shadowbloods moved too. The ones I sensed—and then saw—in the Romanian base I now trace to a spot in Poland. Toni confirmed that Balthazar owns a large plot of land there and had been doing construction on it in recent years.

They aren't all together. I just located Booker off in the middle of Finland. The only one left I know well enough to search out with Griffin's ability is Ajax.

I lean back on my hands for a moment first, trying to regain my concentration. There are too many other considerations niggling at my mind.

It doesn't help that I'm far from sure that mapping out the locations of our younger counterparts does us any good. Balthazar wasn't with Nadia and the others when they left the mountain base. He'd already taken off on his own—he's directing their movements from afar.

I thought it would comfort me a little to know where they are, but instead it's only deepened my sense of helplessness.

I don't know how to get them out. I don't know what Balthazar is putting them through now that their powers are more useful to him.

He's certainly been busy.

One of the other niggling thoughts has me pulling out my phone. When I flick to the news app, nausea curdles in my gut.

There's a hunt for the "monstrous" terrorists going on in Turkey right now, soldiers storming enclaves they've identified as suspicious. I'm guessing that Balthazar has used the shadowkind who work for him under duress to get intel.

The army hasn't been video-recording the assaults, but rumors of smoking carcasses are floating into the news reports. They're hitting their intended targets.

Shadowkind are dying.

Balthazar has continued to spread his efforts worldwide. A couple of days ago, his shadowbloods destroyed Houston's city hall building, killing dozens, and now the Americans are up in arms too.

And not just the military. Roaming squads of citizens, their weapons and vests no doubt arranged by Balthazar, have turned vigilante.

I overheard Rollick on the phone yesterday, ordering his Miami hotel shut down. Recommending that all his employees there either join us at the Spanish mansion or disperse into hiding.

He put on a nonchalant front about it, acting like this was just a momentary inconvenience that would blow over, but guilt winds through my chest when I remember the conversation.

Balthazar has been stockpiling money, property, and weapons for so long. Building his economic and political influence. Gathering information to inform his strategies.

But the key to launching this vast war on the shadowkind now was Ursula Engel's computer. The one we stole from her.

The one I told him how to find.

I inhale deeply and lean over the map again. I'll check Ajax's position, and then I'll search for Balthazar again. If we can pick out one place he's returning to somewhat frequently, that would at least be another start.

I focus my attention on my memories of the slim boy with the near-black skin and thoughtful eyes. The act of concentration has become almost second nature after so much practice, even though the talent isn't technically mine.

An image of Ajax forms in my head. I reach my arm over the map, urging my fingers toward him as if by a magnetic pull.

My hand drops. I peer down at the winding lines of country borders.

Balthazar has him stashed someplace in western China now. I haven't tracked our former captor's movements to any specific spot there before, but he has crisscrossed Asia more than once. For all I know he's made a brief stop that I missed.

Or he hasn't checked in on the shadowbloods there at all since I started monitoring his movements.

As my gaze lingers on the blank territory I touched, more than an inch from any major city, a tingling sensation forms at the top of my skull.

My pulse hitches. I freeze, unsure whether I should try to shake off the feeling or see how it develops.

In the midst of my indecision, a thin but audible voice murmurs through my thoughts as if from right inside my head. *Riva? Is that you?*

It sounds like Ajax, as well as I can remember the solemn boy's low voice. I open my mouth and close it again, not sure how to answer him. If I speak out loud, will he hear that?

His talent was a weak version of telepathy. His original talent, anyway. Has Balthazar expanded the fifteen-year-old's abilities so much that he can project his own thoughts into my head across all this distance?

I think a response as "loudly" as I know how. *Yes, it's me. Are you okay, Ajax?*

The voice wavers, momentarily so quiet that I can barely make out the words. *Kind of. I'm alive. And I can do this now. I had this… this feeling that you were reaching out to me.*

I hesitate. How much should I tell him about what I've been doing with Griffin's powers?

Balthazar couldn't know about our ability to swap talents yet. Even if Ajax doesn't want to help the psychopath, I know far too well that he might not have the choice.

I was thinking about you, I settle on as a vague answer. *You and the other shadowbloods. Are you alone or with some of the other kids?*

Balthazar's people don't let us mingle much. There are adults here who have powers too—they get pretty brutal if we don't listen to them.

My stomach knots. So Balthazar has his new, morally questionable shadowbloods enforcing his rule over the kids when he's not there.

I can only imagine how badly that situation could go wrong for the younger ones.

I'm sorry, I say. *We—the Firsts—managed to get away from him. We're going to do everything we can to get you all out too.*

That promise isn't giving away anything Balthazar

shouldn't already know. I just can't share any specific possible strategies with the boy who's trapped thousands of miles distant.

I get the impression of a sigh. *Well, I'm hanging in there. I'm mostly worried about Devon. I haven't seen him since Clancy's island.*

It doesn't surprise me that Balthazar has been keeping the two separate. He must have realized they were more than just friends. He split up Nadia and Booker once they left his villa too.

Losing his wife seems to be what sent him right over the deep end. I guess he's self-aware enough to realize that we shadowbloods will be even more motivated to fight back if we can see the people we love most in peril.

Unfortunately, I can't offer Ajax much comfort about his boyfriend. *I saw him a few days ago. He was still alive then. Have you been able to talk to him like you are with me?*

Ajax's tone turns mournful. *No. I'm not sure why this worked. Before, I had to be able to see a person to read their thoughts or send my own. Even with the way my power's grown, I haven't been hearing anyone much farther than this building we're in.*

It must be some synchronicity sparked by my use of Griffin's talent. In a way, I was "seeing" Ajax when I found him on the map.

Has Balthazar amped up Devon's powers too? he asks into my pause.

I don't know, I admit, thinking back to our brief confrontation.

Nadia definitely used her light-based talent, and one of the kids I don't know as well must have been responsible for the wind. Devon was able to project heat with his mind—when I was around him before, he could melt very small bits of metal, but that was about it.

Who knows what he's capable of now.

I grimace to myself before going on. *I'm guessing he's done it to all of the shadowbloods he can. He's got a lot of work that he wants done. I assume the other kids with you have had their abilities enhanced too?*

Yeah. Ajax goes silent for long enough that I start to worry I've lost the psychic connection completely. *I hope he's okay. With the others... It hasn't just improved their talents.*

Something about his tone sends an icy finger down my spine. *What do you mean?*

There's this thing we get injected with, and also pills we're supposed to take... I've been able to skip some of the pills without being noticed, so maybe that's why I'm okay. The other kids here have gotten really on edge. Bad tempers. Yelling and getting violent if they're even a little upset. Even their thoughts are all jangly and mean. It seems like more than them just being frustrated about what he's doing to us.

My spirits sink. Yes, it does. It could be that effect explains the aggression I sensed in Nadia's and the others' stances when I encountered them in the tunnel.

Were they standing in our way only because Balthazar forced them to? Or has he messed with their heads as well as their powers to make them feel they need to fight anyone in front of them?

I don't like the sound of that, I say. *Keep doing what you're doing if that's been saving you from the worst effects.*

I'll try. I get the impression of a rough laugh. *Some days*

I actually miss the guardians. Although maybe they'd have done this too if they'd known how.

I know what he means on both points. There's nothing I can think of to say that would really comfort him, and a throbbing pain has formed at the top of my spine.

I rub my neck, measuring out my last words, wishing I had more I could offer. *I'm sorry. We'll get to you as soon as we can. I don't think I can keep talking like this for much longer right now. Do you know where you are?*

No idea, Ajax says apologetically. *We were unconscious when we got here, and there are no windows. Reach out again if you can. I'll see if I can find out anything else.*

Then his voice fades from my head. I rock back on my butt, my mind reeling.

For what might be one minute or several, I stare blankly at the wall across from me. My cheeks cool, and I touch them to find they're wet.

Tears are leaking from my eyes. I drag in a breath that's almost a sob and swipe at them.

I'm not going to give in to the hopelessness. We *are* going to save the shadowblood kids, no matter how hard it is.

Even if some of them aren't clear anymore on whether they want to be saved.

I insisted to our shadowkind allies that we had to protect all of the younger ones. What are they going to do if those teens outright attack them in a fit of temper or misguided aggression?

How the hell do I make this right?

As I stew in my frustration, Ajax's words come back to me. *Some days I actually miss the guardians.*

No kidding.

A bittersweet smile twists my lips—and inspiration sparks in my head.

I leap to my feet, my heart pounding. Could we really — Is it too crazy?

It's a chance, an angle we haven't tried yet, and one Balthazar will never be expecting.

I hurry down the hall to the lounge where I can sense most of my guys have gathered. Their quiet conversation falls away completely when I burst into the room.

Jacob's eyebrows shoot up. "What's going on, Wildcat?"

I brace myself. "I've got an idea. But I don't think you're going to like it."

Twelve

Jacob

When Riva finishes speaking, her words bounce around inside my skull, refusing to totally sink in. Every muscle in my body has tensed as if preparing to fight off the enemies who aren't even here.

"You want us to ask the *guardians* for help?" I spit out, the idea sounding even more absurd when I say it out loud. "The assholes who kept us in cages and treated us like lab rats?"

Riva folds her arms over her chest, looking totally unfazed by my reaction. She was probably expecting me to be at least this pissed off, if not more. "Not exactly asking, and not exactly help. But bringing them into the mix could be useful to us."

Annoyingly, Dominic has to make it all sound reasonable in his usual thoughtful tone. "I can see her point. Balthazar was part of the Guardianship for decades, since they were founded. There've got to be people there who know him way better than we do."

I swivel toward him. "Better than us maybe, but we've got his closest assistant on our side. What could they know that Toni doesn't?"

Not that I like relying on the bitch who stood by while he tormented and killed shadowbloods either, but at least she's admitted she fucked up. And she's already here.

Andreas rubs his jaw. "She saw one side of him, but they'll have seen others. There'd be people there he interacted with more like equals than a superior."

I throw my hands in the air. "Who the hell cares? We can't trust them farther than we can kick them! Didn't we all learn our lesson when we ran to Engel for answers?"

The memory of our creator turning on us merges with all the moments the other guardians hunted us down, and anger crackles through my nerves.

Several of the books hurtle off the nearby bookshelf to smack against the opposite wall.

I close my eyes, my hands clenching. I've got to simmer down. No one's going to pay attention to my opinions if my talent is going haywire like a toddler having a tantrum.

Griffin takes a step closer to me. My twin's voice comes out so gentle it almost makes me angrier. "I don't think Riva has any intention of trusting them. But it makes sense that you'd hate the idea. None of us *want* to have anything to do with the guardians."

"I know," I mutter, willing my body to relax. "I just don't—I don't want to see us make another mistake."

Riva aims a soft smile at me that's worse than Griffin's

reassurances. "We're not doing anything yet. I'm only saying we should talk about the possibilities. They're… a potential resource, like Rollick always puts it. Maybe we could use them like they wanted to use us."

Dominic nods. "Balthazar definitely wouldn't suspect that any contact he gets from them has anything to do with us. He knows that we hate them and that they'd never work with us as allies."

"Exactly." Riva smiles brighter at him. "If we can manipulate them into passing on information or influencing his actions, they might be able to create the opening we need without him or them having a clue that's what's going on."

When she puts it like that, I can understand why she's excited about the possibility. It's not like we've gotten very far against our psychopathic former captor so far.

He has all the resources, all the plans in place, and we're playing catch up. Drawing in the guardians to our benefit could give us a leg up.

Even if imagining reaching out to them in any way makes me want to smash every piece of furniture in Rollick's elegant mansion.

I heave a sigh, expelling more tension with the breath. "Okay. I know we've got to consider every possible plan that could give us an advantage. But I don't think the shadowkind are going to like it either. The guardians wanted to exterminate them just as much as Balthazar does, even if they weren't as ballsy about it."

Riva shrugs. "I guess we'll have to see what they say, then."

If I was hoping that Rollick would see things my way and quash the plan before it even got off the ground, I know I've lost the second a startled but awed laugh spills from his lips.

He leans back in the leather chair at the desk in his mansion's home office, pulling his phone from his pocket. "Of course you'd figure there's a way to make use of even your other enemies. I'd love it if these guardians of yours could lend us a hand against their own interests. Seems fitting."

Zian, who caught up with the rest of us as we searched the demon out, frowns pensively. "Are your shadowkind friends going to be okay with it? A lot of them already seem kind of unsure about working just with *us*."

Riva has brightened at Rollick's approval in a way I can't help appreciating. I'm not in love with her plan, but nothing could shake my love for her.

She bounces on her feet with pent-up energy. It can't have been easy for her spending so much time putting together plans rather than springing into action.

"We wouldn't really be working with them," she says. "We've just got to find a way to get them acting on our behalf without realizing it."

Rollick flashes her a smile. "Exactly. But first we need to locate the people who'll decide on those actions. You said the man who brought you to that island is, ah, no longer in the picture, correct? He was the last of the other founders in this Guardianship?"

Andreas nods slowly. "He was theoretically at the top

of the ladder when he had us running missions for him —but the guardians had other levels of authority. There was a guy who came to visit him… Richmond, that was his name. He talked about a board that I assume he was on, who had the power to take control over the organization if they decided Clancy was screwing things up."

Riva claps her hands together. "Then we need to find the board. They've got to be running things now."

I grimace. "I wonder what they think of all the havoc Balthazar's already wreaking thanks to their experiments?"

"They might not know he's behind it," Dominic points out. "He's been pretending it's monsters making the attacks, right? He hasn't been in contact with them for years—they probably have even less information about his current activities than we do."

Rollick is typing a text into his phone with one hand while the other taps at the keyboard of his laptop. Apparently epic multitasking is among his supernatural skills.

"Your guardians aren't generally secretive enough about their presence to escape shadowkind notice," he says. "It helps that they're so fond of their protective measures, which we can't help picking up on. And having the name of someone on this board… I may be able to dig up contact information and locations they're presently working out of within a matter of hours."

I shift on my feet with a prickle of my own restlessness. "We can't just call them up or barge in and order them around. Why would they pay attention to anything we say or do? If they know who we are, they'll never listen to us. And if we don't tell them, then we'll only be strangers."

"Hmm. There are various methods of persuasion, some more subtle than others." Rollick snaps his fingers and raises his voice at a pitch that makes my eardrums wobble. "Pearl?"

The succubus must have been lurking nearby, because it can't be more than ten seconds before she pops into being next to his desk. "Yes, boss?" she asks with a typically cheeky grin.

My stance starts to tense again. Our grand plan is going to rely on *her*? I mean, the succubus has been nice to us and all, but she never seems to take anything all that seriously.

Rollick clearly doesn't share any of my concerns. "You did a good job getting that lackey of Balthazar's to cough up the info about the hidden route inside the hill," he says. "We might have more intensive need of your skills soon."

Her grin only widens. "Sounds good to me. What's up?"

Riva steps in. "We're going to track down the current leaders of the Guardianship—the organization that all the guardians belong to. That Balthazar used to as well. I'm hoping we can use them to come at him from a new angle, one he won't expect or be ready to defend against."

"The Guardianship," Pearl repeats, and her bright eyes go momentarily distant. "You know, that guy of Balthazar's said something about them when I was working my charms."

Okay, maybe I sold her abilities short. I stare at her,

wishing I could push myself right into the memory like Andreas would be able to. "What? I thought Balthazar had nothing to do with them anymore."

Pearl dips her head in acknowledgment. "Oh, he doesn't. It was—" She glances at Riva, and her smile falters for a moment. "I told you before how when I'm seducing someone, they always seem to end up blabbing their big regrets to me afterward. One of this guy's big failures had to do with the guardians."

Everyone's attention is trained on the succubus now. Rollick makes a circular motion with his hand. "Go on."

Pearl sucks her lower lip under her teeth as she appears to think back. "He was someone in pretty tight with Balthazar. One of his top dudes. But he was worried the big guy would never give him any responsibilities outside of the science-y stuff he was mostly focused on."

Dominic's eyebrows rise. "Wait... Did you manage to get your hands on *Matteo*?"

Pearl blinks at him. "Yeah, that was his name. Is that important?"

A sourness laces my tongue and turns my stomach. Something thumps on one of Rollick's shelves in the instant before I rein in my power.

That fucking smug prick and his sick "procedures." It's his fault almost as much as Balthazar's that we're in this mess.

"Matteo was one of the two employees Balthazar seemed to count on the most at the villa," Riva says quietly. "The other one being Toni. He was in charge of trying to expand our abilities—and he's probably the one who worked out whatever treatment Balthazar's using now to produce his new and stronger shadowbloods."

Pearl wrinkles her nose. "Ugh. He did seem like a creep. We should be looking to take him out of the picture too."

The corner of Riva's mouth curls upward just slightly. "I already did."

Rollick chuckles approvingly. Probably the thing I like most about the demon is the fact that he appreciates my woman's brutal side as much as I do.

Pearl hesitates and then lets out a bell of a laugh. "Well, that's taken care of then."

Dominic clears his throat. "You never told us what he said about the guardians."

"Oh, right." The succubus rubs her hands together. "Apparently a couple of years ago, after Balthazar went off on his own apart from this Guardianship, Matteo figured it'd been long enough of his boss playing lone wolf and that they'd make progress faster if they continued collaborating with the guardians at least a little. So he set up a visit with some of the head honchos, thinking Balthazar would be pleased with his initiative."

I can't imagine that psycho being "pleased" with anyone's inspiration other than his own. "Let me guess. He was wrong."

"Oh, yeah. When Balthazar saw the Guardianship people, he told them off with a bunch of insults and threats… It was so bad Matteo was sure he'd have a hard time coming back even if he changed his mind later."

"And that's what Matteo regretted?" Riva asks.

Pearl shakes her head. "Nope. He was all torn up

about how he'd lost his boss's trust by inviting them in. I guess Balthazar laid into him too in the moment and then never stopped giving him a chilly attitude afterward."

Yeah, that fits my impressions of the guy. Matteo was just as sociopathic as his master and worked his butt off following the prick's insane demands.

Riva's eyes gleam with anticipation. "That's perfect."

My head jerks toward her. "How, exactly?"

She swats my arm in response to my skeptical tone. "The last time Balthazar and the guardians interacted, he treated them like an enemy. All they know is he's gone rogue and he apparently wants nothing to do with them. Don't you see how that plays into our hands?"

Zian's eyes widen. "It might not be too hard to convince them that he's working *against* them. That they've got to take action to save themselves."

"Right." Riva grins. "Now if only we could nudge his new shadowbloods to rain down a little destruction near wherever the Guardianship's top dogs are hanging out to make the threat more immediate, we'd be golden."

Rollick looks up from his laptop. "Who says we need his shadowbloods? We've got perfectly good ones right here."

Andreas glances around at the rest of us. "You're saying that *we* should rain down some destruction?"

The demon shrugs. "Nothing *that* horrible. Just some superficial but suitably unnerving devastation." His gaze slides to… me, before he glances around at the others again. "I've heard your telekinetic prodigy can shake entire mountains. He should be able to shake up the Guardianship too."

Wait, *I'm* the one who has to set this plan in motion?

Everyone else turns toward me expectantly. Zian raises his hand as if he's in class. "I'll go too. I can bash and burn things up a bunch."

"You could borrow my talent for siphoning energy," Dominic says in a subdued tone. "Or I could come along."

And then silence falls as they wait to see what I'm going to say.

I swallow hard. I didn't like this idea when Riva first pitched it, and I still would rather have a million miles between me and any of those fuckers with their helmets and vests.

But there's a plea in Riva's gaze. And where the hell am I leaving us if I say no?

It's not as if I've got a better suggestion. At least this part of the plan involves sticking it to the pricks.

I grit my teeth and then force the words out. "All right. Tell me where to go, and I'm in."

THIRTEEN

Riva

My heartbeat doesn't quite even out until I see Jacob and Zian emerging from the car outside the mansion. Rollick reported that he'd gotten word their covert mission had gone as planned, but after seeing how resistant Jake was to the whole idea, I couldn't help tensing in anticipation of some disaster.

I know all too well how vicious he can be with people who've provoked his rage.

I push past the doors to meet them. Jacob strides over to me with a tight smile that shows he's still not happy about the situation, but he doesn't show any signs of guilt.

"It was fine," he says brusquely. "We bashed up a couple of buildings, left an obvious message, and got the hell out. The worst any of the people got was a splinter."

Zian huffs. "They deserved a lot more than that."

I grab his hand and squeeze it. "Well, there'll be plenty of time to see *that* justice done after we're finished with

Balthazar. Come on. Are you hungry? You've got to be tired after all that traveling."

Rollick sent them in a private jet from a nearby airfield across the ocean and back again. Does jet lag even set in when you're only in the other time zone for a couple of hours?

Jacob shrugs and slings his arm around my waist with a vaguely possessive air, as if he doesn't want Zian to hog all of my physical attention. "We had a four-course dinner on the flight back. And a nap. I feel about like I would if I'd been here the whole time."

As we walk into the mansion, the other three guys come into the hall to look Jake and Zian over. The softening of Griffin's expression reassures me more than my own observations of the duo.

"It all went well," he says. "Good."

Jacob makes a face. "We'll see how 'well' it actually was when those assholes get their butts into gear. I don't know if the Guardianship will definitely fall for the trick—or if they'll do anything useful even if they believe Balthazar has joined up with shadowkind to attack them."

Rollick's smooth voice rings out as he emerges from a nearby room. "We'll just have to wait and see on that score. I have people watching the board members we identified—and Pearl will nudge them in ideal directions as much as she can."

The thought of the succubus having to seduce the jerk currently leading the guardians makes my stomach turn. But I have to admit she didn't look all that bothered about it when she left to make her own trip via portals.

I guess when it comes to meals of sexual energy, all

sources are pretty satisfying. And I know she likes getting to contribute to our war with Balthazar the one way she can.

I sigh, and Jacob's arm tenses around me, pulling me a little closer. *I* haven't been doing a whole lot all day other than tracking Balthazar's movements and brainstorming possible attacks, but I feel as worn out as if I've jetted around the world alongside him and Zian.

Rollick's penetrating gaze passes over us, and a sly smile curves his lips. "I think the six of you deserve a break. You've been through an awful lot—in the past few months, and in your entire lives."

I shake my head to deflect his concern. "We're used to it."

"You shouldn't have to be. And you've been working hard ever since you finally broke free. You *are* free, even if everything else isn't perfect. For once, no one's even hunting you down. Why don't we establish a new normal? It's time you took the opportunity to unwind."

I study the demon warily. "Unwind how, exactly?"

I don't think he'd suggest anything I'd find totally horrifying. Rollick has our best interests at heart. But he is still a sort-of monster. He doesn't see things the same way a human being would.

The demon waves off my question with a carefree air. "However you like. I'll just make it easy for you. Why don't you take a little staycation in the guest cabin across the west garden? It's set up for visitors who want a little more independence. The fridge is stocked, and so's the bar." His smirk grows. "And I'll make sure none of my shadowy companions venture out that way all night, so you don't have to worry about invisible spectators."

It's not hard to figure out what he's suggesting with *that* remark. A wash of heat tickles over my skin, matching the trace of pheromones given off by the guys on either side of me.

"That's very generous of you," Andreas says in a wry tone. His gaze holds mine for a beat, desire flaring in the dark gray depths of his eyes. "A night off from worrying sounds good to me. Why don't we check the place out?"

I'm sure we've all noticed the building at the edge of the west garden before. I'd hardly call the thing a "cabin," though.

As we cross the lawn between the flower beds, the grass whispering under our feet, I study the white-washed walls that match the mansion and debate whether it could even reasonably be called a "cottage" or if "house" is the only fair term.

The place is only one floor, but it's decorated as immaculately and stylishly as the mansion proper. We roam from the sprawling kitchen with its gleaming stainless steel through a living room full of plump leather upholstery and peek into three bedrooms with king-sized beds and the relaxing scent of lavender lacing the air.

I can't help comparing the space to the home I imagined us settling into after we first fled the facility. At the time, I pictured someplace full of old wood and a cozy atmosphere, off in the untamed wilderness.

Kind of like the isolated forest cottage where we found Ursula Engel. Tangling with our creator left me with mixed feelings about that kind of setup.

Rollick's guest "cabin" is expansively airy and bright with daylight-toned light fixtures, but something about the openness makes it easier for me to consider unwinding. Like there's room for me to set aside all of the worries on my shoulders for the night, knowing I won't lose sight of anything I needed to keep track of when I come back to them in the morning.

Back in the kitchen, Andreas starts mixing drinks from the offerings in the bar cabinet and fridge. He slides them across the counter to their recipients one by one with the total confidence of the guy who's always held on to every bit of our history.

Jacob speaks up before Drey gets to him. "I want Riva-style lemonade. If you think you can pull that off."

Before I can open my mouth to say I can make it myself, Andreas grins. "Already had it planned. I can make double." He flicks his gaze to me. "And you can tell me how successful I am."

As he squeezes the lemons, I lean my elbows on the island between the kitchen and the living area, basking in the unexpected sense of normalcy. How impossible is it that after all the torment we endured, all the lies the guardians told and the enemies we've faced, we all ended up here?

Together. Alive. More deeply connected than I could have conceived was possible.

Andreas pushes the first glass of homemade lemonade my way, and I bring it to my lips. Does he have any idea how tart I actually like it?

Apparently so. The sourness hits my tongue hard enough to send a shiver through me, but it's one of delight. All of my tastebuds jitter eagerly as I take another gulp.

I grin at Drey. "It's perfect."

Jacob takes a swig from his glass and shakes himself. "All right, that's got bite. Just like our wildcat, when she's in the right mood." He aims a teasing look my way.

With total maturity, I stick my tongue out at him. And then get back to draining my shockingly refreshing drink.

"Where'd you learn to make cocktails?" Zian asks Andreas, sipping from his own glass. It's a fair question, considering we haven't exactly had access to liquor for the vast majority of our lives.

Dominic chuckles. "You know Drey. He probably taught himself out of some bartender's memories."

Andreas holds up his hands. "Hey, we've got to make use of our talents every way we can, right?"

Griffin smiles at him. "We're nothing without our memories, so you've got a pretty important one."

The casually friendly conversation wraps around me with a different sort of warmth. A lump rises in my throat that I can't quite wash away with the last of my lemonade.

Andreas catches my expression, and the happiness in his fades. "Is everything all right, Tink?"

"Yeah," I say around the lingering ache. "It really is. Even with all the crap we've had thrown at us, even with Balthazar carrying on like a maniac... It's amazing that we're here. That we've got each other. We really made it out. No one's controlling us anymore."

A glow lights in the guys' faces as they absorb those words.

"We made it," Dominic agrees in a soft voice. "Maybe there's more that we'd want to do than we've accomplished yet, but this—this is as far as we ever dreamed four years ago."

Griffin tucks his fingers around my elbow and guides me closer to him, his sky-blue eyes sparkling. "And I think we should celebrate that fact—and the woman who made sure we got here."

I'd protest that all of us worked together toward this goal, but then he's drawing my lips to his. I can't refuse the tender passion of his kiss.

The desire that first kindled at Rollick's suggestive proposal flares low in my belly again. I kiss Griffin back hard and then glance around at the others.

"We should definitely celebrate. It's the first time we've been totally free—let's make it the first time all six of us consummate this crazy relationship together too."

Andreas's gaze turns more intense as he comes around the island. "I'm not going to argue with that suggestion." His attention veers to the other guys, his mouth curving slyly. "We should show Riva just how well we can all work together."

From the rush of desire coursing through the air around me, I can safely assume that the others agree.

Jacob leans in to press a kiss to the side of my neck and then raises his eyebrows at Andreas. "Should we take this celebration to one of the bedrooms?"

Drey taps his lips and nods toward the thick black rug that sprawls across the living room floor. "I don't think any of the beds are big enough for us to put all our skills to optimal use. Rollick said we'd get our privacy."

Jake turns toward the living room's expansive window. At a motion of his hand from afar, the curtain hisses into place, cutting off any outside view of our activities. "Sounds good to me."

"No objections here," I manage to say before he's claiming my mouth himself.

We walk toward the rug with halting steps, pausing as each of my guys steps closer to steal a kiss. Dominic winds one tentacle around my waist and down across my ass. Zian sets a steadying hand on my back, wild relief in his eyes at getting to take part in this shared moment without hesitation.

His kiss is absolutely searing. I give myself over to it, my knees wobbling with the sensation of melting, and he eases with me down onto the thick fibers of the rug.

The other guys cluster close around us. Dominic slips his tentacle upward, tugging my shirt up with it. Andreas grins in approval and adds his hands to help strip the top off me.

"Of course," he murmurs, dipping his head to nibble his way along my bared shoulder, "it's even more fun if we can mix things up."

With those last three words, he brushes his fingertips across my back—with a thrilling prick of claws he must have borrowed from Zian. Pleasure quivers over my skin with a jolt of excitement, and I seek out his mouth to muffle my whimper.

That's all the prompting the rest of my men need to get in on the fun. The next thing I know, Zian is grazing his hand over my hair, sending a ripple of telekinetic force to stroke across my scalp. Griffin's eyes flare with a carefully modulated waft of heat that glides down my chest and licks one of my nipples to a pebbled nub.

And Jacob simply gazes at me. A swell of emotion fills me, heady with devotion and hunger, and I realize he's projecting everything they're feeling into me. Wrapping me up in their eagerness from the inside out.

Dom kisses the crook of my neck. "I think I'll stick to the fun I can't share." He lifts both tentacles to wind them around my breasts, simultaneously plucking at the peaks. Giddy shivers race through my chest.

At my shaky breath, Andreas cups my jaw and captures my lips again. He coaxes them apart with a heated swipe of his tongue.

The feelings coursing through my body meld together as if I'm making out not with five different men but one being formed out of all of them. Their talents dart from one to another at the edge of my awareness.

This hand sprouts claws, then that mouth forms fangs that tease me to delightful effect. Invisible caresses join the regular ones at unexpected moments. My entire being has come alive with the flood of sensations.

But even as Dominic glides one tentacle lower to stroke between my legs and my thoughts haze with a deeper wash of bliss, I know they're more than just one presence. All five of my men have their own damage, their own dreams, their own delights.

And I cherish every bit of the things that make them who they are, no matter how different they might be.

My groping hand tugs Zian back to me. I kiss him hard and beam at him, willing all the adoration I feel into my voice. "I love you."

I turn my head to seek out Dominic's lips next, my hips starting to rock with the pulse of his suckers' attentions. A gasp escapes me, and the words tumble out. "I love you."

I find Griffin next, our mouths melding together. After, he nuzzles my forehead as I whisper the confession he can already feel with every exhilarated thump of my heart. "I love you."

Jacob has bowed down to chart a path of kisses across my belly while he undoes the fly of my jeans. I wriggle to help him peel them and my panties off my legs, and then tilt forward to drag him to me.

His breath scorches my mouth. When I give him his "I love you," his fingers squeeze my side as if to remind me that he's never letting me go.

Finally, I reach for Andreas. He lets his lips linger against mine in the sweetest of kisses, growing hotter with each second. I cling to his shirt. "I love you."

The guys offer my sentiment back to me in echoed words, in the press of their fingers and their mouths. One by one, I peel their own clothes off them, caught up in the growing flames of pleasure.

Dominic adjusts his tentacles so he can kneel between my legs. "It's been too long, Sugar," he says, his eyes glinting, and leans in to lap his tongue over my clit.

Andreas captures my cry with a kiss. As Dom devours me, I rock with the blissful waves flowing up from my pussy and the whirlwind of smaller pleasures sparked all around me.

My hand closes around one erection and then another,

doing my best to spread around pleasures of my own. Then Dominic draws back.

Andreas grasps my waist and pulls me down over him. As he tests the wetness of my slit, he cups my cheek. "How'd you like to go for a ride, Tink?"

In answer, I rub myself against his erection. His groan reverberates into me.

As I sink down onto Andreas, Jacob kisses my shoulder blade. "What do you think about taking two of us, Wildcat? If you'd like to try?"

Both of them at the same time? I've thought about being doubly entered, but we haven't attempted it before.

The idea sets off a flare of lust inside me. I nod eagerly.

Jacob crouches behind me, over Andreas's legs, and teases his fingers over my back opening. A faint pressure forms inside as he must bring his talent to bear to stretch the muscles and warm me up.

I sway into his touch between meeting Andreas's thrusts, caught between two points of pleasure. But as I've discovered before, it isn't enough.

I need all of them.

When Jacob lines himself up and lets his cock gradually sink into me, a moan reverberates from my lips. It doesn't stop me from beckoning the others closer.

I wrap my fingers around Zian's jutting cock and grin at his groan through the haze of own my pleasure. As I glance between Griffin and Dominic, Griffin tips forward to offer a quick kiss and then eases to the side to make room. "Just feeling how much you're enjoying this is getting me off more than you could imagine."

He strokes his hand over his own cock, and my gaze

falls to Dominic's. Sensing my intent, my tentacled lover pushes himself farther upright.

Tipping a little farther forward over Andreas, I slick my tongue around Dominic's shaft. He bows toward me and marks my spine with suckered kisses. "Fuck. *You're* amazing, Riva."

We all are. We're fucking spectacular like this.

I lose myself in the flow of pleasure, in the delicious burn of being penetrated twice at once, in the grunts and groans of satisfaction that carry from all around me and from my own lips. The bliss expands from my core through my chest, carried on my tongue as it swivels around Dom's cock, into my hand as it pumps Zian's erection.

The shadows in my veins dance and stretch to meet my men's inner darkness. I don't know where I end and they begin, and I don't think it even matters.

Andreas sets the heel of his hand against my clit as he bucks up into me, and my control starts to fragment. My moan and the clamping of my lips around Dominic have him jerking in my hold.

As we career toward release, our ecstasy sets off a chain reaction. Moments after Dom spills himself in my mouth, Zian groans and clutches my arm. His cock pulses with his own coming.

Jacob swears through his teeth and speeds up his thrusts, slipping his arm around me to squeeze my breast. Another cry breaks from my mouth, and then his ragged breath courses over my back, his hips jerking.

The feel of them all giving themselves over hurtles me

over the edge. I feel as if I'm plummeting and soaring all at once, tumbling head over heels in a rush of pleasure.

Andreas grips me tight, his exhalation hissing through his teeth as he succumbs to our shared climax. As his movements slow beneath me, I slump down into his arms.

The other guys cuddle close around us. I lift my head to draw Griffin in for one more kiss.

A renewed quiver races through my veins. It isn't just desire that was kindled in me but hope as well.

We have to win. Nothing could be as powerful as the bond we share.

We've just got to figure out how to prove that to our enemies.

Fourteen

Riva

When I pad back into the mansion in the early morning light, my ears catch Rollick's voice in an unusually lilting tone. I pause, torn between discomfort over eavesdropping and my instinct to gather all the information about our situation that I can, even if he'd prefer that I didn't.

"I know you'd rather be in San Francisco," he's saying from a nearby room, lightly cajoling. "But this genocidal menace is hitting a lot of major cities, and he doesn't care who gets caught in his wake. You're safer out of the way while we deal with it."

There's a pause, and I realize he must be on the phone, listening to whatever the person on the other end is saying.

Then Rollick's voice turns wry. "I know, Quinn. I'd rather have a few decades without any more potentially world-ending troubles too. Hopefully we'll have this problem quashed before the latest villain gets much farther. Torrent is providing satisfying company in the meantime, isn't he?"

Quinn. I heard him talking to her before—and also heard him refer to the mortal woman he's devoted to. I guess she's that woman, for both him and Torrent, the kraken shifter we met when we were on the run from the guardians months ago.

The demon is worried enough about the threat Balthazar poses that he's had his lover leave her home. That shouldn't surprise me, but somehow the evidence that even this immensely powerful shadowkind has been shaken by recent events makes my mouth go dry.

Rollick chuckles softly at whatever Quinn says in response, and I walk on down the hall toward my guest bedroom. I spent the night in yesterday's clothes, and I could use a change.

The demon must finish his conversation before I've made it far, because the floor creaks faintly behind me. "Did you enjoy your break, little banshee?"

I will down the blush that flares over my cheeks and glance over my shoulder at him. "It was good to remember how far we've already gotten. But now it's time to get back to work, right?"

A bulky form materializes in the hall between us so abruptly I startle. Steel, the stout demon with the metallic scales, peers from Rollick to me with a scowl.

"What kind of work do you think that's going to be?" he demands. "We're hearing that you've been getting friendly with the mortals who made you again. The ones who wanted you to *kill* us."

Oh, shit. I guess Rollick hadn't bothered to fill all our shadowkind allies in on the new phase in our plans, only the ones he wasn't worried about rejecting it.

I fumble for my words. "We're not—we aren't going to do anything *for* them. We're just using them to get to Balthazar." Or at least hoping that we can do that.

Steel's eyes flash. "What do we need those idiots for? All of us here aren't enough?" He spins toward Rollick. "You're *letting* the hybrids get cozy with the monster-murderers?"

"We're not getting cozy!" I protest, but Rollick is already raising his hand for both of us to shut up.

He aims a level stare at the lesser demon. "I didn't 'let' them. I support and encourage this plan. Why shouldn't we let the mortals who hate us draw out the worst of their kind rather than sticking out our own necks even farther?"

Steel growls in frustration. "You're buying into the hybrids' story. They shouldn't want anything to do with those bastards, not if the ones they call 'guardians' *really* tortured them so horribly like they claim."

My hackles rise at the implication that we've lied about our lifelong captivity. "That torture is why we don't have any problem manipulating them when it benefits us."

Steel swivels back toward me. His furor has drawn the attention of others. Several more shadowkind slip into view from the shadows. Who knows how many are watching from the patches of darkness along the edges of the hall.

And it's not just shadowkind who've noticed. A voice rings out from the direction of the back door. "Hey, what's going on over here?"

Jacob stalks over to join us, his expression fierce and his gaze scanning me for injury and then the beings around us for potential threats. The other guys hustle after him, looking equally apprehensive.

Shanty steps forward with a swish of her dark blue hair. "We think there's something odd about you shadowbloods associating with the guardians again. They should be your enemy."

"And they still are," I say tersely. "Pitting two enemies against each other for our own gain isn't that bizarre a tactic, is it?"

She cuts her gaze toward me. "How can we be sure that's your real motivation? They created you. Maybe they're still manipulating *you* to do their dirty work."

Rollick raises his hands. "Come on now, friends. You might be wary of the shadowbloods, but you know *me*. I'm monitoring the entire situation. I haven't seen the slightest sign that my guests are doing anything other than working to protect all of us."

Steel lets out a huff. "That doesn't guarantee anything. They've got powers as strong as ours that work on us— including you."

Another shadowkind steps into the middle of our cluster, his hands on his hips and his eyebrows arched in an amused expression. It's Ruse, the incubus who's particularly close to Sorsha.

"And our powers work on them," he says in a languid tone. "Would you feel better if I used mine to confirm their intentions?"

Zian lets out a snort he unsuccessfully tries to muffle.

"You're going to seduce us into giving up any secrets we've got?"

Ruse laughs. "No, I don't think any of you would appreciate that sort of tactic. One of the skills most cubi types possess is the ability to get a read on people's internal states—not as detailed as outright reading your thoughts, but more than just your feelings. I'll get an impression of future hopes, past context, that sort of thing. I can do a pretty thorough dive."

Steel shifts on his feet. "And you'll report what you find honestly?"

Ruse's eyebrows lift even higher. "In case you've forgotten, I helped Sorsha take down the jackasses who were experimenting with shadowkind since before these guardians even existed, while most of you all buried your heads in the shadows hoping the problem would go away before it ever affected you. So yes, I'll announce it loud and clear if I see any indication that this bunch is going to conspire with our enemies against us."

Shanty lifts her chin toward us. "If they'll agree to it."

Her voice holds an obvious challenge. My skin crawls at the idea of anyone rummaging around inside my head, digging deeper than even Griffin could, but refusing will obviously be seen as confirmation of their suspicions.

And it isn't as if we do have anything to hide. Why not take this easy opportunity to show our true intentions?

I spread my arms and meet Ruse's gaze. "Go right ahead. Hell, I'd *want* to know if the guardians' influence is still affecting us somehow in any way that could hurt the rest of you."

My guys all gradually nod, though Jacob is scowling

and Dominic's forehead has furrowed pensively. We don't know Ruse very well—but Sorsha obviously trusts him a lot, and she's always spoken up for us. I don't think he'd try to screw us over.

"All right." Ruse rubs his hands together, looking way too enthusiastic about this test that could decide whether the shadowkind kick us out or stand behind us. Of course, that could just be because he's sure we'll pass it. "To make sure any worrisome reactions come out, why don't you give me a hand, Mr. Metal Man? Give them each a threatening lunge, and we'll see what that provokes."

Steel aims a glower at the incubus over the impromptu nickname but moves forward. He pauses and then leaps toward me with a guttural roar.

My nerves jump, and my body jerks into a defensive stance instinctively. But as soon as he catches himself and pulls back a step, my heartbeat thumps back into its regular rhythm.

I didn't even pick up on Ruse's rifling through my mind. He grins at me. "Excellent. A healthy burst of self-preservation, a dollop of frustration at having to go through this ridiculous exercise, and no sign at all that you'd want to do our companion here harm even when he's being an ass to you."

Steel lets out a huff, but a little of the tension seeps out of his stance. "What about the bigger picture, not just in the moment."

The incubus shrugs. "I'd assume that if there's any latent hostility at all, I'd catch some hint of it when you're overtly threatening the shadowbloods, don't you? I didn't get any impression that she's looking forward to seeing you wiped out of existence."

"Fine," Shanty breaks in. "Are you going to check the others?"

Ruse looks as if he's held himself back from rolling his eyes. "As soon as you're ready to let me."

Rollick stands back through the entire demonstration, as Steel and Ruse go through the same cycle with each of my guys. When Ruse declares the last of them free of ill intent, our host draws himself up straighter with a waft of his considerable power and peers over the gathered shadowkind.

"Are you all satisfied that these particular shadowbloods are working *with* us rather than against us?"

A ripple of murmurs passes through the group, varying from enthusiastic to reluctant agreement. Rollick waits a few beats to confirm there are no arguments and then motions for the crowd to clear the hallway. "Good. Then I don't want to hear any more about it. We need to focus on tackling our real enemies, not sniping at each other."

Most of the beings simply vanish back into the shadows. Shanty pauses and dips her head to me with a slight grimace. "I apologize for hassling you."

She slips from view before I can even answer.

The guys gather closer around me, Andreas looping his arm around my waist and Griffin taking my hand. Their presence steadies me.

"What *are* we going to do to tackle Balthazar now?" I ask Rollick. "We faked an attack on the guardians, but we don't even know if they believe he was responsible. And we need to nudge them toward some response that'll help us get to Balthazar as well as whatever they intend to do. Pearl hasn't managed to steer them in a clear direction yet, has she?"

Rollick shakes his head. "She hasn't reported any progress so far."

Dominic frowns. "We could reach out to them telling them directly that we believe he's allied with the shadowkind and is looking to take them out. But I don't know how we'd convince them to believe us. We can't tell them who we actually are."

"I can." Toni strides up to us from farther down the hall, where she must have been watching the confrontation. "They knew me at least a little. They know how closely I worked with Balthazar, and they should have no reason to believe *I've* switched my loyalties. A warning that he's gone off the rails and is going against everything he used to stand for would make sense coming from me."

My heart leaps, but I hesitate at the same time. "Are you sure? He can't know yet just how far you've turned against him. If you speak to them, he could find out…"

Toni gazes back at me steadily. "I said I'd try to make up for all the damage he's done while I stood by, and I meant it. The risk is nothing compared to what the rest of you have been through—it's nothing compared to what Pearl is facing right now."

I hadn't realized Pearl had filled Toni in on her mission. Apparently they've gotten even friendlier than I guessed from the snippet of a conversation I overheard.

"That sounds like a good plan to me," Zian puts in. "You'd know how to talk to people like them better than we would anyway."

The corner of her mouth curls upward. "I certainly hope I do. But we need to be coordinated. What exactly should I be nudging them toward doing?"

Rollick rubs his jaw thoughtfully. "Once they believe Balthazar is a threat to them and needs to be stopped... We decided that our best opportunity would be if they can manage to draw him away from his own territory, at least briefly. Somewhere he'll have the benefit of fewer protections and preparation."

Andreas nods. "Since it's the guardians, I'm sure they'll still make sure there are wards against the shadowkind, but it'll give us shadowbloods a better chance at getting to him."

"The tricky part was that Balthazar won't want to go anywhere that's outside his plans," I say, knitting my brow. "But with all the information the Guardianship must have on him... We're hoping they could convince him that he needs to speak to them face to face, or they'll expose something to the governments he's trying to manipulate that would undermine his true intentions. A little blackmail."

Jacob lets out a rough guffaw. "Knowing that psycho, he'd probably show up just so he could wipe them all out and never have to worry about it again."

A small smile crosses my lips. "That's fine. It doesn't even matter if he succeeds. Two birds with one stone. All we need is to get him someplace where he doesn't control everything around us."

Toni absorbs all that and squares her shoulders. "I'll do whatever I can to direct them toward that outcome." She turns to Rollick. "I assume you have some method for me to communicate with the current leaders of the guardians. We might as well get it over with."

"Might as well," he agrees with a chuckle. "Come on —I'll get you set up."

He lifts his gaze to the rest of us. "And you all should start preparing for the most crucial battle of your lives."

FIFTEEN

Dominic

I'm just adjusting my tentacles around the collar of a fresh long-sleeved tee when a knock rattles against my door. I open it expecting to see one of my friends, not paying enough attention to my sense of our talents to realize that's unlikely.

Instead, I find myself looking at the wild-haired, viciously clawed shadowkind man who's one of Rollick's closer companions. I dredge his name up from my memory: Lance.

"The boss thinks you should do some practice before the big day," the unnerving guy announces with a wide grin.

I hesitate, my fingers curling around the doorknob. "Practice what?"

Lance twitches his claws toward my tentacles. "You suck the life out of things, right? Getting better at it? We want to see how good."

A trickle of nausea winds through my gut. I guess I should have expected this development. Rollick insisted on Riva testing her killing power, after all.

I just do my best to forget I even have a killing power when there's no desperate need for it. I'd rather think of myself as only a healer.

We're not likely to have a more desperate need than taking down Balthazar ASAP, though.

I peel my hand off the doorknob and ease out of the room. "All right. Where's Rollick?"

Lance beckons me to follow him. "He thought outside would be good for this. Lots of plants for you to work with."

Plants? Okay, I can deal with that. I don't love destroying them either—something inside me always shrivels a little watching the leaves curl and the stems crumple—but it's a much lesser guilt. No big deal.

The clawed shadowkind leads me out the front door and across the grounds to a stretch of trees. In a clearing up ahead, the sunlight shines off Rollick's tawny hair.

And not just his hair. Red and silver gleam on either side of him. We emerge from the thicker patch of trees to find the demon flanked by Sorsha the phoenix and Riva.

Riva moves to join me, automatically reaching for my hand. Her bright brown gaze searches mine. "You don't have to do anything you're not comfortable with. You don't have to use this part of your ability at all if you don't want to."

The fierceness of her tone makes me wonder if she's argued with Rollick on my behalf. This is obviously about more than just offing some vegetation.

But what can I say? That one of the other guys should borrow my murderous talent so that I don't have to carry the burden of the guilt?

We've all got our own shit to deal with. We all need to carry our own weight. There've been a lot of times in the past when I felt like I couldn't contribute anywhere close to enough, and that was bad enough without backing away when I actually can.

I give Riva's hand a reassuring squeeze. "It's fine." My gaze slides past her to Rollick. "What exactly are you going to ask me to do?"

Rollick's slanted smile holds a trace of an apology. "I thought we'd start with plants first, to get you warmed up. We should see just how far you can extend your abilities now. Once we're clear on that… Have you ever siphoned energy from a shadowkind or your fellow shadowbloods?"

Somehow, as obvious as the question sounds once he's said it, I hadn't considered it as the logical focus of this training. It's what he wanted to know with Riva too.

My insides recoil so abruptly that my tentacles quiver in turn. I have the urge to spit out an automatic denial, but I hold myself back and think through all the times I've needed to use my power so I can be absolutely sure of my answer.

It remains the same. "Not that I'm sure of. I've mostly relied on plants. The guardians and Balthazar's people made me experiment on animals. And a few times I've drained regular human beings when I had to. Once I took one of the younger shadowbloods hostage, and I think I might have absorbed a little of her energy without meaning to, but it was hard to tell at the time and I didn't take any on purpose."

That moment with Celine during our failed escape from Clancy's island facility was the first time I realized that my powers might be starting to work from a distance. Back then, I got the impression from only a few feet away.

After all Matteo's procedures at Balthazar's command, how much farther has my ability expanded? Under Matteo's supervision, I never revealed the new dimension I'd discovered to my talent, and he never stumbled on it.

"I can't use my powers to *heal* shadowkind," I add. "Not totally. When Billy… was hurt, I could patch him up a little, but that's it. It felt completely different from healing a person—or a shadowblood."

Rollick nods. "I suspect melding someone back together properly would be significantly more complex than unraveling them. But it will be good to determine your limits regardless. For this next and hopefully final scheme against Balthazar, disabling beings of various sorts from a distance may be the key."

I roll my shoulders, attempting to loosen both my muscles and the ball of tension in my stomach. "It makes sense. I probably should have tested myself sooner so that we'd know."

Riva hooks her arm right around mine. "I know how much you hate this part of your powers. No one's going to blame you for not pushing yourself to use it more."

The smile I manage to offer her is tight. "I'd blame me. Let's get this over with."

Riva steps back, and my four observers drift to the side of the clearing under the shade of the trees. Rollick points to the other side, where orange ribbons catch my eyes in stark contrast with the green vegetation. "I've marked bushes at three-foot intervals going as far as thirty feet. If you can make it farther than that, I'll add some more. I'd suggest starting with the closest and moving on from there."

That sounds like a reasonable strategy. I drag in a breath and focus on the nearest marked bush, more relieved than I'm comfortable with at the temporary reprieve from using my talents on actual people.

My tentacles snake around my arms and extend toward the line of bushes. The warm breeze tingles over the suckers.

A quiver of the life energy in the nearby plants touches my awareness. I hone my attention to that—and pull.

It's more of an effort than I'm used to, a jerk of my own energy before a flow rushes into me from the shrub. But once I'm locked on to the target, I drink its life force in as easily as if I had my tentacles wrapped around it.

The bush sags, its leaves browning. A heady thrill courses through my veins with the extra energy, and hunger for more coils in my chest.

I yank my focus away, sweat breaking out on the back of my neck that has nothing to do with physical strain. My skin tingles where my tentacles stretch a fraction of an inch farther from my back.

It isn't the ability itself that I really hate. It's the temptation that always grips me when I activate this particular talent.

But I didn't kill even the shrub. I held myself back. Whether because the distance slowed the flow enough that

I couldn't get too caught up in it or because I'm actually getting better at moderating myself is a question I can't bring myself to look at too closely.

One by one, I work my way down the line. Each greater distance requires a bigger initial jolt to latch on to the target, but nothing I can't handle.

It's not until the seventh bush, a little over twenty feet away, that I fling my power forward and grasp nothing.

I steady myself, refocus, and lash out again. This time, I manage to snag hold of the bush's energy enough to start draining it, but a prickling ache forms in the back of my skull at the same time.

After what amounts to a few sips, I let go and turn to my audience. "I almost couldn't reach that one. I don't think it'd be worth trying to go any farther—it'll take more out of me than I'm getting back."

Rollick rubs his hands together. "Still, a reach of twenty feet—that's not bad at all. Especially when you started out needing direct physical contact."

"Yeah." And the last time I stretched my abilities, I'm not sure I could have grasped on to energy more than a quarter that distance away.

Balthazar does excel at turning people more monstrous than they already were.

Lance clicks his claws together. "Is it my turn now?"

Rollick chuckles. "Are you really that eager to lose a little essence?"

"If he can steal it." The shadowkind man grins at me in challenge.

This is the part of the test that I was least looking forward to.

I swallow hard. "I wouldn't have to take very much, right? Just enough to know whether I can take any at all. If I can absorb some energy, then there's no reason to think I'd run into any obstacles taking a larger portion later."

"I definitely don't want you draining my associates to oblivion," Rollick says dryly. "Have a little taste—see how quickly you can take hold. That should tell us plenty."

Lance positions himself several feet away and watches me expectantly, his striking violet eyes looking more amused than anything. "Ready when you are."

Careful and controlled. I'm the best at those virtues out of all of us shadowbloods—at least, among the Firsts.

I inhale slowly and aim my tentacles toward Lance. The hum of energy that emanates from his body gives a different sensation from what I'm used to from plants, animals, or humans. It's a little airier, wispier, like the haze that spills from their bodies instead of blood.

I have to concentrate harder to latch on to the ephemeral impression. My tentacles sway in the air, my nerves jitter—and there, I've got it.

A waft of life force, ten times as giddying as what the plants can offer, sweeps into me. A shiver runs through my body, welcoming it.

Lance shivers too, his jaw flexing. The subtle signal of discomfort chills me.

I let go with a jerk of my tentacles back toward my body as they emerge another tiny bit farther. The extra energy dances through my chest and limbs, but I feel sick at the same time.

"You were right," I say to Rollick. "I can take from

shadowkind. It was a little hard getting started, but I think it'd be easier now that I know what to expect."

"Good to have the confirmation, although it seems unlikely that our main foe will have many if any shadowkind still on his side." Rollick glances at Riva. "The most important test is how quickly and effectively you can drain a fellow shadowblood."

My pulse stutters. Of course Riva isn't here just to offer moral support—she's another target.

The thought shouldn't horrify me as much as it does. I didn't flinch when I watched her inflict her talent on Jacob and Zian. But then, *she* obviously balked at doing it.

I once pieced this woman back together from the brink of death. I've refused to sacrifice any part of my talent or the monstrous appendages that come with it so that I can be ready whenever she needs me again.

Nothing could feel more wrong than to steal any of the life I've preserved so carefully away from her.

Riva takes the same spot Lance did. She smiles at me without any sign of concern. "I'll be fine. I've got lots of strength. And every time I use *my* power, I replenish it."

I don't really think I could hurt her badly by accident. My mind can't even wrap itself around the idea. But nausea bubbles in my gut just at making myself pretend that I'm going to attack her.

I close my eyes for a second. This is *for* her too, isn't it?

To make sure I'll be prepared to defend her from every enemy we might encounter in the days ahead… including the ones with shadows in their blood like us.

I hold on to that justification and fix my gaze on Riva. My tentacles extend toward her.

Memories of much more pleasant encounters tickle up in the back of my mind. The first time she kissed one of my suckers... The way she's accepted my tentacles right inside her...

I shut down that line of thinking before my face can flush too much and yank myself back to the present. All I need is a little tug of energy out of her. Just enough to tell if it'll be much more difficult than I expect.

I'm aware of her presence in multiple ways—the quiver of connection through our marks, the tingle of the talents she could lend me, and the pulse of life resonating through her body. I narrow my attention down to the last of those and ever so tentatively pull.

Energy flares into my chest with a hitch of my heart. I drop my tentacles before Riva can do more than rasp a breath, my throat choking up. "I'm sorry—it was even faster than—"

"Hey, I'm okay." Riva hurries over to me and grasps my arm. There's still color in her cheeks; her eyes still shine as vividly as I'm used to. "It was just a little jab. I've felt *way* worse."

Rollick cocks his head. "You drew on her energy more easily than with a regular human?"

I nod. "That felt more natural than even siphoning from the plants, especially considering the distance." I pause in queasy contemplation. "But I don't know if that's because we're both shadowbloods or because of the other connections we've formed."

Sorsha, who's watched most of the demonstration in silence, raises her eyebrows. "The six of you who grew up together are all pretty tightly connected now, aren't you?

We don't have any other shadowbloods like you around, but you could give a different sort of hybrid a try." She spreads her arms.

She talks as casually about it as Lance did, but I can't help asking, "Are you sure?"

After seeing her phoenix fire consume Balthazar's villa in a matter of seconds, I definitely do not want to piss this woman off.

Sorsha laughs. "That's what we're here for. I'm kind of curious how it feels."

She walks over to the target spot, and I cautiously lift my tentacles again. The warble of her body's energies does feel pretty similar to Riva's, although with a deeper crackle of power that sends goosebumps rippling up my arms.

I reach and take an even smaller gulp now that I'm prepared. Sorsha gives her body a little shake. "That wasn't bad at all."

Rollick is studying me. "Still easier?"

"Yeah." I look down at my tentacles as they coil closer around my shoulders. "I guess the shadowblood energy matches the best with my own, so it's the simplest to take in."

"Sounds like as good an explanation as any." Rollick gives me another crooked smile. "Somehow I'm guessing you'd rather not extend the practice beyond our initial experiments."

God, no. "I think I've got a pretty good idea of what to expect just from that," I say diplomatically.

"All right. There's one other matter I'd like to talk with you about, just the two of us."

Riva shoots him a curious glance, but she heads back

to the house without complaint. Rollick's done more than enough to earn all of our trust.

Sorsha ambles off with Lance, motioning toward his clawed hands. "So, I'm assuming you don't attend a whole lot of tea parties…"

Rollick waits until they're all out of hearing. I assume he can tell whether there are any shadowkind nearby in the shadows too, although maybe he doesn't care about some of them overhearing.

"I've been thinking about the problem of your tentacles," he says.

I instinctively reach toward my shoulder, toward the spot on my back just below where one of the two tentacles spouts. Something about his phrasing, calling them a "problem," itches at me. "What about them?"

"It's odd that the others haven't experienced any kind of growth when they've experimented with borrowing your power. From what I've gathered, you didn't always have those appendages, did you?"

I shake my head. "They emerged about three years ago."

Rollick taps his lips. "And you could draw energy to heal before that. They weren't necessary."

"Well, no." I hesitate. "But my powers got stronger after they came out. I don't know if that's because of them or if it would have happened anyway."

"They do make a regular life blending in among mortals difficult," the demon says. "Nearly as much as those claws of Lance's. I told you before that we could attempt cutting them off but that there was a reasonable chance they'd simply grow back."

The itch expands into a creeping sensation over my skin. "I decided it wasn't worth trying."

"Yes. But having worked together some more with our phoenix, it occurred to me—I think it's likely Sorsha could use her supernatural fire to permanently burn them away. If you wanted that."

My heart all but stops. It takes me a few seconds to recover my voice. "I—I mean, I might need them in the battle—"

Rollick waves his hand dismissively. "Yes, of course. I didn't mean right away. But after we've dealt with this Balthazar and whatever's left of the Guardianship if necessary, when I'd hope you six can go on to lead relatively peaceful lives... I thought you should know the option is on the table. So you can take your time considering it. It sounds as if you could assume you'd keep some—if not all—of your actual powers."

To shed this very literal weight off my back—to feel fully human again on the outside if not the inside... There's no energy I could siphon that could bring the same thrill as that thought.

But it comes with a starker uncertainty that sinks through my abdomen. Without the tentacles, I might only be capable of the relatively minor healing I could pull off as a kid and teenager.

Would that be so awful, if we weren't fighting battles where my friends might take near-fatal injuries?

Can I even really hope that we'll finally get the kind of peace where giving them up wouldn't feel like a huge risk?

Before I can prod at that question much further, a curvy figure bursts out of the shadows with a jostle of blond curls. Pearl grins up at Rollick with an eager but urgent air.

"Toni gave them the push they needed!" she crows. "We've got them! The Guardianship is making their plans for Balthazar—and he's agreed to meet them tomorrow."

Sixteen

Riva

I lean against the tree trunk, the tang of pine scent tickling my nose, and will away the knots in my stomach. Knots that aren't only because of the perilous mission we're here to carry out.

In every direction around my perch about ten feet off the ground, trees loom close together. Their branches—some bare, many sprouting needles so dense they look like a chillier version of palm-tree fronds—crisscross overhead, filtering the late-afternoon sunlight.

A faint dusting of snow coats the forest floor and the winter-wizened vegetation between the trees, which is why I'm up in the air. Turning invisible doesn't do us much good when our footprints will still be seen.

Everything about this place washes over me like an echo from the past. The only thing missing from the memories it stirs up is the dark walls and sloping roof of Ursula Engel's cabin.

We aren't anywhere near our creator's final home, the site of her death. It turns out—maybe not surprisingly, considering they owned an entire tropical island—that the Guardianship has a little property in Europe too. Including several dozen acres of undeveloped forest in northern Wales.

Balthazar agreed to meet them here, on a slab of concrete the size of a tennis court that's the only sign of human intervention here so far. It's just beyond the limits of my vision through the trees up ahead.

Whatever the guardians planned to do with this territory, they haven't gotten very far yet.

We didn't want to approach that site too closely until Balthazar arrived. We don't know how carefully the guardians are patrolling the woods... or whether our greater foe might have sent some of his own people to make an advance survey of the terrain.

He's definitely bringing some of the shadowbloods with him. We'd briefly hoped that we might be able to end the confrontation before it even started, with Sorsha blasting his helicopter out of the sky. But in my most recent drowsing for his location, I determined that Nadia, Booker, and Devon are in the helicopter with him.

We have no idea how many of the other shadowblood kids he might be bringing along. Sorsha has managed to get her sights on it from a distance and reported it's a large one that could hold at least twelve people as well as the pilot.

She didn't argue when I insisted that we had to wait until we could strike at Balthazar without murdering the kids too. Neither did Rollick.

I should probably be glad that most of the demon's allies didn't come along this far on the mission, since the Guardianship has prepped the forest around their future building site with numerous deposits of silver and iron. I can only imagine what the other shadowkind would have to say about our hesitation.

It shouldn't be a problem. Balthazar will get out of the helicopter, and all I need is to set eyes on him to project the killing shriek already vibrating at the base of my throat. Or maybe Jacob or Dominic or Sorsha will get a clear enough line of attack first.

Our former captor isn't leaving this forest alive, one way or the other. Not as long as we're alive to have any say about it.

An icy breeze winds between the branches. Our supernatural concealment shields us from sight but not the nipping chill. My fingers curl inside the gloves I'm ready to tear off the instant I need my claws.

The slimmer branches sway around me. Everywhere I look, images float up from our stealthy trek to Engel's isolated home.

I can't help thinking back to the deceptive welcome she gave us while she was plotting our deaths the whole time. To the words she hurled at us as her mercenaries burst into the house.

You're monsters of the worst kind. Abominations. Now I can end the catastrophe I set in motion.

I lower my head and gather my resolve, ignoring the pained thud of my heart. Our creator didn't end us. She was wrong.

I'm not going to let the Guardianship *or* Balthazar

doom us and the other shadowbloods, as much as they might want to.

A high-pitched bird call peals through the forest, and my gaze darts up. It's a whistle we're using as a signal—Zian is alerting us that it's time to close in.

I shed my gloves and dart along the branch I'm perched on to leap to the tree ahead of me. My feet land with only the softest patter. My clawed fingers dig into the bark to steady me.

Over the rustling of the wind through the pine needles, the distant warble of helicopter blades reaches my ears. Zian's heightened senses will have picked it up before the rest of us.

With another few careful jumps, I can make out the stretch of bare pavement through the interlaced branches. I can also catch the slight movements of several figures in military-style camouflage lurking on the forest floor between me and the landing spot.

Immediately, I can tell they're with the Guardianship, not Balthazar. Their helmets and vests may be painted in greens and browns to help them blend in with the vegetation, but the style is unmistakably familiar and the texture gives away the metal underneath.

Protections against shadowkind. We did convince them that Balthazar has allied with monsters in his supposed quest to bring down humanity.

From Pearl's questioning of one of the Guardianship board members under her seductive spell, we've gathered that Balthazar left evidence to suggest we shadowbloods fled to freedom after killing Clancy. The guardians have no idea that he rounded us up.

There's no way they could imagine that he not only has their former tools at his beck and call but can also manufacture more shadowbloods to his specifications.

Apparently, the guardians are hoping to take him prisoner—or kill him if that's their only option. I don't think they're remotely prepared for the fight he'll actually give them.

But that's okay. I can't summon any sympathy for the organization that shaped us through clinical brutality.

All that matters is finding our opening to destroy the man in charge. If we can do that, then the other shadowbloods will be free of his genocidal ambitions.

None of us can figure out how to build real lives for ourselves until he's gone.

I cross the short distance between two more trees even more carefully, curling my fingers around branches and easing my feet across rather than risking a small jump. Thankfully, Wales doesn't get huge snowfalls, so there isn't enough of a dusting under my boots to do more than stick to the soles.

When I have a reasonably clear view of the concrete surface, with only a couple of trees hiding any movements the branch under me makes, I sink into a crouch. The whir of the helicopter blades grows ever louder.

Through the tingle of energy in the marks along my collarbone, I touch base with each of my men. Zian and Jacob have crept up to the edge of the landing spot in trees several yards on either side of me.

Dominic has settled onto a branch almost directly across from me, where he was set by Sorsha as planned. Without supernatural strength and speed or Jacob's telekinetic ability to help him along, we figured it was safer to have her carry him into place.

Andreas has hung back about a quarter of a mile away. We decided his ability to confuse our enemies wasn't worth the possibility of him getting caught, since agility isn't his strongest suit either. But he's ready to race in and help however he can if it sounds like we need it.

And he's already given us a huge advantage with the invisibility he cast over us.

Griffin, who's never been much of a physical fighter, stayed with Drey. He'll be casting calming vibes over the guardians and Balthazar from a distance to help the beginning of the confrontation go smoothly.

We're all in this together, working toward the same goal. Connected not just by blood but by love and trust as well.

Living proof that we're so much more than the monsters Engel saw us as.

Below me, the patrolling guardians come to a halt. The helicopter glides into view, stark black against the cloud-hazed sky.

I think of Balthazar's smug face on the villa's TV screen. Of his demands that I take his side as his daughter against everyone I care about.

Of his casual slaughter of Lindsay and Sully—just kids, just shadowbloods like us.

My shriek burns in my throat. My muscles tense in anticipation.

It doesn't really matter who takes him down in the end, as long as we destroy him. But I can't deny that I'll be happiest if it's me.

He insisted on being a part of my existence from the moment of my conception, in ways I'd never have asked for. So now I'm going to excise him from my life with as much compassion as he deserves: none.

As the chopper descends to the ground with a slight sway in a gust of wind, three men and a woman emerge from the trees on the other side of the concrete clearing to meet Balthazar. In their midst, I recognize the dour face and slumped shoulders of the man who scolded Clancy: Richmond from the board.

I assume the others are fellow board members. How large is their organization anyway? It seems like every time we pick away at their numbers, more spring up like heads on a hydra.

Their authority and their resources have dwindled, though. They've lost every member of their founding families, one way or another. They've lost all of the shadowbloods they've created.

Without us, they're nothing. They can't even track us down without one of our own.

The helicopter settles onto the concrete surface. The blades slow and go still, leaving an eerie hush in their wake.

Any second now, he'll step into view—

A door opens with a faint squeak, but it's on the opposite side of the chopper from me. I grit my teeth in frustration.

My jaw clenches even tighter when Balthazar makes his appearance in front of the helicopter.

At least, I assume he's part of the cluster I'm seeing. Six tall men, each as brawny as our leonine former captor himself and at least half a foot taller, form a tight circle that Balthazar must be in the center of. He's brought a literal human shield with him.

Is he only worried about physical attacks, or has he considered that we shadowbloods might be involved in this confrontation after all? Or maybe he isn't completely sure that he has grabbed all the Guardianship's test subjects, and he figures it's better to take precautions about being seen.

Either way, I can't inflict my shriek on him while those thugs are in the way.

Thugs seems like the right word for them. They're wearing heavy coats that amplify their bulk, and a couple of them have shaved heads revealing the tattoos of skulls, daggers, and other violent imagery that decorate their skin. Another has a scar carved across his protruding brow from some past fight.

They must be some of his new shadowbloods—the criminals he stole from various prisons. One of them lifts his hand to scratch his neck, and I get a glimpse of a metal band around his wrist beneath the cuff of his coat.

My pulse thumps hard. I could shriek his bodyguards' deaths and then move on to him, but as soon as any of them start to falter, he'll know something's wrong.

He might have that concentration-shattering device on him. We have earplugs in our pockets, but we felt it was more important to be able to follow the initial conversation when he shouldn't know we're here. I might miss an opening if I can't hear what's going on.

And who knows what other strategies he's come up with?

No, I can't attack yet. We wait until we have a clear shot at the man himself. That was the plan.

Although if this meeting goes far enough to shit that he heads back to the helicopter without any of us getting that chance, all bets are off.

As Balthazar's huddle comes to a stop about ten feet from the board members, I let my gaze dart to the helicopter for a split-second.

I know I traced the three younger shadowbloods' location to the same path that Balthazar's presence was moving along. They *had* to be in the helicopter with him.

He's left them and maybe other shadowbloods inside —why? If he doesn't want his former colleagues seeing their "property" in his hands, why would he bring them at all?

A whiff of adrenaline reaches me from the lurking guardians below. They're already preparing to launch themselves at Balthazar just like we are.

But Richmond does still offer the last remaining founder of the Guardianship a brief chance to talk. He lets out a slight scoffing sound. "What's this, Otto? You're not even going to let us see your face in person? You'd think we were the ones who attacked you."

Balthazar's ominous baritone carries from his ring of bodyguards. "I know you think I'm just a problem to be solved. There's no need to play friendly."

Richmond sighs and makes a swift flick of his hand that could be dismissed as fidgeting—except at the next second, a squad of some twenty armed and armored guardians step from the trees, surrounding Balthazar's group and cutting him off from the helicopter.

Richmond lifts his chin. "You can force your men to die for this, or—"

If Balthazar gives a signal of his own, I don't know how anyone sees it. But before Richmond gives his second option, a surge of movement explodes from the forest.

Five more shadowbloods spring from the helicopter, all of them teens—Nadia, Booker, and Devon among them. A much greater force charges from between the trees where they must have used their own talents to allow them to prowl unseen.

It only takes the space of my heart's stutter for chaos to erupt across the concrete field. Blinding light sears through the space, blue lightning sizzles in its midst, and gunshots thunder.

Another second, and the screams start splitting the air. Bodies thud to the ground amid a fierce bellow that sends ripples all the way to my perch, shaking the branch beneath me. Other figures dash around the mass of attackers at supernatural speed.

And in a pause between two streaks of Nadia's blazing light, my gaze comes to rest on Balthazar himself.

Now that they've seen how easily they can take down the guardians, his bodyguards are easing away from him to deal out their own attacks. One's eyes flare with an unnerving green light; another lashes out with an arm that stretches to twice its normal length.

Between them, they've left a gap straight to their master.

He looks exactly as I remember: the mane of silver-and-gold hair, the square jaw, the coldly intent eyes.

Exactly like the psychopath he's proven himself to be over and over again.

I called him Dad once, but only to save my guys. His presence doesn't stir the faintest hint of a familial bond.

I don't hesitate. The moment I recognize what I'm seeing, I'm propelling my mental shriek straight into his skull.

In the midst of the bolts of energy and the cacophony of the battle, maybe my concentration isn't perfect. Just as I feel the vicious energy hit its target, Balthazar flinches—and wrenches his hand toward his pocket.

It's possible he does have the device he used to interrupt my previous attack on him. It's even possible he'd have managed to activate it before I lanced my scream into him with even more force, if I were alone.

But I'm not.

Before Balthazar's fingers quite brush the surface of his jacket, his wrist snaps sideways as if twisted by an invisible force. His forearm cracks in a different direction, the bone raking through the fabric.

And with the extra second Jacob earned me, I throw everything I have into my shriek.

There's no time for lingering in the torment, as much as I might like to pay this man back for what he did to us like I got to with Matteo. I channel all of my brutal power into the wrinkled organ within his skull.

The neurons cleave apart; the tissue shreds. The bony dome fractures into a thousand pieces.

Life sputters out.

Balthazar's knees buckle, a single searing jolt of pain

resonating from him into me. As he topples over, his body jerks.

It slams into the ground, and his face crumples in. Bloody dents burst across his flesh, smashing his features.

I can picture Zian's fist pounding into our former captor. Zee is still invisible, but his supernatural strength shows in every break of Balthazar's skull—until all that remains is a bloody pulp framed by crimson-streaked hair.

Relief sweeps through me, knocking the breath out of my lungs. It's done. We did it. Balthazar is actually… gone.

I hurl myself from my tree and race to the concrete yard, needing to see the proof up close to confirm it. Needing to taste the tang of our tormenter's blood in the air.

Skidding to a stop just a foot away, I stare down at Balthazar's mutilated and undeniably dead form. The man who called himself my father only as another way to control me. The man who forced himself into all our lives even more viciously than the guardians he once helped lead.

He can't hurt anyone else ever again.

As my heart thumps hard in my chest, a sense of triumph that has a shocked edge to it fills my chest.

We *really* did it. I almost didn't believe we could—

The impression of being stared at yanks my attention away. I glance up and find the nearest of the scattered shadowbloods gaping at Balthazar, looking totally bewildered.

Right. They can't see me or Zian to know what even happened to him.

That thought has just passed through my head when Nadia lets out a cry and hurls a blast of her blazing light our way. It smacks into me with an unnerving prickling sensation, as if I'm sloughing off my skin like a snake.

No, not my skin—Andreas's invisibility. As I blink the burn from my eyes, Zian wavers into sight beside me.

He's fully wolf-manned out, muzzle jutting and fur sprouting down his neck to the collar of his coat. Gore smears his clenched fists.

"You…" Nadia says in a shaky voice.

I touch Zian's arm in solidarity and raise my voice to peal out through the clearing. "Shadowbloods! Balthazar is dead. He doesn't control you anymore. It's over."

More of the figures who were still fighting the remaining guardians swing toward us. Only a few continue the battle—nearly all of their enemies have fallen anyway.

Bodies litter the concrete surface, but nearly all of the dead wear guardian uniforms. Balthazar's bodyguards have smashed right through the four board members who stood nearest, their corpses lying crumpled and distorted on the ground several feet away from where I stand.

One of those thugs, the one with the scar across his brow, stares at Balthazar's battered form. He lifts his gaze to me, and his lips curl with a snarl. "*You* did that?"

I blink, my throat momentarily closing up. "I—"

All around us, pairs of shadowblood eyes have narrowed. Hostility crackles on the crisp breeze.

The man who spoke cracks his knuckles and steps toward us. "You're going to pay."

SEVENTEEN

Riva

As the scarred shadowblood thug strides toward us, Zian jerks closer to my side, more visible by the second just like I am. His lips pull back to show his wolf-man fangs.

My pulse is racing so fast my chest rattles with it, but I hold up my hands. "Wait! We're on the same side as you. We got rid of Balthazar to set you free."

I can't tell if the hulking shadowblood even registers my words. Fury flashes in his eyes—and a figure outlined in fire descends from the sky to plant herself by my side.

Sorsha's phoenix flames sear away the invisibility Andreas had cast over her. She takes in the swarm of shadowbloods around us, a ball of fire hovering over one hand and her scorching wings unfurled from her back. "Back off. The fight is over."

The several shadowbloods who'd been watching the confrontation freeze. Even the man who was stalking toward us hesitates, sizing Sorsha up. Through the tears in his coat from the fighting, I see his muscles flex.

One of the other former inmates, one with a tattoo of a skull in a snake's embrace emblazoned on his shaved scalp, pushes toward us. Thick, bone-like blades protrude from his shoulders—they ripped through his clothing as they emerged from his body.

He jabs his hand at us. "You were working with the Guardianship—the fuckers who made all you young ones. You turned on our own people to help *them*."

A few gasps from around us tell me that the kids in the crowd hadn't thought the situation quite that far through yet—and find the revelation even more shocking than our accuser does.

I raise my chin, keeping my voice loud and steady. "We *used* the guardians. When we tried to get at Balthazar by ourselves before on his own territory, he was too prepared."

A thin, scratchy voice wavers out from my left. "You tricked him. You tricked *us*!"

My head jerks around. Tegan has come up beside Nadia, her hands clenched at her sides, her pale face gone even more sallow with horror within its frame of fawn-brown hair.

Oh, God. I didn't even realize she was here. The kid is *twelve*, for fuck's sake. What was Balthazar thinking?

I already know the answer to that question, so sure it turns my stomach. He was only thinking about his ends, his goals, and to hell with how it hurts anyone else.

"We killed him for you," Zian protests, looking more bewildered than threatening now.

I motion to my bare wrist. "The manacles don't matter anymore. Sorsha can burn out the mechanisms. You don't have to do any more fighting for—"

"Why the hell wouldn't we want to fight for him?" the tattooed man interrupts. He holds up his meaty hands, the thin leather gloves he was wearing splashed with blood. "*He* freed us from life behind bars. He gave us the power to do whatever the fuck we want."

A figure drops from one of the trees at the edge of the pavement—Jacob, his form hazy as his own invisibility has started to fade with the passing of time. "He used you like tools, just like the guardians always did with us. He *was* one of them and only left them so he could be even worse."

"Now they're all dead," I add, motioning to the bodies strewn around us. "Like Sorsha said, it's over."

The scarred guy close to us aims a sneer my way. "I don't think so. I liked the work he gave us. And it sounds like you expect us to stop."

My heart lurches. But maybe I shouldn't be surprised that the hardened criminals Balthazar picked out to do his dirtiest work are the kind of people who'd enjoy bashing up buildings and leaving carnage in their wake.

I always knew we might have to fight his new shadowbloods as well as the man himself. I hadn't expected it to go down quite like this, though.

My gaze darts to Nadia. She's still poised with her hands raised as if ready to blast us with another bolt of light. As if she thinks she might need to.

The taste of ash coats my mouth. "Nadia, you know

what Balthazar was like. You saw what he did to Lindsay —to Sully—what he always threatened to do to you."

She shakes her head with an odd twitch of her eyes, as if they refuse to totally focus. "He cut out the weak ones. He found a way to make us stronger."

"Yeah!" Tegan says, stirring restlessly from foot to foot. "He made us as powerful as you Firsts are. Maybe more! Like we always should have been."

Nadia rolls her shoulders with another twitch, and her tone turns harsh. "You're jealous. He said you probably would be. You liked being the strongest shadowbloods, seeing the rest of us so weak and pathetic. You wanted to always be in charge of us. Now we can fight back for ourselves."

Her voice takes on a fiercer rasp with those last few words, and ice forms around my gut. I can imagine Balthazar indoctrinating the kids, telling them lies over and over that fed into their insecurities and regrets.

During the time when we all lived together, some of them admitted to me that they longed for more power. That they felt useless, expendable. And it wasn't as if they could see any chance of living like a regular human instead.

They had the worst of both words, too monstrous to be normal but not monstrous enough to fight their way free, and Balthazar gave them a little flame of hope.

I'd like to think that his manipulations wouldn't have worked on the kids I knew back on the island. But Ajax told me that the process for bringing out their stronger talents has riled up something else in the younger shadowbloods.

Has Balthazar not just expanded their powers but made them as insane as he was too?

Not all of them. Ajax sounded normal.

And another familiar voice, if a little hoarse, carries from the other side of the clearing. "You've got to know that's not true, Nadia."

I yank my gaze in the opposite direction. Booker stands tensed near the tree line, his shaggy blond hair damp with sweat and maybe a little blood, no sign of carefree surfer dude attitude in him now.

His supernatural ability was reading auras. I have no idea how Balthazar's treatment might have warped that talent.

"The Firsts always looked out for us," he adds. "They did everything they could to get us away from the guardians. Of course they'd do the same with Balthazar."

Nadia's eyes flick to her boyfriend—if they still have that kind of relationship—but only for a second. Her expression tightens.

"He could have given us more," she says, her voice rising. "He found ways of making us better that no one else managed to. They took that chance away from us."

Sorsha folds her arms in front of her with a skeptical glance. "From what I've seen, this Balthazar guy didn't give you anything except a whole lot of crap to weigh on your conscience. If he wasn't sending you kids out to destroy and murder already, he would have soon."

The tattooed man with the bladed shoulders snorts. "There's nothing wrong with teaching a lesson to the people who never thought we'd amount to anything anyway."

Tegan glares at Sorsha. "We don't even know who you are. What does it matter what you think?"

I summon all the patience I can. "Sorsha's with us. She's as close to blood as anyone who wasn't created by the guardians can get, and she wants what's best for you too. If we could just talk this through, I'm sure we could figure out a way to go forward that—"

"They're going to try to take our powers away!" a youthful voice cries out from closer to the helicopter. "They want to crush us like they did to the boss."

"No!" My jaw clenches for a moment before I can speak through my frustration. "We're looking out for you just like Booker said. We can set up new lives free from anyone ordering us around or forcing us into awful situations."

The tattooed man who appears to be the most outspoken of the criminal shadowbloods sputters with derisive laughter and starts striding toward us again. "I don't think so. Sounds like you pipsqueaks figure *you* can give the orders now. No fucking thank you. Get out of my way. We've got so much more to do."

I don't like the awful implications of his statement—and obviously neither does Sorsha. She steps forward to meet him, her wings flaring brighter. "Stop right there."

His face flushes with anger. "I'm getting back on that chopper to go where I feel like, and I'm taking whoever wants to come with me. Unless you really are trying to call the shots for us now."

"You can't just take off," I protest. Not to do whatever it is he and the other shadowbloods are planning—we can't leave these super-powered criminals running rampant.

"Oh, I think we can," the tattooed man growls, and springs forward to lunge past Sorsha toward the helicopter.

A yelp of dismay breaks from my throat. Sorsha spins, her hand whipping back to fling fire toward him—and a streak of blinding light sears from Nadia's hands straight into the phoenix's eyes.

Sorsha gasps, and her spurt of fire flies wide, singeing the back of the tattooed guy's coat before smacking into a nearby tree. The flames roar up the trunk with a wash of heat.

Suddenly, everyone seems to be yelling. I whirl around, reaching out toward Nadia and Tegan, but the two girls dash toward the helicopter. Other shadowbloods race off into the forest or follow them to the chopper.

Zian looms over me, his head swiveling as if he's hoping to protect me from all sides. My throat aches with a futile scream I don't know how to let out.

Who should I be attacking here, if anyone? Technically Sorsha attacked them first; Nadia was only defending someone she apparently sees as a friend.

Jacob charges toward the helicopter too, lifting his hands. One of the propeller blades is already bending with a metallic groan when a shadowblood thug hurtles into Jake.

They thump to the ground and roll on the concrete. Barbs jut from the older man's hand and wrist, and he rakes them across Jacob's face.

As I scramble to help, my lips parting with a shriek I

might emit after all, the thug shoves himself away from Jacob with a stomp of a foot that's grown abnormally large and a crack of Jacob's forearm.

The first squeak of sound breaks from my lips, and another body slams into me from behind. I topple face-first toward the pavement, only just throwing out my hands in time to catch myself with a scrape down to my elbows.

I buck at my attacker with all my supernatural strength, but they're already heaving away off me. Zian barges toward him with a wolfish snarl.

Devon has clambered partway into the helicopter. He raises his hand toward the warped blade as another of the former inmates hauls himself right onto the top of the aircraft to reach it.

As heat flares from Devon's hands with a ruddy glow, softening the metal, the guy up top wrenches the propeller back into its proper shape.

I push myself toward them. If they get that thing in the air—if we can't even try to talk sense into them—

Then Tegan leaps between us Firsts and the chopper, her mouth opening wide.

I've seen the twelve-year-old use her power once before —to help us escape the guardians on the island facility. Then, she only emitted a puff of noxious smoke just large enough to cover a narrow path.

Now, a rippling haze billows out of her with a heave of breath. It rushes toward us, stinging my eyes and burning my lungs in an instant.

"You don't get to stop us!" she shouts. "No one gets to hold us down ever again."

I crumple, coughing and wheezing. Zian slumps beside me.

And the rumble of the helicopter's propeller reverberates through the clearing.

I hear Sorsha muttering curses, but no more fire streaks through the air. Between Nadia's light and the toxic haze, she's probably afraid she'll end up incinerating us rather than the escapees.

I'm not sure I'd even want her to try. The adult shadowbloods might be hardened criminals, but the kids… There's got to be a way to shake them out of their madness.

A soft pressure wraps around my wrist—the curl of a tentacle. As the whir of the helicopter fades into the air, a breeze gusts through the smoke, washing the worst of it away.

Dominic kneels beside me, his other tentacle extended toward Jacob's sprawled form, a bush he must have uprooted clutched in his hands. With a surge of tingling energy, the pain in my lungs recedes.

The second Jacob's bones have melded back into a regular arm shape, Dominic reaches toward Zian and Sorsha. His mouth tightens, and the shrub in his hands withers even more.

Jacob rolls into a sitting position, swiping at the blood left on his face from the healed cuts. "Fucking hell." Then his gaze fixes on something across the clearing from us, and his stance goes rigid.

Booker hurries over, his eyes wide. He motions to a girl who looks to be about fifteen, who's hugging her skinny frame tightly.

The teens hesitate several steps from our cluster. Booker's gaze darts between us. "We—we can come with you, right? I didn't want— I don't know what they think they're going to do— Those guys scare me."

From the way he talked to Nadia, I suspect even she scares him right now.

I swallow against the dryness of my throat. "Of course. That's what we wanted from *all* of you."

My gaze travels around the concrete yard, taking in the corpses of the guardians and Balthazar, the streaks of blood and ash, and the aching absence of all the shadowbloods we meant to save. A wave of despair crashes down on my spirits.

The battle was supposed to be over. We destroyed all our enemies. So why does it feel like we only created more?

I wet my lips, the flavor of cinders filling my mouth. "And now we have to figure out where we go from here."

EIGHTEEN

The door for the cell Riva directs me to is locked. But the dim building in the middle of nowhere, northern China, has looked abandoned from the moment we showed up. Griffin confirmed that he couldn't sense any human emotions inside other than the boy we're here to save.

So I aim my searing vision at the door without any concern about triggering an alarm. Really, after walking through the silent hallways where the air is almost as still and icy as outside the grim gray walls, I'd *welcome* a chance to actually fight.

Riva's apparently been talking to Ajax since well before we arrived, in her head. He directed us to his cell.

He must be able to see my progress, but he doesn't risk breaking my concentration until the narrow slab I've carved out of the steel door topples out into our waiting hands. The light catches on his dark brown face amid the thicker darkness beyond, and his voice slips into my mind without any movement of his lips.

You made it. Thank you.

Even his inner voice sounds exhausted. Bags have formed under his eyes.

As Riva extends her hand to help him ease his slim form through the opening, Andreas peers in over the boy's head. "They didn't even leave you any food?"

Ajax shrugs and opens his mouth. I guess it's been a long time since he spoke the regular way, because his regular voice comes out all creaky. "I don't think they saw much point. Balthazar never got much use out of me anyway. I ate yesterday."

"That's not enough," Dominic says with a strained note, and beckons Ajax over. "Here, let me give you a quick energy boost—and I've got some protein bars. There are a bunch of snacks on the jet once we get there."

While we tramp back through the dreary halls, the fourteen-year-old chomps through three protein bars and uses his telepathy to give all of us the account he already passed on to Riva. *Balthazar only had a couple of staff people here. They found out he died last night. Right away, they took off. They might have forgotten I was even here. Balthazar came to round up the shadowbloods he actually wanted to use the day before.*

Jacob scowls, his hands flexing like he'd welcome a fight or two himself. "That's no excuse. That fucking psychopath. And the other shadowbloods talking like —like—"

He cuts himself off with a growl of indignation. I can't tell whether he stopped there because he can't bear to put the praise we heard from the shadowbloods in the forest into words… or because he's worried *Ajax* won't be able to bear it.

But if the kid's been able to tap into the minds of everyone in the building with him, if he's noticed his fellow shadowbloods getting unhinged, then I'm pretty sure he'll have picked up on their shifting attitudes toward their captor too.

We pass a gymnasium obviously used for training and a few other rooms that jolt me back to images from our time in the guardians' facilities. Balthazar didn't leave the basics behind when he abandoned the Guardianship.

At one smaller room where a desk is visible, Riva pauses. She waves the rest of us onward. "Get Ajax to the helicopter so he can rest. I want to take a quick look in here."

Griffin dips his head. "I'll help him relax."

Though the whole building has been nothing but empty gloom other than Ajax's cell, I hang back automatically. I'm not leaving Riva alone, not on our greatest enemy's turf.

Even if just yesterday I pummeled that enemy's head into a pulp.

My jaw clenches at the memory. It should come with a rush of triumph, but instead all that floats up is the echoes of horror and fury from when I watched the people—even the *kids*—we came to save complain at us like the maniac we killed was some kind of hero.

It's been almost a full day since the ambush in the forest. We haven't had any contact from the other shadowbloods.

Riva has used Griffin's seeking talent to check the location of the teens she was friendly with a few times, but all that's told us is they've stayed in Europe. They're roving around, maybe using whatever vehicles Balthazar left behind like that helicopter.

I don't like the sense of the other shadowbloods prowling across the continent, stewing in the brutal wildness they showed against the guardians—and against us. Especially the assholes who don't even know what it really means to call yourself a shadowblood.

Riva paws through the desk drawers and the jumble of items left on the shelves before letting out a rough sigh. "Well, there wasn't much chance we'd find anything helpful here. Even if Balthazar left some clue behind, it'd be about his plans, not theirs."

I don't need to ask which "they" she's talking about. "Maybe they'll simmer down after they get used to him being gone," I suggest as we hustle to catch up with the others. "Lay low and just live, the way we wanted anyway. We don't even know if the stuff Balthazar did to give them powers will wear off after a while."

Riva shoots me a grim smile. "That's a nice thought, anyway."

As we reach Rollick's helicopter, she falls into a tense silence. I don't think I've seen her relax since we set out to face Balthazar yesterday.

It isn't the same barely restrained rage that was smoldering inside her for days in Balthazar's villa. As the chopper flies out to the landing strip where the jet waits for the longer trip back to Spain, she manages to speak gently with Ajax about where we're heading, and she leans into Andreas's arms when he offers a quick embrace.

I'm not afraid she's going to explode with anger like I was back then. But every time I look at the tightness of her jaw, the rigid set of her shoulders, my heart aches.

She wanted Balthazar's death to be the end of our problems. She wanted this long, awful journey to be over so badly—maybe more than any of the rest of us.

And now we have no way of even *knowing* when the catastrophe is really over.

Rollick is waiting for us on the jet. He watches Riva without saying much, but I think he can pick up on the same vibe I can.

When we're getting close to our destination, I motion him to the back of the jet to talk to him quietly. "There's something I could use…"

When I explain, a small smirk creeps across the demon's lips. He gives me a quick nod. "I can arrange that."

The flight leads to a short drive from the local landing strip to Rollick's estate. Ajax drifts into a doze in the back of the SUV, and Riva glances back at him with a sad smile before shifting restlessly in her seat.

"When we get back, I should check the others' locations again. Maybe Booker will have thought of something that the other kids or the criminal shadowbloods mentioned that'll point us in the right direction…"

As we get out of the car outside the mansion, I touch her arm. "Nothing huge is going to change in the next half hour. Meet me in the lounge room with the fireplace?"

Riva knits her brow, but after she meets my hopeful gaze, she nods. I've realized one of the benefits of not asking much of her is that she understands how important it must be when I do ask for something.

The other guys glance at me with obvious curiosity, but I put them off with a subtle shake of my head. I don't think she needs a crowd hovering around her right now.

There are a few things I've proven I'm good at with her all on my own.

I take a quick detour to the mansion's massive kitchen and walk into the lounge carrying a tall stack of sandwich-size plates—with nothing on them. Riva takes one look at me and laughs. "You were so hungry you forgot to add the food?"

I join her by the fireplace, set the plates down in front of us, and give her a gentle nudge with my elbow. "Things have been kind of shitty. I thought you might feel like breaking something."

Understanding lights in her bright eyes. When she was at her worst in her helpless rage at Balthazar, we flung flowerpots off the side of the hill.

It helped then, and I can already see the idea loosening the tension in her now. She exhales shakily, like a ragged release, and grins at me. "And Rollick won't mind us destroying his dishes?"

The corner of my mouth crooks upward. "I already got his permission, as long as I clean up the mess afterward. He had this stack set out for us."

There's nothing in the broad, stone-lined fireplace right now except for a smattering of ashes left by the last actual fire lit here. I tug the protective grate to the side and heft a plate, but I let Riva take the first shot.

Her fingers clench around the smooth china. She glares at the blackened stones. "That fucking asshole screwed the kids up even more than they already were."

She flings the plate. It smashes against the stones at the back of the fireplace with a satisfying *crack*.

As the pieces rain down into the ashes, I ready my own. "I wish I could have pummeled him for twice as long while he could still feel it, just for that."

Bam. Bam. Bam.

We hurl plate after plate into the fireplace, muttering our frustrations and then simply pouring them all into the jerk of our arms. With each throw, a little more tension seeps out of Riva's expression.

She lobs the last plate with a little battle cry. We stare at the heap of broken shards for a moment before I will the heat into my eyes to char all that pottery into dust.

Then Riva spins toward me and wraps her arms around my chest.

My pulse hitches with pleasure just at the knowledge that she feels comfortable enough to hug me without hesitation now. That I've shown her she's earned that comfort.

My happiness swells more at her words, muffled in my shirt. "Thank you. I needed that."

I scoop up her small frame easily and sit us both in the nearest armchair. Nothing could feel as good as having the woman I love cuddle deeper into my embrace as easily as breathing.

I lower my head over hers, drinking in the crisply

sweet scent of her hair. "We'll fix this. There's got to be a way." Even if I've got no clue what that is at the moment.

Riva grimaces. "I know Balthazar's gone, and everyone important in the Guardianship probably is too. But everything still feels so messed up, and I don't know how to help the other shadowbloods. They don't *want* to be helped."

"They haven't had much time to really think about it," I point out.

"But they're stuck with the criminals Balthazar picked out. Who knows what those jerks are going to be telling them?" She rubs her forehead. "They're just kids. They shouldn't have to deal with any of this crap."

"I know." From the moment Riva found out the younger shadowbloods existed, she's always cared so much about looking after them. Wanting to save them from having to go through as much torture as we did.

Even with all the crap the guardians did put us through, they couldn't stop her from knowing instinctively how to act like a big sister. Or even...

The stray thought wriggles through my brain and sends a strange sensation that's both giddy and terrified washing over me. I stroke my hand up and down Riva's arm from shoulder to elbow, but the idea doesn't drift away. It only grips me harder.

I hesitate and hug her tighter. Riva glances up at me as if sensing there's something I'm grappling with.

I might as well spit it out. If she laughs or recoils, well, then I'll know.

"Do you think... I mean, we don't even know if it's possible for us... but way down the road, when everything is okay and we have regular lives… would you want to make the family the six of us have a little bigger?"

Riva stares at me. Her hand drops to her belly. "You mean like—"

Heat flares in my cheeks. "I just—I know how much you care about the kids, so it's easy to imagine—obviously it would be *way* in the future if it happened at all—"

She reaches up and touches my face, letting the softer warmth of her palm cool my blush. "I haven't really thought that far ahead. It's kind of scary letting myself imagine a future that normal. But I could see wanting that and being ready for it someday." A coy smile curves her lips. "And you'd make a great dad."

My skin flushes even hotter. "I'm not sure—I'd have to work on a lot of things."

Riva does laugh then, but it's one of the sweetest sounds I've ever heard. "I've seen you with the kids too. When you were carrying George around on your shoulders while we were hiking through the jungle, giving him pep talks, you practically looked like you were *his* dad."

The reminder sends a pang through my chest. George was a good kid.

And he died on the last mission the guardians sent us into.

I press a kiss to her temple. "I guess it's silly to think about that stuff when we don't even know what we'll be doing tomorrow."

Riva snuggles even closer. "No, I think it's good to have some kind of dreams. Even if I'm too scared to really hold on to them just yet. I'm glad… I'm glad that we've gotten to a place where we can have dreams like that."

My throat clogs with emotion. "Yeah. Me too."

I might have tipped up her chin to really kiss her then, but as the words are leaving my mouth, Billy bursts into the room with his curly hair flying wild around his faun horns.

"Riva, Zian, you need to come. We've just seen—the other shadowbloods are attacking the mortals."

NINETEEN

I don't realize that I seem to have forgotten how to blink until a burn spreads across my eyes. I shake myself, but my gaze veers right back to the computer screen.

I'd thought watching the destruction Balthazar orchestrated was awful. Somehow the scenes playing before us now are even worse.

We started with the official news broadcasts on the TV. Like with Balthazar, those images showed only the aftermath of the attacks.

The footage veered across a squad of soldiers reduced to a jumble of bodies, silver-and-iron helmets streaked burgundy with dried blood. More corpses, wearing civilian clothes, sprawled in a haphazard ring with weapons intended for shadowkind—crossbows with iron bolts, blades formed out of silver—jabbed into their bodies at odd angles like some kind of horrific modern art installation.

It was after the third scene like the latter when Sorsha made a rough sound where she'd been scrolling through less-formal news sources on the laptop at a nearby table. All of us—Firsts, our few rescued younger shadowbloods, Rollick, Billy, and a dozen materialized shadowkind with who knew how many more peering from the shadows—turned toward that.

As the first shaky video recording from the cellphone of a nervous witness played across the screen, I found myself flanked by Andreas on one side and Griffin on the other. Jacob's outrage vibrated from his rigid frame where he'd positioned himself behind me.

Drey's arm is still tucked around mine, Griffin's hand on the small of my back. Maybe to steady me; maybe just to remind me that they're here with me.

But it's not me I'm worried about.

The cellphone footage might be crude, but it shows the story of the attacks well enough. We can hear the panic in the rasped breaths as one near-victim huddles in the hasty shelter they found, their chest hitching as the shadowbloods who've descended on the amateur militia snap bones and stomp flesh. We watch the video tremble with another's muffled sobs.

There's no mistaking who the attackers are. They appear to have started their attacks yesterday in what was the early evening in the United States—past midnight for us here in Spain. But even as the dusk darkened into night for the later assaults, the glow of security lamps or fallen flashlights catch off the faces.

I catch glimpses of the thug with the skull-and-snake tattoo, the one with the scarred brow, and a couple of the others who formed Balthazar's human shield. I spot Tegan's pale face, and other kids whose names I never learned.

Then Nadia's statuesque frame rushes by, flares of searing light yellowing her brown skin. Devon's teeth flash somewhere off to the side as he lets out a vengeful cry.

We don't even need to ask why they're doing it. The criminal shadowbloods bellow their accusations between bursts of violence.

"You thought you could destroy the monsters, huh? You never met monsters like us."

"You wanted this fight—now you're getting it."

"This fucking country belongs to us as much as it does to you!"

"I'm done with getting shot at."

A few steps away from me, Zian shakes his head in hopeless confusion. "But… all those people were hunting *shadowkind*, not shadowbloods. And Balthazar told them to do it!"

Dominic's mouth has flattened into a stiff line. "Who knows what he told the shadowbloods to encourage them to launch the first attacks? And technically those squads *did* want to kill the shadowbloods—they wanted to destroy the 'monsters' that bashed up their cities."

An ache has clogged my throat. My voice rasps before I can force any of it out. "If the shadowbloods had just stayed hidden for a while—if there hadn't been any more attacks with Balthazar gone, the hostility would have died down. Everyone would have dismissed the idea of monsters again."

Rollick is leaning against the back of the sofa in a typically disaffected pose, but his tone holds none of its usual nonchalance. "I don't think your counterparts wanted the violence to die down. They're reveling in the excuse to deal out punishment."

I swallow hard, the images of the younger shadowbloods flashing through my mind. The hatred and the fury showing in every expression, every motion...

I know how much anger a person can bottle after a life full of imprisonment and torture. I remember how easy it was for me to extend that anger beyond my immediate captors to all the regular people who turned a blind eye to Balthazar's machinations, to the spectators who came to watch me forced into cage fights.

We've been treated like monsters since we were born. Like slaves only worthy of fighting other monsters. We haven't been taught to do a whole lot *other* than fight.

When we were on Clancy's island, I tried to give the kids visions of a different future to reach for. A dream of freedom and peace. But I failed to get us there, over and over.

Then Balthazar swept in and fueled their rage. Enhanced their abilities so they could fight and win against anyone. Didn't give a shit when his gift frayed their tempers and messed with their sense of reality.

He lit a different flame of hope for them, yes—a hope that they could conquer anyone who'd ever want to hurt them. And now that fire is burning out of control.

As queasy as it makes me to see the results, I can't

claim I'd have been immune. There was a time in the villa when I felt so helpless and enraged that even my guys were scared of me.

I *did* slaughter an entire audience of cage-fight fans, most of whom had never done anything at all to me other than show up to watch that night's battle.

Billy shivers where he's hugging himself off to the side of the crowd around the laptop. "Why did they go back to America to do all this?"

I can understand that motivation too, more than I like. "That's where we were raised. I think where Balthazar took the criminals from too—the ones I've heard talk all sound American. The people back home are the ones who fucked them up or failed them the most."

Steel spins toward Sorsha with a glint of his metallic scales. "Why didn't you destroy them all when you had the chance, phoenix? They were right there in front of you."

Sorsha gives him a firm look. "Between all the powers getting thrown around, I couldn't see what I was doing. I might have burned up our friends here too."

Fang lets out a growl, his lips drawing back from his jutting teeth—which I now know belong to his monstrous bear form. "You should have incinerated the helicopter with the maniac and the rest before it even landed."

"Balthazar had some of the kids on there," I protest.

Willow the nymph swivels to face me, her thin face tight. "Does it matter? It looks as if the young ones are enjoying the destruction just as much as the grown-ups."

My stomach churns. I can't deny that. But... "They *are* kids. They've been screwed over their whole lives, and

Balthazar's messed them up even more. It isn't their fault. We've got to help them snap out of it."

Steel lets out a dismissive huff. "I think it's gone past that. Who knows what they'll do or who they'll target when they're done with the hunters? Balthazar wanted to kill all of *us*."

Shanty appears from the shadows with a jerk of a nod. "Yes. These hybrids seem to be so fond of him now. They could take up his cause."

Snap glances around at us from his position next to Sorsha, his green eyes gone wide. "And even if they're only attacking mortals now, that isn't okay either. The mortals are only hunting shadowkind because they're scared—because of what Balthazar told them and did—right?"

Crag's rocky gargoyle jaw works as if he's chewing over his thoughts. "Whoever the shadowbloods are hurting, they've got to be stopped. It's bad for everyone."

Fang nods with a jerk. "We have to do what should have been done to begin with. Find them and blast them all away."

"Hey!" Booker breaks in with a quaver in his voice but his expression fierce. "My *girlfriend* is one of those shadowbloods you're talking about. She wouldn't be doing any of this if Balthazar hadn't injected her with his crazy serums. A few weeks ago, she was one of the kindest people in the world."

Beside him, Ajax is still staring at the laptop screen, even though the current video is paused on a muddle of indistinct shapes. His dark eyes look haunted. "I never saw Devon purposefully hurt anyone the whole time I knew him."

He yanks his gaze away so he can frown at the shadowkind. "This isn't who they are. It's like... like they're sick. You have to give them a chance to get better."

Shanty throws her hands in the air with a shake of her dark blue locks. "With what cure? We don't know how to fix them."

I lift my head. "We have to try. We owe them that much. The criminals—it seems like they were horrible people before Balthazar took them. I'm not saying we try to reason with them. But the kids are victims here just like the people they're attacking, just like they've always been."

Willow fixes me with her penetrating gaze. "You've been saying that all along—that the kids need to be saved. This is where it's gotten us." She waves toward the screen. "How much more harm are you going to let them do?"

Jacob pushes forward to glare at her. "None of this is Riva's fault. We're all doing the best we can—at least, the six of us have been."

I grasp his arm to get him to back down. Guilt condenses in my gut.

The nymph isn't wrong. I'm the one who's advocated for the younger shadowbloods the most, who's argued the loudest whenever any of the shadowkind expressed doubts about rescuing them.

If I hadn't insisted so adamantly that Sorsha be careful and avoid the kids, she probably *could* have ended this catastrophe yesterday, when it would have been so much less of a disaster. When the dozens of people now dead were still alive.

But I still can't quite convince myself that it'd be better if the many dead had included Nadia's charred corpse—

and Devon's and Tegan's. And all the other kids, some not even in their teens yet, that Balthazar transformed into his greatest weapons.

"We haven't really tried to fix things," I say. "Not since we realized how badly Balthazar messed with the younger shadowbloods. We know what we're dealing with now. There has to be a way to stop them without murdering every shadowblood other than us."

Fang snorts. "And how do you figure you're going to find that way? How long are you going to let them keep rampaging around while you think about it?"

I square my shoulders, my heart thudding faster. "We know where they are now. It looks like they're sticking together—the attacks were all at different times, following a fairly straight path across the country, weren't they?"

By the computer, Sorsha nods. "It looks like they're traveling from one place to another as a pack, tracking down the groups of hunters."

Her expression is tense, but she holds her posture steady, looking ready to leap into action when *I* say how I think we should handle this—regardless of what the shadowkind think.

If we still have her on our side, that's something.

Girding myself, I seek out Rollick's gaze at the edge of the crowd. "The six of us—and anyone else who's willing to help and follow our lead—will head back to the States. We can predict where the other shadowbloods are headed. We'll stop the attacks, take out the former inmates, and do whatever we can to get through to the kids."

The corner of Rollick's mouth lifts in a slanted smile. "It sounds like you have your plan all worked out. You don't need permission from me. But I assume you could use a method of transportation."

I shrug awkwardly. "Unfortunately, we can't just leap through a portal."

"My private jet is getting quite a workout these days." He dips his head to me. "We can set off as soon as you say the word. I wouldn't mind getting back to my usual turf myself."

"I'm in," Sorsha says without hesitation.

Snap sets a possessive hand on her shoulder and looks toward his friends. "We go where Sorsha goes."

I turn to check with my guys. Every one of them looks back at me with total resolve.

"We're not going to let those kids down," Zian rumbles, his dark gaze stormy.

Please, may that be true—and may we save them without letting down a whole lot of other people who don't deserve to die either.

TWENTY

Griffin

By the time we get within ten miles of the wayward shadowblood group, Riva doesn't need to borrow my locating talent for us to keep track of them. I can taste their erratic fury even from that distance, like wavering blasts of a scorching wind.

The caustic emotion prickles through my awareness, setting my nerves on edge. I'm used to picking up on other people's feelings, and I've absorbed some horrible sensations, but nothing that eats at my insides quite like this before.

It's like acid, burning away at my thoughts, at every gentler feeling inside me.

What must it be doing to the people who are experiencing it firsthand?

From where I'm sitting next to Andreas at the front of the SUV that's carrying us, Sorsha, and a bunch of ephemeral, invisible shadowkind on our quest, I point to the right at an intersection. "They're that way."

The glow of streetlamps and late-night bar windows streaks over our vehicle through the darkness. A giggle passing between a swaying group of friends filters through my window from the city street.

Riva stirs impatiently in the seat behind me. "How do the shadowbloods feel?"

"Angry." The word pops out before I can shape it into something fully accurate. It isn't a fraction enough to convey what I'm picking up on.

As another prickling wave washes over me, I swallow and try again. "I didn't realize how angry they were when I was sensing the fight with you and the guardians in the forest. Or maybe they weren't that angry yet, when they'd only just seen Balthazar killed. It's like... like there's no room for anything else in them. It doesn't stay the same— it shifts and takes on different flavors, but everything is tainted by it."

In the rearview mirror, I see Jacob's mouth twist. I catch the hitch of guilt that hits him.

"That sounds like how I felt," my twin says. "When I thought you were dead and that Riva had set you up for the guardians and turned on us. I did horrible things when that rage was gripping me. If I... if I could be that harsh with people who were my friends, who knows how far they'll go against strangers they never cared about at all?"

There's a rustle of movement—Riva taking Jacob's hand. Compassion and pain mingles with those memories, but a whisper of relief passes through my brother at her gesture.

Dominic leans forward from behind the driver's seat. "Can you calm them down with your powers?"

My stomach tightens. "I tried in the forest, and you could see it didn't work very well then. But it might be easier closer up."

With each surge of fury that sears into me, I believe in that possibility less.

Sorsha rolls her shoulders where she's sitting in the very back next to Zian. "Maybe we should have brought along the kids we already freed. They grew up with some of the others—they might know what to say."

"No," Riva says firmly before the phoenix's last word has faded from the air. "Booker tried to talk Nadia down last time, and she didn't listen at all. The others might even be angry that the three of them came with us. The powers they have can't protect them from an attack. This is *our* fight."

Sorsha nods, but I taste the tendril of doubt that winds through her other emotions. She's letting us call the shots when it comes to our fellow shadowbloods, but after what's already gone down, she isn't totally convinced we're right.

I don't think Riva is completely sure either. She's just desperately hoping to find a way through this mess that doesn't involve slaughtering children.

I point the way at another crossroads. "We're almost there. A few more minutes, I think. They haven't attacked yet. They're agitated but not the way it'd feel if they were in the middle of actually fighting."

As soon as Riva determined what direction the wayward shadowbloods were heading in, it wasn't hard for us to figure out their next target. The internet holds plenty of accounts of a group of anti-monster vigilantes who gathered together here in Memphis, Tennessee to patrol the city.

They got a lot of publicity after a couple of them riddled someone's pet wolfhound full of silver bullets, taking it for a supernatural beast in the dark. But with the current atmosphere after the "monster" attacks on other cities, the backlash wasn't enough to shut the vigilantes down completely.

They'll be out sweeping the streets with the tools Balthazar arranged for them to get, and the shadowbloods are hunting them in turn. Just as we're hunting the shadowbloods.

Thankfully, it looks like we got here before the bloodbath. The shadowbloods are moving slower as they search, giving us time to catch up.

We leave behind the bars and sounds of late-night revelry for quieter streets with wide-spaced houses behind sprawling lawns. The sense of anger thickens until I can almost see it clouding the air.

"Just—just a couple of blocks farther and I think one street to the right." I clear my throat, the swelling emotion choking me. "Drive another five blocks and then double back so we can meet them head on. I'll try to settle them down."

As Andreas pushes the engine a little faster and my friends ready their stances to spring into motion, I extend my senses outward. Rather than simply absorbing the emotions around me, I focus on the most calming memories I have and push the feeling out toward the raging presences nearby.

Softly lilting music. Petting my now-lost cat, Lua, while she curled up on my lap. Waking slowly in the same bed as Riva, drifting out of sleep with her contentment twining with mine.

There hasn't been a whole lot of peace in our lives, but my talent lets me amplify those impressions and intensify them. I pour all the serenity I can summon in a deluge toward the forty or so figures stalking the suburban roads.

The wave of calm sweeps toward them, propelled by my will—and smacks into their fury as if their anger is a solid wall of flame. The rage disintegrates my efforts before the emotions I'm projecting even start to penetrate it.

I close my eyes and push harder, maintaining the delicate balance between holding on to my own inner calm and bringing the necessary force to bear. My awareness tickles across the inferno in search of a gap, a momentary lapse.

Nothing. I try to expand the sense of calm even broader, to turn it into a tsunami large enough to overwhelm the flames, but the feeling of peace starts to fragment. I'm stretching it farther than I can sustain.

I jolt back into the physical reality of my seat and find my breath coming with a rasp, my forehead damp with sweat.

Riva reaches around the back to touch my arm. "Are you okay, Griffin?"

I manage a shaky nod. "Yeah. But I can't—I can't get through the anger. It's too much."

Jacob shrugs, his voice terse. "We do things the other

way, then. Take out as many of the criminals as we can. Then the kids will have to listen to us, however long it takes."

That's the plan. But picturing it sends a lurch of nausea through my gut.

I have trouble seeing how it'll all come together without some kind of disaster. The best we can hope for is a better disaster than the one that's already in motion.

"Here we go," Andreas murmurs, and swings us around a corner.

As we hurtle toward the mass of rage, my queasiness grows. I motion to the intersection up ahead. "That street. No more than a hundred feet away."

Riva stiffens. "Park right in the middle of the road so they can't keep going."

The SUV jerks to a halt at the intersection, blocking any traffic from the street beyond my window. Headlights gleam across the dark asphalt.

Without speaking, we ease out of the vehicle. No one wants to be confined to that small space when we're not entirely sure of all of our opponents' supernatural abilities.

Several shadowkind materialize around us. Rollick glances at the darkened windows of the shadows around us and appears to judge it safe to shift into his massive, ruddy-skinned demonic form. Steel's metallic scales ripple across his entire bulging body, and Thorn whips out his wings, his eyes glowing red.

Staying sheltered behind the van, Billy—who insisted on coming along even though he isn't a fighter—brings his panpipes to his lips and starts to play a soothing tune. It's a nice thought, but I doubt it'll settle down the rampaging shadowbloods any more than my efforts could.

The silvery notes spill out into the night and are swallowed up by the growl of the approaching cars. An assortment of vehicles—an SUV, a couple of vans, a station wagon, and a pick-up truck—roll to a stop a few houses down from where we've set up our blockade.

For the first tense minute, we get nothing more than the low thrum of the still-running engines. The shadowbloods must be communicating with each other—flashes of confusion, frustration, and even starker anger flare through the roiling impression of continuing fury.

There's a creak as the back doors on one of the vans swing open. We all brace ourselves. Sorsha hasn't lit any balls of fire yet, but a sharp heat wafts off her skin as if she's restraining herself.

A bunch of the shadowbloods must have been crammed in the back of that van. Several figures move toward us between the vehicles. I recognize a few of their faces from the island facility, including Riva's friend Nadia and the scrawny girl who isn't even quite a teenager yet.

The whole group is kids, I realize. The new adult shadowbloods have sent out the ones they know we're least likely to kill.

No silver bands show on their wrists. They must have figured out how to get Balthazar's manacles off.

Nadia steps to the front of the group, her chin high, her hands balled at her sides. "What are you doing? Get out of our way."

Riva shakes her head. "You can't go around killing people all across the country. That's just as wrong as what they were doing—and you're going to make everyone else even more scared of 'monsters.' How does that fix anything?"

A tremor runs through Nadia's body with a strange mix of revulsion and irritation. "Maybe we don't want to fix anything. Maybe we're tired of being expected to be a solution, and we just want to break everything that's wrong in this world."

"Which is a fuckload of things!" one of the other kids snaps from behind her.

Next to me, Zian scowls. "So, what, you're just going to break everything as things get even worse?"

"If we want to," Nadia retorts. "We have the power now. We can do whatever we want."

Riva splays her hands pleadingly. "Nadia, you know that's not the life you wanted before. You could still have something normal. We want to make that happen for all of the shadowbloods."

I catch just a flicker of hesitation. Then the girl's eyes narrow. "Really? Even the new shadowbloods Balthazar made? Cutler and them have been looking out for us, you know. They could have ditched us, but they didn't."

"Because you make a convenient shield," Rollick remarks in the deeper, eerily resonant baritone of his demonic form.

Nadia shivers when she looks at him, but she draws herself up straighter. "Why would any of us need a shield? What are you really here to do?"

"They want to slaughter us all like we're the real monsters," someone hollers from the pickup truck.

Sorsha crosses her arms over her chest. "We don't want

to hurt you. We only want to stop you from hurting anyone else."

Nadia's eyes flash. "And what happens if we say no? *Then* you kill us?"

I raise my voice. "Not if we have any other choice. That's the last thing we want. We're angry too, shadowbloods. But we *are* blood, all of us—the six of us Firsts have always said that. We only need you to meet us partway."

Jacob lets out a hoarse laugh. "Yeah. And then we can destroy whatever needs destroying together."

A firm command rings out from the SUV. "Get back in the van, kids."

Nadia glances over her shoulder, uncertainty darting across her face. "Are you sure, Cutler?"

I get a brief glimpse of the man she's talking to behind the wheel when he leans toward the open window—the shaved head with the skull-and-snake tattoo. The guy the others described to me who seemed to be leading the criminal shadowbloods.

He pulls back into the shadows behind the glow of the headlights before Riva would have had a chance to latch on a killing shriek. And any larger attack on the SUV would risk everyone inside.

Given their strategy so far, I'd be incredibly surprised if they didn't have at least a couple of the kids in each of the vehicles as leverage.

"There's no point in talking with these assholes," Cutler says. "We'll just get on with business."

Nadia only hesitates for a second before hustling back to the van with the other kids. We all exchange a glance.

Are they figuring they're going to smash right through our blockade?

Riva lifts her voice in what serves as a warning. "We're not going to let you keep rampaging around. The slaughter stops now."

The teens keep clambering into the van. I don't see any sign that the wayward shadowbloods care about her implicit threat.

I breathe slow and deep to steady myself. We *can* stop them. We've got the shadowkind on our side here when they couldn't help Riva and the others in the forest. There's no way this group can match the power our allies can bring to bear.

I just hope we don't have to hurt many of the kids in the process.

"Take out the tires," Jacob mutters under his breath. "Fuck up the engines. That way they can't get anywhere but we're not murdering anyone."

Riva nods. Without another word, most of my companions leap forward.

Metal screeches within the hoods of the closest vehicles. Flames shoot up beneath their tires, hot enough to meld the rubber to the asphalt.

As Zian slams his fist into the hood of the van that's at the front of the line, hard enough to crack the steel and dent it down toward the components inside, our opponents burst out the backs of their cars. Some are simply fleeing toward the farther vehicles we haven't touched yet, but others are launching their retaliation.

Streaks of painfully bright light rake through the air. The pavement lurches beneath our feet. With a bellow, all the lamps and headlights nearby shatter, casting the road in total darkness.

Grunts and thumps reach my ears from all sides. And then, with a shine in a few windows along the sides of the street, jabs of fear lance through the chaos of emotion I'm drowning in.

Fear—from the residents waking up at the clamor of the battle, having no idea what madness is going on just beyond their doors. If the rogue shadowbloods decide to take out their anger on those innocent people as well…

The thought hasn't even fully formed in my mind before I spot a tall, muscle-bound man heaving away from the road onto one of the dimly lit lawns. The scar scraping across his brow makes his harsh features look even more threatening in the hazy light.

I've got no weapons, no talent that's much good against brawn. I don't want to steal any of my friends' talents in case they need them right now. But panic shoves me toward the running man with the vague idea that I've got to protect the people who have no part in this fight from whatever he intends.

Maybe he wouldn't have done anything to the residents at all. Even as I sprint toward the scarred man, he veers along the edge of the lawn, racing as if to charge past our blockade rather than to head to the houses.

"Griffin!"

My brother's voice tears through the night. And the man's knee buckles.

He falls to the ground with a groan and a hissed curse when his broken leg smacks the lawn. I stall in my tracks just a few feet from where he fell.

His head jerks up so he can glare at me, and a blast of cold air freezes the grass around my feet hard enough to grip my shoes.

"You have to let me at those fucking hunters," he growls, his gaze darting past me to the darkness beyond our car. "Those assholes, you don't even know—I saw what that one prick did to the kids at our halfway house. Death is too fucking kind for—"

Another form dashes toward us so fast I can't make out whether it's male or female. Male, by the hoarse voice that rasps out, "Omar, I've got you!"

The man with the scarred forehead rolls, and the supernaturally swift figure hefts him right off the ground. They disappear into the fray farther down the road, leaving me with an ache in my gut.

It wasn't just anger I sensed from that man—Omar?—when he talked about the hunters they'd wanted to attack, about the one man he knew... He was full of enough anguish to knock the breath out of me.

Did he grow up around here? He recognized one of the hunters from the news footage?

It isn't difficult to believe.

Fire streaks through the air. The ground shakes with a monstrous roar—and a different kind of roar reaches my ears from behind.

Engines. Several vehicles are racing toward us from the opposite direction. Are there more shadowbloods who split off from the first bunch?

No. As the vehicles screech to a halt and their doors fly open, the figures that charge out are holding weapons *I* recognize from the newscasts—crossbows and odd guns and eerily glinting knives.

We caught the rogue shadowbloods by tracking them to where they were looking for the hunters. And now the monster hunters have found us. Shit.

With shouts that sound a little panicky, the hunters hurtle into the fray. Bullets and crossbow bolts zing through the air.

A few shadowkind who were focusing their attention on rounding up the rogue shadowbloods cry out when the weapons puncture their conjured flesh. As they spin around to face the new threat, streams of smoky essence trickle up toward the sky.

My gut lurches. Somewhere to my left, Jacob lets out an epic string of curses.

Supernatural light blazes across the street, hazing my vision. I stagger, and my brother catches my arm.

"Those idiots are ruining everything." He swipes at his eyes, which must be just as spotty as mine are right now. "Damn it."

More yells and yelps cut through the night. I stumble toward the SUV, knowing I'm a liability out in the open rather than a help.

Then Zian's holler cuts through the rest of the chaos. "I hear sirens coming! Someone called the cops."

At the urgency in his voice, I hustle faster toward the car.

Riva catches up with me after a few steps, grabbing my arm. Her voice is raw with frustration. "There's nothing else we can do. We've got to get out of here."

"What happened to the other shadowbloods?" I ask as

we scramble into the back of the SUV, the others clambering in around us.

Dominic crashes into the seat just in front of us and peers past it as whoever grabbed the driver's seat guns the engine. "The other shadowbloods stole some cars farther down the street. A couple of them must have talents that let them hotwire the things easily."

"And one of the vans took off before we could get to it." Riva sighs and slumps in her seat, deflated. "Jacob managed to shatter one of the new shadowblood's skulls, and Sorsha torched at least one. I think the other shadowkind killed a couple of the criminals. But I don't know if it'll make any difference. The rest of them are going to be even more pissed off at us."

As the van lurches around, I debate with myself. But I don't want to keep any more secrets from the woman I love or the brother I nearly lost.

"I don't know if we should want all of the criminal shadowbloods dead either," I say quietly. "The one guy who ran my way—he said something, he was *feeling* something…"

Jacob raises his eyebrows. "What are you talking about?"

I grimace. "I think he had a personal reason to want to attack the hunters here. I think he'd actually seen that at least one of them had hurt a lot of people in the past—not monsters, only troubled kids. He wanted to protect everyone from that guy, not just kill for the sake of killing. I don't know about all of the inmates Balthazar picked out, but they're still human. They're not only out to do evil."

Jake scoffs. "That one wasn't, maybe."

But Riva's brow has knit. "We really don't know about any of them—what they've been through, what they'd really want if they thought they had a real choice." She tips her head back against the seat. "Fuck!"

I scoot closer to her and slip my arm around her waist. She leans her head against my shoulder. "I wish it wasn't so complicated," she murmurs.

I kiss her forehead, reveling in the ease with which she relaxes into my embrace. "People are complicated. We're trying. At least we gave them something to think about tonight. Maybe some of them will decide to back off once the things we said sink in."

"Maybe." Riva sounds as doubtful as I have to admit I feel too. She tucks her head right against the crook of my neck. "Stay right there. Don't let me go."

A lump rises in my throat, all affection and agony for the woman I love. "Never."

After a while, with the rumble of the engine and the gentle rocking once we get onto the highway, Riva's breaths slow into a doze. I think Jacob drifts off too where he's leaned his head against the window. Next to him, Andreas leans forward to carry out a hushed conversation with Zian up front.

My own eyelids are sinking when Billy emerges from the shadows, perched on the seat next to me.

He peers at me and Riva with his wide eyes and scratches at his head just below one of his horns. His voice comes out in a whisper. "You two are very close."

I can tell he's not just talking about our current physical position. The corner of my lips curls upward. "Yeah. All six of us are."

"I mean… You told her something that upset her. But she still wanted to be near you."

I blink, considering the implicit question. "She knew it wasn't my fault—I was just passing on information. And being with each other makes us feel better."

The faun cocks his head, studying Riva's face again. His mouth forms a smile that looks pained. "I don't know what that's like. I have friends, but it isn't normal with shadowkind—most don't really get attached like that."

Curiosity shines in his eyes. The offer comes out of me automatically. "Do you want to see what it feels like?"

Billy stares at me for a second before his lips part in understanding. "You can do that. Your talent. I— If you wouldn't mind…"

"Of course not."

I focus on the warm emotion that glows inside me when I've got Riva in my arms, the tenderness and the adoration and the sense of shock that I've managed to earn a love like this at all. A few of the more passionate impulses, I edit out of the feelings I convey, but the rest I let flow through me into the slim shadowkind man.

He sits very still as if soaking in the impressions I've passed on. Then his gaze darts to meet mine again with an almost giddy cast to his features.

"That is… That is something that shouldn't ever be lost. I'm glad I've been helping you, even if there isn't much I can do. I won't let anyone ruin what you've found with each other."

The conviction in his words brings an ache into my chest, even after he's slipped back into the shadows. I tip my head against Riva's and shut my eyes against the tears that prick at the backs of them.

There's sadness in those tears—for the problems we're still facing, for the complications we don't know how to handle yet. But there's sweetness too.

I might not have a talent that can win a skirmish for us, but my powers can do more than manipulate. I can learn and reveal and teach, make things clearer not just for my friends but everyone else we want on our side too.

That power might not sway any fistfights… but it could get us one step closer to winning this war.

TWENTY-ONE

Riva

I can't stop prowling through the hotel room. Every luxurious feature my gaze passes over somehow sets off my annoyance all over again.

When we first got to enjoy Rollick's opulent tastes, I appreciated the indulgence. It was thrilling to experience that kind of extravagance after a lifetime of tiny prison cells and tasteless food.

Now, the fluffy duvet and elegant furniture of the place where he got us rooms just remind me of how little I fit in here.

I *was* raised in prison cells. I should know how to get through to the other shadowbloods, both the kids and the former inmates.

So why are they still out there, driving around in stolen cars, launching crazed attacks, while I'm roaming around this pretty bedroom?

Andreas looks up from where he's been scrolling

through his phone while propped against the mahogany footboard. "It looks like there are only a few dead. It could have been a lot worse."

The guys all tramped in here to join me about ten minutes ago after seeing the morning news. It's playing on the huge TV mounted on the wall now: scenes of smashed signs and shattered glass, crumpled cars and blood-splattered sidewalks.

Our fellow shadowbloods were only more furious after we deflected their attack on the hunter group they meant to slaughter, however badly the confrontation fell apart in the end. They took out their anger on downtown Memphis.

There might be only a few deaths so far, but the text scrolling across the bottom of the TV screen mentions more than twenty hospitalized for their injuries. If it'd been any earlier in the night—more restaurants open, more people on the streets…

As I imagine the carnage, I shudder.

Jacob is pacing too, near the door, with a scowl darkening his face. "It will be worse if those fuckers keep this up. Who are they kidding, saying they're just destroying the things that are wrong? They're bashing up whatever the hell they feel like."

Dominic swipes his hand across his weary face where he's sitting on the chair by the executive-style desk. "Maybe they think everyone and everything except them is broken. This is the world the guardians came from, after all. Every 'normal' person is afraid of monsters."

Zian looks like he's considering kicking the foot of the bed in frustration but then thinks better of it, maybe because of how expensive the bedframe looks. He growls under his breath. "They can't just kill everyone in the whole world."

Jacob lets out a raw laugh. "They can try."

Griffin has perched on the edge of the desk itself. He casts his gentle gaze across all of us. "We'll get through to them. They've got more going on inside them than just anger."

I drop down on the side of the bed, my head drooping. "But how are we going to do that? We weren't even strong enough to get them under control with a bunch of the shadowkind there to back us up."

We couldn't have known that the hunters would notice the fight and charge in before we'd finished what we started—but where can we catch the rampaging shadowbloods that we won't risk being interrupted?

It's not as if I can blame the hunters for trying to protect their communities from the violence we brought down on them.

My gaze veers to the TV screen again, to worried bystanders with panicked eyes being interviewed by a reporter. Terrified of beings like me.

The words that've been solidifying in my head over the past several hours—possibly the past several days, if I'm being honest—tumble out. "Maybe Engel was right."

Jacob's head jerks toward me as his feet jar to a stop. "*What?*"

I can't quite stomach the disbelief I know will be etched on all the guys' faces, so I stare down at my lap instead. "She thought we were too dangerous. That the guardians should get rid of us rather than trying to keep using us, because we'd end up doing worse things than the monsters they wanted us to fight. Aren't the other shadowbloods proving her point right now?"

"That's the rest of them, not us," Zian says with a wave of his hand toward the screen. "And Balthazar made them like that after Engel was already gone."

My throat constricts. "Kind of. He used her formulas to make whatever injections and pills let him give the criminals their new powers and enhance the ones the kids already had."

I pause and force myself to lift my head. If I'm going to say this, I have to be brave enough to face the reactions I'll get. "Haven't you ever wondered if we could end up becoming just as unhinged as the others are? What if Balthazar just sped them along on a path we're heading down too?"

Griffin blinks at me as if he really hadn't ever considered that possibility. I guess that's reassuring, considering he has the deepest access to our inner states.

Dominic's pensive expression suggests that he *has* thought along those lines before, though, and he doesn't like where those thoughts have taken him.

Jacob and Zian just look peeved.

Andreas reaches across the bed to rub my back reassuringly. "I don't think it does us any good to speculate about things that haven't even started to happen. We've had stronger powers than the kids for our whole lives, and even when we were pushed to our limits, we didn't lash out like they are now."

Zian speaks up carefully. "Balthazar must have added to whatever Engel was doing, right? I mean, if she could have turned grown-ups into shadowbloods rather than having to raise us the whole way from when we were babies, it'd have been a lot faster."

I sigh and let myself lean into Andreas's touch. "I don't know. *We* can't really know for sure. But we can't let the other shadowbloods keep going like this. And talking to them hasn't gotten us anywhere so far."

Griffin tips his head to the side, studying me. "You're not really thinking that we should kill all of them after all."

I grimace and shake my head. "I don't like the idea of killing *any* of them, especially after what you said about that one guy and what you felt from him. Is it fair for us to decide that all of the adults Balthazar changed must be evil just because they were criminals? That's exactly the same way so many people would look at *us* because of our powers! We've done criminal things too. No matter how it happened, we're all blood."

"We can't keep trying to reason with them," Jacob puts in. "They'll just take off, no matter what we do."

"I know."

A sound like a cleared throat carries through the room. As I startle, Rollick appears by the door, the shadowkind version of stepping inside.

From his solemn expression and his opening words, I suspect he didn't just arrive. He sweeps his gaze across all of us, his hands slung in his pockets but his posture tense. "You definitely need to come up with a solid new plan soon."

My stomach clenches. "Are the shadowkind complaining again?" Or worse, outright abandoning ship?

I don't know how we're going to stop the shadowbloods who've gone rogue, but I'm sure we can't do it just the six of us on our own.

The demon sighs. "No more than usual. They understand that last night went wrong due to circumstances beyond your control. But with each additional assault from that pack of shadowbloods, you're risking an even bigger problem on your hands."

A chill washes over my skin. "What do you mean?"

The corners of Rollick's mouth tighten. "I was hoping we didn't have to worry about this. They've been quiet and detached from events in the mortal realm for years since a rather uncomfortable incident they'd prefer everyone forgets."

"Who's 'they'?" Jacob demands.

"I'm getting to that." Rollick brushes his hands together as if he wishes he could wash himself clean of the issue that easily. "Among the shadowkind, there are a few particularly ancient and powerful beings we call the Highest. No one can remember them coming into existence—they were around before any of us. They never leave the shadow realm, but they do try to control what happens on both sides of the rifts, mostly with an eye to making sure they won't be disturbed."

Dominic's forehead has furrowed. "What does that have to do with us and the other shadowbloods?"

"Well, the Highest are even less fond of hybrids than any shadowkind you've met before. They spent a few decades trying to track down Sorsha and exterminate her before she managed to convince them that she was a greater help against potential threats than one herself. And they don't like any disruptions in the mortal realm that could draw attention to our existence."

My heart sinks. "Crap. That ship has already sailed."

Rollick gives a curt nod. "It seems word has finally reached them that something has gone amiss over here. I had one of their errand beings approach me earlier this morning wanting to know if I had any information about the current turmoil."

Zian turns a bit green. "What did you tell them?"

The demon shrugs. "That it appeared to be a bunch of mortals playing at being monsters, and I was working on dealing with it. But I'm not sure if that lie will cut it for very long."

I swallow thickly. "And what happens if the Highest decide to intervene?"

Rollick meets my eyes with an apology in his gaze. "Extermination is their usual go-to strategy."

A groan of frustration escapes me. I rub my temples as if I can jostle a useful thought out of the turmoil that's going on in my own head.

After a moment, I glance up at Rollick again. "How do you handle it? There are destructive shadowkind, and ones who act out for good reason. You don't like seeing your own kind destroyed, do you?"

He makes an awkward gesture, and I can't help remembering that I've seen him threaten and maim beings who betrayed him before. For all I know, he kills other shadowkind on a regular basis.

But even if he does, from what I've seen of the demon, I don't think he's happy about it.

"I have to be firm," he says finally. "I can't maintain

authority if the beings who deal with me don't believe there'll be consequences for stepping out of line. But I do try to adjust those consequences depending on the circumstances and motivations of those involved. I understand why you want to simply rein your fellow shadowbloods in rather than outright murdering them."

Something about those words, *rein them in*, sparks the inspiration I was searching for. I sit up a little straighter. "That's it."

Andreas shoots me a curious look. "What?"

"We can't get the other shadowbloods to listen to us when they're roaming around, and as long as they're on the loose, they'll keep attacking people. So we'll just have to restrain them. Capture them and hold them someplace where they can't do any more damage while we figure out how to get through to them."

Jacob frowns. "Stick them in a sort-of prison. Like the guardians were always doing. Like Balthazar did."

The truth of his words makes my stomach churn, but I barrel onward. "It isn't the same. We'd be doing it so that we can *save* them, not to use them. And the fact that the guardians could do it without any powers of their own proves that we should be able to round the rogue shadowbloods up too, especially with help from the shadowkind."

And it's a lot better than asking Sorsha to simply incinerate them all.

Dominic nods slowly. "We'll need to figure out a place where we can catch them where we shouldn't be interrupted like last night. And we'd need to go in looking to disable them or knock them out right from the start, no trying to talk and giving them the chance to prepare for an attack."

"How *are* we going to capture them?" Zian asks. "They're pretty good at fighting back. Even if we can surprise them…"

I turn back to Rollick. "We'll need to come up with a plan with any shadowkind allies who have abilities that would allow them to overpower people without doing major damage."

The demon rubs his chin. "I can think of a few already who'd be well-suited to that task."

I glance around at the guys. "I'm not sure how useful the rest of us will be toward that goal… Andreas could confuse them with projected memories, but Griffin hasn't been able to impose any emotions on them before. I guess Zian and Jacob and I could slow them down by breaking bones, but… that'll just make them angrier, and it won't get in the way of a lot of their powers."

"There are a lot of them," Griffin points out. "It'll be difficult to tackle them all at once effectively."

"Yeah." I hesitate, my mind spinning, and then the idea hits me like a punch to the chest. "Balthazar managed it, though. He stopped all of us and Sorsha when we came after him at his mountain base—with the device that made that awful sound. It was impossible to concentrate enough to aim our talents. That should work on the other shadowbloods too."

Zian cocks his head. "And the rest of us… wear earplugs?"

I can't restrain a laugh. "Whatever works. They'll need to be really good earplugs, but we already thought of that when we were worried about Balthazar trying it on us again."

A pleased gleam has come into Rollick's eyes as he watches us pull our scheme together. He motions toward the TV. "You'll also need a means of determining where your fellow shadowbloods might go next—and I think we may have that right here."

A group of silver-helmed figures have appeared on the screen. As I shift my attention to the interview being conducted, one of them pumps his fist in the air.

"We won't be knocked down, no matter what those fiends try to throw at us! Just let them try any of that BS in Chicago."

A shiver runs down my back. "You think the rogue shadowbloods will see that and take the challenge?"

Rollick offers me a small smile. "I wouldn't be surprised. They do seem to be rather impulsive. And Chicago is along the trajectory they were already on. I'd imagine our best strategy would be to check for other similar declarations in the area and then monitor which direction the kids you can track start heading in."

And then we attack. I drag in a breath, repeating to myself that we're doing the right thing, that this is the best option we have.

Then I reach toward the bedside table for my phone. "I'm going to call Toni and see what she can tell us about Balthazar's tech. He used us in plenty of ways. Now we might as well use whatever we can from him."

Twenty-Two

Jacob

I'm starting to realize that I have a love-hate relationship with watching Riva in action.

Nothing can compare to the fire that comes into her bright brown eyes when she focuses all her determination on a goal. She lights up with the energy that carries through every brisk movement, turning her seemingly delicate body into a force of nature.

It's a hell of a lot better than the deflated hopelessness that's come over her at the worst of times. Seeing *that* always makes me want to tear the rest of the world apart until I reach whatever's hurting her.

But gearing up for a fight involves more than just determination and energy. As she stalks through her new hotel room, tension hardens the set of her shoulders and the curl of her fingers. Her eyes burn with worry as well as resolve.

This woman cares so much about so many people. I

can't complain about that, since I'm lucky enough to be one of those people.

But the stress of wanting to protect them all, save them all, digs into her with each passing minute when she hasn't accomplished it yet.

Now, she spins on her heel toward the door with a swing of her braid. "I should check in with Rollick's people again. Go over the plan one more time."

That'll just remind her of how much time we still have to wait before we can actually do anything. And how little we can be sure that what we're going to do will work out all right.

I get up from the chair where I was studying a map of the city on my phone. "You just talked to them a half hour ago. They probably won't like it if you act like you think they're all idiots."

The shadowkind seem to be a pretty sensitive bunch for beings that've existed for hundreds or even thousands of years.

Riva lets out a strangled sound that brings up both Dominic's and Griffin's heads where they've been sitting on the end of the bed, checking the latest news reports on the TV. "I don't like just waiting around. Maybe I should confirm the shadowbloods' location again."

"You just did *that* fifteen minutes ago," I remind her, as gently as I can while staying firm. "They've barely moved since they got to the city a few hours ago."

Dominic nods. "They've never attacked before it started to get dark before. The hunters don't even start patrolling until then."

Riva sighs, but she knows he's right. We figured out

that the rogue shadowbloods were heading to St. Louis, presumably to target a vocal group of hunters who've made the news recently here, and made it to the city ourselves this morning. But even after solidifying our plans for tonight, we've still got hours left before evening.

Despite that, Riva starts eyeing the door again as if she's inventing other reasons to go stalking through the halls. An ache that's both love and frustration reverberates through my chest.

She always takes so much onto her shoulders, as if it's her job alone to conquer every evil in this world. To make sure the rest of us are where we need to be to help that happen.

She isn't alone, though. She's got all of us and the allies we've gathered. If we win, a lot of it will be thanks to her —but if we lose, there's no way it's her fault.

I know she trusts us to stand beside her and have her back. She just needs to get better at letting us take care of her as much as she watches out for us.

My mind trips back through time to a much more anguished moment when I came to her and she needed me. When I helped her shake all the guilt and worry that was gripping her.

Riva steps toward the door, and I move to intercept her. "Nope," I say. "You're staying right here. Sit down on the bed."

She narrows her eyes at me. "Are you giving orders now?"

I smile and wave my hand to usher her in the right direction. "Only because you obviously need them. You have no jobs to do right now. So I'm making it my job to protect you from stressing yourself out."

Riva folds her arms over her chest with a defiant expression, although the gleam in her eyes looks more like a challenge than real irritation. "I don't feel like sitting down."

"You haven't tried it yet." I aim my gaze past her to the other two guys in the room, who are watching us in bemusement. "A little help, anyone?"

Dominic lets out a soft chuckle and gets to his feet. As he walks over to Riva, he unfurls his tentacles from their usual coiled position against his back.

He reaches out one tentacle and wraps it around Riva's forearm before giving a little tug toward the bed.

She glowers at him next. "Ganging up on me now?"

The corner of his mouth quirks upward. "Only because you need it."

"You definitely need it," Griffin pitches in from where he's swiveled around on the bed. "If you stay that tense all afternoon, you'll be worn out before we even get started on the important stuff."

Riva releases another little growl, but she lets Dominic pull her over to the bed. As she clambers on and settles cross-legged in the middle of the duvet, I climb after her.

I sink down right behind her and rest my hands on her back, just below her shoulders. Carefully, I extend my supernatural touch beneath her skin.

Once, in a vengeful moment it makes me queasy to remember, I used my power to test her muscles and joints for tracking devices in a purposefully painful way. Today I'm aiming for the opposite effect.

I keep the telekinetic pressure as light as a feather, no more than wisping over her muscles to identify which hold the most tension. Then I add it as a faint additional massage while I circle my thumbs against the tightened spots.

If you want to make up for how brutal you were before, Riva said to me once, *why don't you show me how gentle you can be now?* And I've been following those instructions in every way I can for her, whenever I can, over and over since that first fragment of trust she offered me.

Our woman has been through so much—all the same horrors we experienced under the guardians' and then Balthazar's control, and the shit we threw at her when she came back to us on top of that. Any generosity we can give her, any way we can pamper her, she deserves in spades.

As I deepen the massage, Riva hums in a much more approving noise and lets herself lean into my touch. The sound and the whiff of her sweetly sharp scent shoot straight to my groin. Just like that, I'm half hard.

She can probably tell with her own supernatural senses how she's affecting me, but she doesn't shift her position. I ignore the clamor of my baser instincts and work my hands down her back through her thin cotton tee.

With a vaguely amused air that reminds me that Griffin is perfectly aware of my internal state too, my brother decides to get in on the action. He slides off Riva's sneakers, slips her socks off in turn, and then applies his thumbs to the arch of one foot.

Her head tips back with a deeper hum that's almost a purr. Desire crackles through my nerves, and *half*-hard is a thing of the past.

With a small smile playing on his lips, Dominic sets her other ankle on his thigh and gets to work himself. He lets one of his tentacles caress her calf while he rubs his thumbs into the tendons of her foot.

Riva licks her lips. The vibe in the room is definitely heating up, even if none of us is acting on that awareness yet.

A brief pang of guilt hits me—maybe we should find some way to call Andreas and Zian over. Drey went off to his own room to meditate on the memories he could use to distract the shadowbloods in our ambush tonight, and Zee was going to do some sparring in wolf-man form with a couple of the shadowkind to figure out most effective uses of his increased strength.

But to reach out to them, we'd have to burst the bubble of peace we've already formed here. It's not like there's anything wrong with a few of us enjoying a somewhat more private interlude with our woman.

I hope to hell that I still get occasions when it's just me and Riva, as much as I appreciate what the other guys can offer her.

As I reach the small of her back, she arches into my touch. I can't resist leaning in to brush my lips against the crook of her neck.

Her gasp sends a giddy hitch through my pulse. I add a little teeth before murmuring, "I think we could take care of you even better than this."

Riva turns her head to seek out my mouth, and that's all the answer I need. I claim her lips while sliding my hand around and under her shirt.

My fingers stroke upward to the band of her bra.

Through her warm skin, her heart thumps a heady rhythm against my palm.

Our shadows thrum in unison. I kiss her harder, pouring all the passion I have into the meeting of our lips.

When I ease back to tug her shirt right off, Griffin scoots over with a sly smile. The second her arms are free, he unclasps her bra.

Riva tugs my brother into a kiss and then reaches to help undress him. I catch her arm before it gets very far.

"Nope," I say, nudging her down on her back. "You do so much for everyone. Let us do all the work for once. Just lie back and enjoy."

She gives me a skeptical look, but Griffin is already peeling his own shirt off. As he tosses it aside, Dominic and I follow suit. Can't leave her alone in her nakedness.

Dom teases both his hands and his tentacles farther up Riva's legs over her cargo pants. He aims one of his quietly pensive smiles at her, but his hazel eyes shine with eagerness. "Would it be so bad to take for a little while instead of always trying to give?"

Riva lets out a faint huff, but she sinks down on the bed. "It's more fun when you're all enjoying yourselves too."

Griffin laughs. "Oh, we're already enjoying ourselves. You don't have to worry about that, Moonbeam."

My grin widens. "And we're going to enjoy it even more when you're writhing and moaning."

A perfect flush colors Riva's cheeks. She rests her hands on her abdomen just below her pert breasts as if she's not totally sure where to put them.

"Hmm. How about up here?" I grasp her wrists gently

and lift them over her head so her arms sink into the pillow. Then I trail my fingers down from her hands to her shoulders, so delicately she shivers in anticipation.

Dominic is undoing her fly. Griffin and I lift Riva's hips so he can strip her pants right off her.

I allow myself one brief glance over the nearly naked, gorgeous planes of my lover's body before lowering my head to flick my tongue over the peak of her breast.

Just like that, I earn a whimper—one step down from a moan. We can build up to the real symphony.

Riva reaches for me this time, unwilling to stay still. As her fingertips graze my hair, Griffin catches them and presses kisses across her knuckles.

"Take," he reminds her. "Tell yourself you'll have more to give everyone else later this way."

Riva snorts, but the dismissive sound breaks with another gasp as I test her nipple between my teeth. Griffin trails his kisses down her arm while Dominic charts a path up her thigh, a course I totally approve of.

When he hooks his tentacles around the sides of her panties, Riva gives a little wriggle that's both encouragement and assistance. He drags them down and then dips his head to lap his tongue over her pussy.

There's our first moan. It vibrates from her chest into my mouth, and I suck her pebbled nipple with more force, ignoring my jealousy that I'm not the one tasting her arousal.

It's enough to hear it, to have orchestrated it, to be part of this delicious encounter that's completely about showing our woman how much we worship every part of her.

As Dom eats her out, his tentacles keep stroking over her skin—her waist, her hips, farther down her legs. Griffin cups Riva's other breast with his hand and glances toward our friend.

"Give her your monstrous side too. She wants it just as much." His mouth curves into something that might be a smirk, as un-Griffin-like as that expression is. "Maybe even more."

Riva lets out a little growl of agreement, her hips rocking to meet Dominic's mouth. He raises his head slightly, his face as flushed as hers is, but he doesn't hesitate more than a second before teasing one tentacle over her mound and between her folds.

Holy hell. I've never seen him actually fuck her with his extra appendages before. But there's no denying Riva's ecstatic response.

As he eases the tentacle deeper inside her, she lets out another moan and squirms as if urging him onward. Her breath breaks into little pants that I want to drink right off her lips.

My cock is practically tearing through my boxers now. I smother a groan of my own by bringing my mouth back to Riva's breast. I lap and suckle while her body trembles, knowing my twin is giving her just as much attention on the other side.

With a cry, her torso goes taut as a bowstring. She digs her fingers into my hair, and this time I let her, reveling in the force of her coming as it radiates through the pinpricks of pain she presses into my scalp.

Then I pull myself down her body. I nip the skin over her ribs and then lick her belly.

"My turn for a taste," I mutter when I reach her hip.

Dominic eases aside with a rasp of breath and no argument. I catch a glimpse of him applying the suckers of his slickened tentacle where my mouth was working over Riva's breast before, and then I dive in.

She's so fucking wet, her pussy searing hot in the aftermath of her orgasm. I lap up her juices and suck hard on her clit, loving the way her hips jerk for me. Absorbing every mewling whimper that tells me I'm doing my job well.

With each sound of her satisfaction, something releases inside me too, even though my cock is still hard as a goddamn crowbar. The love she first woke up in me years ago and stirred back to life in the past few months flows into every particle of my body, washing away the last prickling bits of anger.

I'll never forgive the guardians or Balthazar for how they messed with us. I'll never think it was remotely okay. But how can I keep raging about it when without them, I'd never have had the woman before me at all?

Their fucked-up plans brought us together, and I can't regret that, no matter how much I hate the rest.

Riva bucks into my mouth and growls in frustration. "I need more. I need you all to be coming with me."

My dick twitches at those words, but my newfound benevolence has me pushing myself upright. I catch my twin's gaze across the bed and tip my head in invitation.

Like he did for me, the first time we were with Riva together. I can share too.

I *want* to.

Griffin beams at me so brightly I'm even more satisfied

with my choice. As he kicks off his pants and positions himself over Riva, I free my own cock to pump it in my hand.

Riva smiles up at Griffin with that softer brilliance she's always reserved just for him—and I find I don't mind it even a little. She's a bit different with all of us, and she's also the same, and that's part of the magic of what we have together.

As Griffin slides into her, she raises her knees to give him better access. Her hand creeps across the covers to fondle my balls while I jerk myself off.

I groan at the contact, dipping forward. A tingle shoots through my dick with the sense of my impending release.

Dominic has both of his tentacles plucking at Riva's breasts now. She strokes one of them with her other hand while he pumps his erection.

It's a crazy picture—but this is us. This is where I want to be.

I wouldn't have any of them without the shitty life we came from—not my brother, not my friends. No matter where we came from or how we were made, I can't imagine a better family.

No psychos or assholes can change that fact or diminish what we've become.

Riva squeezes my balls again, and my hips jerk with a heady surge of heat. I spill myself onto the pale skin of her belly just as Dominic tips over the edge.

Riva bows up to meet Griffin's thrusting body, and another keening moan escapes her lips. They come together with ragged breaths mingling and a giddy relief so potent it flows from her shadows into mine.

As Griffin eases back, Riva tugs us all toward her. We cuddle around our woman in a nest of living heat, and she snuggles into our joint embrace without a single comment about all the things she could be doing to see tonight's plans through.

I did right by my love, by my family. This time.

If I can keep doing that, over and over again, we all might come out of this catastrophe in one piece.

TWENTY-THREE

Riva

"Are we sure that Nadia and the others will show up here?" Booker whispers to me through the dark as we crouch by a sawdust-streaked window.

I pause to bring up the glowing map on my phone and concentrate on my sense of her: the confident, wry teenager I knew on Clancy's island and the being of blinding light and anger she's become.

The fall of my finger is proof enough. "They're coming closer. She is and whoever's with her, at least. Last time I checked, Devon and Tegan were there."

I slide the phone into my pocket. I shouldn't check again—they're less than ten minutes away at the pace they've been setting so far.

We don't know exactly how far they'll have spread out or how quickly they'll keep moving. I don't want anyone catching a glimpse of my face in the glow.

We didn't bother with invisibility for this ambush, not

when we need Andreas's talents for other purposes. It wasn't worth tiring him out for a small benefit. Both the siren sounds and Nadia's glow have shattered the concealment he can offer us before, so the effect probably wouldn't have lasted long enough to make a difference anyway. The darkened buildings we're hiding in should be shelter enough until the rogue shadowbloods arrive.

And the rogues have every reason to venture into this part of the city. Ruse and Pearl visited the local vigilante group this morning and used their persuasive skills to cajole them into making a couple of public comments online about the site they planned to sweep tonight, supposedly to warn regular folks away.

And then the incubus and the succubus cajoled the same monster hunters into deciding to go to a totally different part of the city so they won't actually get in our way.

Booker frowns as he studies the rain-slick pavement outside, gleaming under the security lamps. The drizzle stopped an hour ago, but everything's still pretty damp.

"What if people come wanting to see the 'monster hunters' in action?" he asks.

I put on my best reassuring voice. "That shouldn't be a problem. Ruse and Pearl and a few of the other shadowkind who wouldn't be much help in a fight are patrolling the edges of the construction area. They'll send off anyone who tries to come right in."

The setting we've chosen for our ambush should be the perfect venue. The university is building a new set of dorm buildings, the outer shells complete but the innards still mostly raw wood with occasional stretches of drywall.

The construction workers all went home for the day before dinner time. Pearl coaxed the security guard into staying in his office at the edge of the site. There should be no one here but us monsters, hybrid and otherwise.

We have all the details worked out. I should feel confident. But uneasiness creeps over my skin. I find myself reaching for my cat-and-yarn necklace as if holding it will somehow make things more likely to turn out right.

My discomfort is partly from not being sure just how far the raging shadowkind will go to see through their rampage. And partly from the claustrophobic feeling the unfinished buildings give me.

That's a benefit, really. The strip is set up like a cul-de-sac, a row of townhouses on either side of the narrow road with one more set at the dead end farther down. Once the other shadowbloods drive in, it'll be easy to block them off.

But I can't help thinking of the other university campus we hid out on, back when my guys and I were first on the run. The one where *we* were ambushed in the night by a squad of brutal guardians.

It didn't look much like this. Those townhouses were dull concrete rather than the ruddy bricks that cover these outer walls. They were shorter and broader.

There were the little patios in the back, in the alley where the guardians launched their attack. Patios that held planters where Dominic tended to a tiny garden.

The angles of the shadows and the tight press of the buildings feel familiar, though. When I blink, memories flash through my mind of Brooke, the student next door who did her best to make friends with me. To protect me from the tensions she picked up on between me and the guys.

The girl who died with the stab of a guardian's blade just seconds before my outstretched claws could save her.

No one has to die tonight. We'll interrupt the other shadowbloods' powers, knock them out every way we can, and cart them off in the truck that Rollick's parked nearby. His people have spent all day outfitting a warehouse to hold the rogues, contain their powers, and keep them subdued.

Among the shadowkind lurking in the buildings around me, there's a being called a lamia who can put any of our opponents to sleep with a touch. Steel—the scaled demon—revealed that he can shoot out a paralyzing force from a short distance that'll last a few hours.

If that's not enough, I can temporarily freeze the rogues with my shriek; Jacob can lock them in place with his telekinetic power. Willow the nymph volunteered to send the roots of the saplings spaced at even intervals down the street shooting from the patches of earth to bind them.

That'll buy us the time to use the powerful sedative in the syringes we're all carrying. Toni gave us the name of the drug the guardians found most effective for using on us.

It's necessary, even if turning to yet another of our former captors' tactics turns my stomach.

I'm not super keen on having Booker here either. His aura-sight hasn't developed into any kind of talent useful for self-defense. But he and the other two shadowblood kids we rescued insisted on coming along.

They know the rogue shadowbloods better than we do —a lot better, in the case of the other kids. After some arguing, Rollick put his foot down and pointed out that we should give them the same kind of choices we wanted for ourselves.

I still don't like it.

One of the kids has ended up playing a crucial role in the ambush. As I shift restlessly on my feet, a quiet voice forms inside my head.

Griffin says the nearest ones are just a minute or two away, Ajax says. *We should put our earplugs in now.*

Once we've sealed our ears, he'll be the one passing on all communications between us using his telepathic talent. If any of us needs to say anything, we'll think it at him first, and he'll relay the message on.

I know he's said the same thing to Booker, because the teen next to me reaches to his pocket for his plugs. His face looks yellowed in the dim light, and I don't think it's only because of the jaundiced security lamps.

His girlfriend is on her way, and he can't be any more sure than I can that we'll save her this time. Or that she won't do something horrifying while we attempt to.

As I pull out my own earplugs, distant, raucous laughter reaches my ears from somewhere behind me. I freeze, tracking the sound as it filters through the walls.

One risk of an ambush on a college campus: drunken partiers roaming around.

One of the patrolling shadowkind must redirect the wanderers. The sound fades away. I take a few slow, steadying breaths and shove the plugs into my ears.

The industrial-strength brand we found is incredibly

effective, but they don't give me total silence. Shutting out all external sound only heightens my awareness of what's going on inside me.

My breaths woosh in and out. The thud of my pulse quickens.

I curl my fingers around the device we picked up following Toni's specifications. With one jab of a button, it'll flood the street with a piercing wail that should shatter the focus of anyone who can hear it.

We got three of the devices, just in case one fails or one of us is attacked before we can activate it. Sorsha holds hers where she's waiting as backup by an unfinished window on the third floor of another partly-constructed townhouse. Crag the gargoyle carries a third where he'll be perched on one of the nearby rooftops.

Backups upon backups. We can't let this confrontation go wrong.

I move to the doorway where we've left the door ajar and scan the street through the gap. Maybe I'd be able to make out approaching motors by now if I could hear any sound outside my body.

It should be an increasingly urgent approach as the rogues chase the illusion of monster hunters. Andreas watched all the video footage he could find of the vigilante groups so that he could project accurate images from those memories into the rampaging shadowbloods' minds.

If it all worked out, they'll have caught glimpses of their prey ducking out of view up ahead here and there, leading them on toward this construction zone. Confirming the story that the hunters thought the site was ideal grounds for an extermination.

Ajax's voice peals into my head again, sounding louder amid the outer silence. *We can see the first of them now. They're just coming into the cul-de-sac. There's a minivan... A big pickup truck with a bunch of them sitting in the cargo area... A little delivery truck it looks like they stole from a flower shop.*

As he rattles off that list, the first of the vehicles creeps into view. The black minivan looks like a shadow itself on the darkened street.

It rolls to a halt by the curb only a couple of buildings into the dead-end area. Of course, the rogue shadowbloods still think they're hunting the hunters. They'll need to be on foot for their main attack.

Which also works in our favor. We don't want them close enough to their vehicles to make a run for it like last time.

Of course, it won't be long before they can't get anywhere on those wheels anyway. As soon as they've left the vehicles behind, Jacob will be applying his ability to the engines, snapping and cracking vital components so the motors won't run.

I suspect he's looking forward to breaking a few things, even if none of them will be skulls.

The figures gather around the vehicles before prowling forward as one large mass. I make out facial features here and there as they pass the pools of lamp-glow.

It looks like the criminal shadowbloods are still using the kids as a sort of shield. Nadia, Devon, and Tegan walk on the edges of the group alongside other teens and preteens.

I catch sight of the skull-and-snake tattoo emblazoned

on the scalp of the group's apparent leader, who we now know is named Cutler. The hazy light glances off the scarred brow of the man Griffin spoke to briefly, who he said another of the shadowbloods called Omar.

There's a lamppost with neon orange caution tape wrapped around its middle, about two thirds of the way down the cul-de-sac. That's our tipping point—when the last of the shadowbloods is past it, we launch our attack.

Most of them are staring into the shadows at the dead end of the street. They pick up their pace, maybe seeing another projected memory that suggests the hunters are in the buildings down there.

My palm turns clammy against the siren device. I wet my lips, keeping my body tensed and motionless.

The group moves past the marked lamppost—the first several figures, then more, then the last forms bringing up the rear...

I wait until that last foot steps past the post's thin shadow. At the same moment, Ajax's voice rings through my mind. *Now!*

I hit the button with more force than it probably needs. The device shivers in my hand.

Its siren wail splits through the night, so loud and piercing I can make out a faint screech even with the industrial earplugs blocking the sound. I can only assume that Sorsha and Crag have set off their devices too.

The mass of prowling shadowbloods breaks apart. Kids and criminals alike stumble, their hands clutching their ears, their faces twisted with agony.

A few of them swipe at their eyes too. Andreas will be

filling their heads with a jumble of other remembered images now, a nonsensical mishmash designed to confuse.

I bolt past the door and race toward the group of them, setting the siren device down on the curb. My hand reaches to the syringes hooked on my belt.

The faster we can get them all knocked out, the safer we'll all be—them included.

The shadowkind are doing their part too. Stretching roots ripple across the pavement from where Willow has appeared by one of the saplings. One body and then another crumples to the ground as Steel and the lamia send out their talents.

The plump woman with sleeping powers is just reaching toward Devon when a massive figure looms in the middle of the chaos. My heart lurches.

One of the criminal shadowbloods has morphed into an unnerving blend of giant man and snake. His hairless scalp gleams with mottled scales—which cover his head like a shell except for his slit-pupil eyes and tapered muzzle.

He's got no ears. The siren isn't affecting him.

In the instant I realize that, he aims a contraption that looks like a blend between a crossbow and a gun at Steel. I've seen those before—in the hands of the would-be monster hunters.

A gleaming metal bolt that must be silver and iron shoots from the weapon and stabs straight into the demon's broad forehead.

Twenty-Four

Riva

Smoky essence plumes up as Steel's bulky form crashes to the ground. The demon's body sprawls lifelessly on the asphalt.

A cry breaks from my throat that I mostly hear from inside my head. I whirl toward the shadowblood shooter with his reptilian face, the sound condensing into a killing shriek in my lungs.

But before I can heave it from my mouth, searing light lances into my eyes. A voice that must be Nadia's hollers as loud as the siren as she flings her blinding power in all directions, even harsher than I've felt it before.

With my vision whited out, I stagger and bump into a body beside me. I can't tell if they're friend or foe.

My men are around me—I feel their presence through the marks on my chest. The little quivers of emotion that reach me echo my disorientation.

The rogue shadowbloods must be blinded too, but

how much does that matter when they were already put off balance by the piercing sirens and Andreas's projected memories? Nadia isn't hurting them so much as putting the rest of us on an equal playing field.

Ajax's voice careens through my thoughts. *Sorsha wants to know what's going on down there. Do you need her to step in?*

Do we? At that point it'll become a barbeque rather than a rescue mission.

My heart stutters with the sense of our plan falling apart. *Not yet,* I think at Ajax. *We might still be able to pull this off.*

I swipe at my eyes and grope through the scene that's alternately blotchy and completely hazed with more bursts of Nadia's light—and the sirens dwindle.

With my dulled hearing, it takes me a second to realize that they haven't all gotten quieter. It's just that one has cut out completely. A victorious shout rises from the stumbling crowd of shadowbloods, telling me the destruction was purposeful.

I don't know how they did it, but one of our opponents managed to use their power to cut off the device.

It's true that we don't know where all of them came from before they were turned into shadowbloods or what they're really feeling under the anger. We also don't know most of the powers they can wield.

We thought we orchestrated this battle with every advantage, but in some ways we were going in blind from the start.

My vision clears enough for me to make out one of the

shadowblood teens just a couple of feet away from me. I jab the syringe I'm still clutching into his back and squeeze.

He spins around, making me lose my grip, but the effects are already kicking in. Even as he tries to spring at me, his knees buckle under him. He topples over unconscious on the ground.

One more down, God knows how many more to tackle.

Ajax's voice reaches my head again. *She says it looks bad down there. She's heading in.*

No, wait—

Before I can finish my protest, fiery wings flash against the sky above us. Sorsha's voice rings out. "Clear the crowd! Give me room!"

Room to burn them all. My gut lurches in recognition of her meaning, but I heave myself backward instinctively. No part of me is interested in getting incinerated.

But I can't help letting loose my protest aloud at the same time. "No!"

Where's Nadia—Tegan—Devon? Can I at least pull them to safety? If they were away from the former inmates' influence for a little while, surely—

Sorsha swoops lower, her phoenix fire sweeping an orange glow and a waft of heat over our milling bodies. Has she hesitated because of my protest?

She raises her hand to fling out a stream of flames. At the same instant, a feral bellow like I've heard during our past fights with the rogues careens through the air.

In the milling crowd, I catch sight of the man with the skull-and-snake tattoo—the one Nadia called Cutler, who seems to be the leader of the rampaging shadowbloods. His head is tipped back and his mouth stretched impossibly wide.

His roar must carry a supernatural force. Something invisible smacks into Sorsha, snapping her head to the side. Her body sways off-kilter.

"Sorsha!" With a roar and a swish of black feathers, Thorn hurtles out of the night. He catches the phoenix woman in his arms before she can drop from the sky.

I don't know what that jolt of power did to her, but it's obviously disabled her for the moment. And as I whip back toward the crowd of wayward shadowbloods, the second siren cuts out.

More silver bolts flash through the night from the crossbow-gun the snake-man is wielding. Some rattle against the asphalt, and a couple strike his own allies, but in the space of a few heartbeats, one carves a smoking path through Crag's gargoyle thigh as he plummets to join the fray.

Another bolt slams into Willow's temple where she's waving her summoned roots onward. Bits of skull and locks of hair fly out with the billow of essence. She's thrown into the sapling and sags down its frail trunk.

Another blast of Nadia's light blurs my sight. A cacophony of yells and snarls and grunts reverberates around me.

Then a sudden sense of silence despite the din, as the final siren crackles and stops.

Oh, no.

With a louder bellow of rage, the shadowbloods we were trying to contain erupt into more purposeful motion.

They lash out at our ring of Firsts and shadowkind with every power at their disposal.

Some speedy form dashes through our forces with a flash of a blade. The shadowkind he passes blink into the darkness to dodge it or hunch over with gushes of essence from the stab wounds.

The tang of Tegan's toxic smoke reaches my nose. I swivel to see her exhaling a vicious cloud toward Zian and a few of the shadowkind.

My hand leaps to my remaining syringes. Grasping it, I leap toward her.

Not quite fast enough.

A huge, brown-furred form barges at her from the other side. Fang pummels the girl who's less than a third his shifted bear size with one of his massive paws and tears into her neck with a wrench of his brutal teeth.

No—please, no. But even as my wordless plea tumbles from my mouth in a gasp, Tegan crumples, her head lolling from her shoulders at an angle that makes it clear no life will ever come back into her vacant eyes. She hits the asphalt with a splash of her blood.

My lips part wider. I suck the air into my lungs, a scream bubbling up my throat.

I don't know how to pick apart allies and enemies in the chaos around me, but I can freeze them all. I can halt the carnage in its tracks.

And then what? How the hell are we going to disentangle ourselves? At some point, we have to move.

A burly figure charges into view, another of those crossbow-guns clutched in his hands. It's one of the teenaged shadowbloods, a vengeful laugh hitching out of him as he pelts the shadowkind with silver-and-iron bolts. More cries and grunts ring out.

Was that Lance's voice? Pearl's?

Tears sear up behind my eyes, but I have to protect *someone*. The shriek that was building inside me tears up my throat, and I propel it toward the boy with the gun.

My power socks him right in the skull with more force than I probably needed to use even against a fellow shadowblood. A swell of pain surges from him into me as the bones splinter and pierce the flesh around them, as his nose crumples in and his jaw cracks.

Nausea hits me along with the punch of energy. I'm not here to torture, only to protect whoever I can.

I yank at the energy coursing through my scream and jab one of those splinters deep enough into the boy's heart to sever his life.

The sensations flowing from him blank out. He topples over to join the other corpses now littering the ground.

I don't have time to wallow in the guilt that clutches my chest. Gulping another breath, I prepare to cast out my shriek again.

Before the first hint of sound can pass from my lips, a body slams into me from behind. I fly forward, just barely catching myself with my hands before my face smacks into the pavement.

My chin still catches on the gritty ground, a slash of pain spreading through the skin. I swallow a sob and shove myself up and around to face my attacker.

Whoever shoved me has already moved on. But through the melee, I see something worse.

Booker has emerged from the building where I left him in supposed safety. He's walking toward the battle with nothing at all to protect him from the weapons and powers being flung around.

His face has gone pale, but it's set with resolve. There's no sign of the easy-going surfer-dude attitude in him now.

Somewhere in the fighting, one of my earplugs popped out. So I hear his voice perfectly clearly when he raises it over the clamor of the fray.

"Nadia! Nadia, please, you've got to help us stop this craziness. Please, come talk to me."

I step toward him. "Booker, get back into one of the buildings. It isn't safe for—"

He swipes his hand through the air to dismiss my concerns. "I only want to talk to Nadia. Nadia, where are you? Please. I love you. You know that, right?"

A lump rises in my throat—and Nadia's statuesque frame sways into view through the grappling bodies. Her pixie cut sticks up in tufts between strands slicked to her scalp with sweat or maybe blood. Her eyes look wild, the pupils over-dilated.

She stares at Booker. "You're here."

He nods, a gentle smile spreading across his face that's totally at odds with our surroundings. "I'll always be here. I miss you. If we could just—"

Something hisses through the air. Booker's plea is cut off in mid-sentence with a bloom of red in the middle of his throat.

A bloom of blood around a glint of metal. Someone's shot him with one of those crossbow bolts.

Booker staggers and coughs. More blood sputters up over his lips to dribble down his chin.

With a cry, I dash over to him. My call for help vibrates up my throat as forceful as any scream. "Dominic! Anyone—we need a healer!"

Nadia gets to Booker first. He collapses into her arms, his jaw working but no more sound than a ragged gasp escaping his mouth. More blood spurts across her dark gray sweater.

"No," she mumbles. "No, no—Booker, no."

His head slumps forward. His eyes glaze. Nadia's fingers clutch at his back, but when his legs give, she has to sink with him to the ground.

I come to a halt over them, not knowing what else to do. He's gone. I'm not sure even Dominic could save him if he got here now.

Anguish for both the boy I couldn't save and the girl grieving him clogs my lungs. For a few seconds, I can't breathe.

Nadia strokes her fingers over Booker's cheek with a choked wail. She stares at the blood that's still pulsing from his throat to soak into her clothes.

Then her gaze jerks up toward me.

Fury hardens her features. She lurches upright, her lips pulling back from her teeth to bare them.

"You brought him here! You got him killed! You don't care about any of us!"

My jaw goes slack. I don't know what to say in the face of her rage. Can't she see that it was one of her allies' bullets that killed him?

But Booker couldn't have taken that bullet if he hadn't

come here with us. If we hadn't been trying to stop her and the other rogue shadowbloods.

"I—I'm sorry," I stammer out. "Nadia, I swear, I only want to help you. I—"

She lets out a scream that's pure agony and flings out her hands. Light so sharp it gives off tangible heat blazes out in all directions, not just from her palms but every inch of her skin.

She's close enough that her fingers slash across my cheek. In the instant before I flinch backward, my skin sears with a physical burn.

"No!" she screeches. "You're all the same. You're all against us. You fucked us up and you screwed us over and you should all fucking die!"

I'm not sure who all she's talking to right now. From the groans and yelps around me, she's hurting her fellow shadowbloods as much as the rest of us.

But she definitely means me. Girding myself, I reach for her again, but she whips her hand straight toward my face.

An even sharper spear of light spikes straight through my eyeballs. My forehead and cheeks sting with the sensation of scorching. The pain echoes the agony that laced her voice, shooting straight into my brain with the fizzling of my vision.

The pit of my stomach hollows out. In every way that matters, I think my friend might be gone too.

Then a heavier force rams into the back of my head, and the blazing light gives way to total darkness.

TWENTY-FIVE

Riva

Sunlight pierces through my eyelids and wakes up a dull throbbing at the base of my skull. I wince before I've opened my eyes, and clothing rustles nearby.

Dominic's voice reaches me, soft and soothing. "Hey. You're okay now."

With a thin line of pressure, one of his tentacles slides along my arm. A waft of warm healing energy washes through my body, and the lingering pain in my head melts away.

I blink and stare up at him—at all of my guys, who are standing around the bed I'm lying on. *They're* all okay and wearing matching expressions of concern.

With a lurch of my pulse, I shove myself upright. We're surrounded by the muted beige walls and chic furnishings of a hotel room, though not one I recognize from before.

The last thing I remember before waking up is the battle. Crossbow bolts flying, cries ringing out, light blazing—Booker, Nadia...

My voice comes out raspy. "What happened? How did we get here? The other shadowbloods..."

Griffin sits down on the bed by my other side and rests his hand on my shoulder. A faint caress of calm seeps from his palm through my mind—not really changing my emotions, just helping me focus despite the sudden swell of anguish.

Jacob is gripping the oak footboard, his fingers clenched as tight as his jaw. "It was a shitstorm. After you fell, we pulled out as fast as we could. Zian grabbed you. The assholes took off down the street as soon as they had the opening. I messed up their vehicles, but we know they can steal new ones."

He sounds almost annoyed that the rogue shadowbloods decided to prioritize staying alive over continuing the fight.

"We did get a few of them," Zian says in a hopeful tone that clashes with the unhappy cast to his face. "We picked up three of the shadowbloods we managed to knock out—a couple of the kids and one of the criminals."

I swallow thickly. "Some of them were more than knocked out. And the shadowkind they attacked—I saw Steel get shot, and Willow..."

Andreas nods, not even his normally animated eyes managing to offer any light. "I think six or seven of the shadowkind didn't make it out. It's hard to keep track when we didn't know for sure who all was going to come out of the shadows. We lost about as many of the other shadowbloods too, in the fighting. Mostly the kids and a couple of the criminals. Tegan and Booker…"

His voice trails off raggedly. My fingers curl into the covers beneath me. "I know. I saw them."

And the kid *I* killed, whose name I didn't even know. I'll never get the chance to find it out.

I don't think the shadowkind will see their deaths as a loss, though. Not when they lost so many of their own to the rampaging hybrids.

I rub my forehead, still working to piece together everything that happened. "They were carrying weapons like the hunters were using—for fighting shadowkind."

Dominic strokes the tip of his tentacle back and forth over my wrist. "They saw the shadowkind working with us when we confronted them in Memphis. We figure they wanted to be prepared in case we came at them again."

It makes a sick kind of sense. In the most horrible of ironies, our attempts at shaking our fellow shadowbloods out of Balthazar's influence have pushed them into becoming the monster-murdering soldiers he wanted.

Fuck. I feel hollowed out inside, as if all my inner organs have sunk to the bottom of my belly.

"The shadowkind must be pissed," I murmur. "They didn't really want to help us anyway. They thought the other shadowbloods weren't worth saving, too much of a threat."

A tawny-haired figure wavers into view by the door beyond the foot of the bed. Rollick has his arms folded loosely over his chest, his expression serious but otherwise unreadable. "I asked my associates to leave you undisturbed while you recovered, but I think you should talk to them directly about how they're currently feeling. It's good to see you with us again."

I have to resist the urge to cringe under the demon's penetrating gaze. It was my plan that sent his people into the fray—and ended some of their normally infinite lives.

I can take responsibility for my decisions. I can face the people my mistakes hurt the most.

With a wiggle of my legs to make sure they're in working order, I shove myself toward the side of the bed. "Let's go do that now."

Rollick dips his head in acknowledgment. He leads the way out the door.

It turns out we're not just in a hotel room but a whole penthouse suite. I halt in the doorway, staring at the sprawling living room with its floor-to-ceiling windows giving a view over the surrounding city from above. The hazy light that's creeping over the buildings and the burnt gray of the sky suggest dawn has just arrived.

"We needed the space—and not to be interrupted," Rollick says in brisk explanation.

My gaze lands on a body-shaped form draped in a white sheet, lying on the floor beyond the sofas. I freeze in place. "Who—"

"Booker," Dominic says softly. "One of the shadowkind managed to grab his body and carry him here through the shadows—I guess that's possible for a mortal once they're dead."

Rollick nods. "She saw how upset you were by his death. She thought you'd want to give him a proper burial rather than leaving him to your crazed counterparts or whoever else would have found him."

"Yeah." My arms come up to hug myself. I can't see Booker through the sheet, but the image of his sagging face after the crossbow bolt hit him is emblazoned in my memory.

The rogues killed him—a shadowblood just like them, simply because he was trying to get through to Nadia in the most peaceful possible way.

I don't like considering what that says about them and how far gone they are.

I turn to Rollick. "Will you be able to help us with that? We don't have the money or the contacts to arrange any kind of regular burial."

The demon offers a small sympathetic smile. "We'll sort it out."

He motions for us to follow him to one of the other bedrooms off the common room. As we walk over, several shadowkind materialize to trail after us.

Among them, Shanty sweeps her deep blue hair back over her shoulders, her features pinched with what looks like grief. Fang lumbers forward, his muscular prowl making my limbs tense with the memory of his bear form tearing into Tegan.

Crag brings up the rear with a steady stride that reassures me that the injury I saw him take didn't do any permanent damage. Even so, his harsh face with its rocky jaw looks even grimmer than usual.

The room we step into holds two queen beds. One appears to be empty. Sorsha lies on the other, her head tipped back against the pillow, but she pushes herself into a sitting position at our entrance.

And promptly sways as if she can't find her balance.

Beside her, Snap catches her shoulder with a noise of concern, his bright green eyes wide with worry. Across from him, Thorn looms taller as if he can intimidate whatever's bothering the phoenix into submission.

My heartbeat stutters. I dart forward to the foot of the bed. "Are you all right? What happened?"

Sorsha rubs her temple and offers me a crooked smile. "Those friends of yours have quite the assortment of powers. One of them hit me with something that seems to have rattled my brain around. If I move at all quickly, I get very dizzy."

Jacob speaks in a growl. "They're not our *friends.*"

"She's got vertigo," Rollick clarifies from where he's positioned himself by the wall. He glances at me. "We're monitoring the condition. Your tentacled friend hasn't been able to identify a physical source to fully heal it, but we're hopeful it'll clear up with rest."

Nausea wraps around my gut. If Sorsha can't even sit up without getting dizzy, there's no way she'll be able to fly.

The rogue shadowbloods managed to disable our most powerful ally with one blow.

With a shifting of the duvet, a figure pops into being in the other bed, her legs tucked under the covers. Pearl grins at me as if oblivious to the thin trail of essence trickling up from her arm. "And I'm going to be okay too."

I dash to her bed, my throat constricting. I'd almost forgotten that I thought I heard her yelp during the fight. "Pearl…"

A bunch of other shadowkind have emerged with her

arrival. Billy is among them, closest to the bed. He shakes his head at her with a swish of his dark brown waves and yanks a roll of gauze from his pocket. "When you jump in and out of the shadows, you lose your bandage."

The succubus glances down at her arm while her friend wraps enough gauze around the wound to suppress the flow of essence. "The cut is almost all healed up anyway." She meets my eyes again and lets out a laugh. "You should have seen how it looked last night. *That* was scary."

She doesn't sound scared, but guilt chokes me anyway. The shadowbloods *I* insisted we try to capture could have killed my closest friend among the shadowkind.

This is all my fault. How do we come back from this?

My skin prickles with my awareness of the other shadowkind who've joined us in the room, the small crowd scattered around the two beds. They're all watching my reaction.

"I'm sorry," I say to Pearl, pushing the words past the lump in my throat, and turn toward the others. "I'm so sorry. I didn't know they'd have those weapons, or that they'd be able to use their powers against the devices emitting the sirens—I never wanted any of you to get hurt."

I brace myself for accusations and recriminations. Instead, surprise ripples across the shadowkind faces before me.

Shanty speaks first, in a low tone. "One of the young ones like you nearly shot me. I saw you finish him before he could hurt anyone else. You killed your own blood to protect us."

Lance pipes up from where he's hopped up to perch on the room's dresser. "Jacob took down one of the other shadowbloods too. You fought for us like you wanted to fight for them."

Fang peers at me with a wary air. "I thought—I wouldn't have wanted to kill that girl, but I saw her attacking the others, and… Aren't you angry with me?"

I gulp air, overwhelmed by the response so different from what I expected. "I mean, I wish she was still alive, but I can't blame you for protecting your people."

"You protected us too," Billy says. He flickers through the shadows to emerge at my side and takes my hand tentatively. There's nothing but genuine appreciation in his big faun eyes as he smiles up at me. "Even when shadowkind have attacked *you*, you've never wanted to see us hurt unless there was no other choice. I should know that better than anyone."

Tears hit me like a punch from inside my skull. I swipe at my eyes. "I hurt *you* before. You didn't—"

Billy's smile doesn't waver as he cuts in. "You stopped. I felt you pull back—I felt how quickly you yanked away the moment you realized. It was foolish of me to leap into the middle of the fight. We all make mistakes. I might not have much experience with the mortal realm yet, but it seems to me that what should matter is what we do about our mistakes when we see the problem."

For the first time, I fully believe that he doesn't blame me for aiming my power at him. I've known all along that I never meant to do it, but it still felt like a vicious act. Like proof of my monstrousness.

What if it's actually a sign of how human I am, that I could screw up so badly… and regret it so much?

Rollick clears his throat. "My associates aren't looking to cast you out. But we do need to come to a decision about what to do about your fellow shadowbloods who are still out there on their rampage. Last night only culled their numbers by about a quarter."

"Right," I say, still grappling with my whirling feelings. "I heard we captured a few of them. What happened to those three?"

The demon tips his head toward the doorway. "We've got them in another room. You can come see them."

Something about his tone makes my stomach sink. The guys join me as we head out the door—where we nearly run into Toni, who's rushing over to the bedroom with a paper bag clutched in her hand.

She pauses and swipes at her now-rumpled bob with a slightly self-conscious expression. "Are you all right, Riva? You must be feeling better if you're walking around. I just got into town a few hours ago—I was out grabbing something Pearl said she wanted for breakfast."

At the mention of the succubus, a hint of a flush colors Toni's cheeks. Huh. I can't help remembering the little kitchen interlude I saw between the two of them back in Rollick's Spanish mansion.

"I'm doing fine," I say with a quick smile. "I'm sure Pearl will appreciate the food." From what I understand, shadowkind don't *need* to eat in the usual mortal way, but a lot of them seem to enjoy the act all the same.

As Toni hustles by, Rollick leads us to the third bedroom. He pauses outside the door. "All three of them have been… difficult any time they start to come to. Lull has been keeping them unconscious with her powers to avoid any violence."

The lamia. I guess that's a little better than constantly drugging them up.

I cross my arms over my chest, just shy of hugging myself. "What have they been doing when they wake up?"

Zian rubs his shoulder. "One of the kids tried to tear my arm right off when I went to talk to him. I could barely hold him down—whatever his powers are, they include a lot of strength. He wouldn't stop yelling long enough for anyone to get a word in."

Rollick eases open the door and motions us into the room. Three cots are set up with the dozing figures, who are pinned to their beds with heavy chains.

The one girl has a gag tied across her mouth. The man is blindfolded.

Before I need to ask, Andreas points to a large black splotch on the wallpaper. "The older guy has some kind of rotting power he projects with his eyes. He nearly disintegrated a hole in the wall."

The plump woman with a silvery sheen to her skin wavers out of the shadows near the teenage boy—the one who attacked Zian, I guess. She looks at Rollick in question. "He's starting to wake up. Should I send him back under?"

Even as she speaks, the boy's limbs twitch. I square my shoulders. "I'd like to see how he is. At least as much as you can let him wake up before he's a real threat."

Rollick inclines his head to give his agreement. Lull

stations herself near the boy's head in anticipation of using her powers.

A tremor runs through the boy's body. He jerks against the chains before his eyes have even opened.

Then he thrashes his head from one side to the other, but the movement is still a bit sluggish with sleep. "Let me out of here! I'm going to rip you all to pieces, you freaks. If I—"

The lamia brushes her fingertips over his hair, and his voice falters. His eyelids droop again, but they don't fully close.

I dart to the end of his cot. "We want to help you. But we can't do that if you're trying to fight us. If you could just listen for a minute or two—my friends and I are shadowbloods just like you—"

"Nothing like us," the boy mumbles out in a thickened voice. "Deserve everything you get. I hope Cutler finds you and chops you all to—"

His arms have started to slam against the chains again. With an apologetic pursing of her lips, Lull presses her whole hand to his head, and he trails off into slumber.

I take a step back, my posture deflating. How the hell can we get through to him when he's still so caught up in his rage, even separated from the rest of the group?

There's obviously nothing more to see. Rollick ushers us back into the living room.

I walk to the sofa and then back again, my nerves jangling. "And the other rogues—the ones that got away? Do we know what they're doing?"

"It seems like you shook them up some," Rollick replies. "They bashed up a few things—and people—on their way out of the city, but they didn't stop to revel in the destruction. They were in a hurry. I don't think they liked how close you got to overpowering them."

"Not close enough," Jacob mutters.

I swallow a choked laugh. Not close enough by a long shot.

One of his colleagues appears on the other side of the room and points to the bedroom where I woke up. "The wild shadowbloods are on the TV again."

My stomach sinking, I hurry over with the others. The TV mounted on the wall across from the bed emits a reporter's clipped but slightly frantic-sounding tones.

"No one's quite sure who the culprits are or what the motivation for this massacre was. Police are pursuing every possible lead. We can't help speculating that it may be connected to the recent string of attacks attributed by some to 'monsters.'"

The imagery on the screen shows a city park. Shrouded bodies too much like Booker's scatter the blood-stained grass. Paramedics are loading some figures onto stretchers as quickly as they can.

My throat clogs with a lump of nausea. I want to shut my eyes against the images, but I can't let myself.

The reporter is still giving her commentary. "The only message officials assume was left by the murderers was a few words carved into one of the paths: *We won't be tamed.* What that has to do with the slaughter of more than fifty seemingly random pedestrians, it's impossible to say at this point."

"Fifty." I repeat the number raggedly. "Oh, God."

Andreas looks as sick as I feel. "'We won't be tamed.'

Do you figure that message is directed at us?"

Zian's eyes widen. "They killed all those people just to get back at us for trying to stop them?"

Jacob scowls. "From what I've seen of them, I wouldn't be surprised."

"They are… very, very angry," Griffin puts in quietly.

The newscast has switched to a different story. Dominic picks up the remote and turns off the TV. Then he glances at me. "We obviously can't leave them out there still on their rampage. What are you thinking, Riva?"

I finally allow myself to close my eyes, ducking my head and rubbing the back of my neck. Feeling the fine chain of my necklace shift beneath my fingers. The symbol of family and connection Griffin gave me all those years ago.

Yes, we have to do something about our fellow shadowbloods. We can't let them keep wreaking havoc wherever they go, killing dozens upon dozens of people out of pure spite, for who knows how long.

It's not even just the already awful threat to all those innocents. We have no idea what the Highest beings Rollick mentioned might do if they feel they need to intervene.

I've been the one calling the shots when it comes to the younger shadowbloods, demanding that we give them a chance to stand down. Which means if that was a mistake, I need to be the one to say so.

It all comes down to me.

A wave of loneliness sweeps over me, absurd when the five men I'm closer to than anyone in the world are standing right there.

My thoughts must be louder than I realize, because another familiar figure slips past the bedroom door and approaches. Ajax offers me a soft smile and a voice inside my head. *Whatever you decide, I'll help you do it. You've tried so hard. We all know that.*

Suddenly, tears are pricking at my eyes again. Griffin eases his arm around my waist, and Andreas strokes my cheek with the back of his fingers.

Dominic studies my expression with his usual pensive air. "We'll talk it through. We'll figure it out. We still have options."

Not many. But the sense of their solidarity pulls me out of my momentary despair.

We are blood. We are family. So are the shadowbloods carving a path of destruction across the country... but that doesn't mean they can't be wrong.

What does it say about the rampaging rogues that they've made mistake after vicious mistake, and all they want to do is keep at it?

They're our blood, yes. That doesn't just mean we should save them if we can, but also that we have a responsibility to stop the damage they're doing.

We don't owe them infinite patience when they're leaving bodies of other people who deserved to live just as much in their wake. We're the only ones who have a hope of ending the devastation.

I glance toward the room where Sorsha and Pearl are recovering. All those shadowkind are waiting for my answer too. Trusting me to lead them.

"I want to save everyone," I say quietly. "But what... what if we can't?"

Jacob's mouth twists. "If anyone could figure out how, it'd be you, Wildcat. But even superheroes can't win every battle."

If I even am a superhero by any definition. What would I do if I was?

That answer is shockingly easy. I gird myself before I say the words. "Then we have to do what's best for the most possible people. What'll save the most lives."

Even if I hate it.

Rollick doesn't ask me to spell out what I mean. He simply cocks his head with a glint of sympathy in his eyes. "Any preferences for how we get started on that?"

I think about the past battles—how the other shadowbloods defied us, struck back at us, escaped from us. The injuries and losses we've taken.

What are our best chances at ending this once and for all without another mistake?

I raise my chin. "Sorsha and I can take them out the fastest from a distance. But Sorsha can't be moving around right now. And we don't want to leave the rogues any avenues for escape."

Dominic's gaze goes distant in contemplation. "Trying to pen them in with just our powers hasn't worked out all that well. If we could get them into an enclosed space where you and Sorsha could focus on them all at once and they couldn't attack anyone else in the process..."

The idea comes to me with a queasy lurch of my stomach, but I can't deny how perfect it is.

A shaky laugh spills out of me. "I think I know just the place."

Twenty-Six

The fence with its barbed wire topping doesn't look as intimidating as I remember. But then, it's been nearly five years since I was last back here, and I've endured a lot in that time.

Andreas picks up a stick from the forest floor behind us and tosses it at the chain-link face. A brief crackle of electricity makes him grimace. "Still electrified."

The guys around me all look as uncomfortable as I feel. They left this facility not long after I did, under equally traumatic circumstances.

Jacob folds his arms over his chest. "The guardians don't want anyone stumbling on their secrets even if they're not using the place anymore."

Rollick shifts his weight on his feet, his stance all typical smooth confidence but the lines of his own face tauter than usual. None of his shadowkind allies accompanied us this close to the guardians' territory. The silver and iron protections laid down around the facility are wearing even on the demon's immense power.

"We haven't seen any sign of mortals coming and going or patrolling around the place," he says. "It appears to be abandoned. But I can't say for sure that no one's been working inside without leaving during the short time we've been able to monitor it."

Griffin tilts toward the fence, his gaze sharpening with intentness. "I can't sense any emotions from inside. But I don't think we should go through with the plan without making sure."

Rollick glances over at us. "This is the place where you were held for most of your lives."

I nod. "There's a lot more to the building than you can see. It goes at least a few floors underground."

The demon's tone turns dry. "Ideal for keeping shadowbloods contained. Even by other shadowbloods."

"Yeah." I hug myself, my nerves creeping just looking through the fence.

I can't completely suppress the memories, as much as I'd like to. The small concrete building stands in the middle of the fenced-off clearing, with the solid steel door Griffin and I burst out through when we made our escape attempt all those years ago. The span of asphalt between the gate and the building holds no cars now, but it did back then.

Back then, when I pulled him into our first kiss under the star-flecked sky. When I watched his body jerk with the impact of a bullet from an unseen sniper.

When I thought I watched him die, bleeding out on

the pavement while the guardians swarmed me and dragged me away.

Griffin's memories will be similar to mine. The other four guys have two. The version I told them about, and the one they saw on a tablet's screen, doctored by the guardians to make it look as if I walked away from Griffin's crumpled body willingly. As if I'd set him up to die in exchange for my freedom.

The horror rolling through my gut is bad enough. I can't imagine the clash of emotions that must be gripping them.

On the other side of the building sprawls the field where we had our occasional outdoor training sessions. After so much time out of the guardians' clutches, it's strange remembering how much of a novelty it used to be to breathe this fresh air, to take in forest scents rather than the dull, heavily filtered air of the underground rooms.

Zian flexes his shoulders, looking both determined and uncertain. "We've got to go in, right? Make sure it's empty so we can use it."

I swallow thickly. "Yeah. Where are the controls for the electricity?"

Jacob makes a dismissive sound. "We don't need to worry about the controls. All I need is the wire…"

He prowls along the edge of the fence with his gaze fixed on the ground. He must be prodding the earth below with his powers, because as he comes around the left side of the facility, he pauses and smiles. "There it is."

Jake closes his eyes. His arms twitch with the invisible effort he's extending.

A faint sputter is the only sign that anything has

changed. But when he steps back with an air of satisfaction, the next twig Andreas tosses has no effect at all.

As Jacob stalks back to the gate to coax it open, I study Rollick. "Do you want to stay out here?"

His mouth tightens, but he shakes his head. "If we're going to use this place to make this our last stand, I want to know exactly what we're working with—and be able to make suggestions to craft that plan as carefully as we can. I think I'll follow you from the shadows from here on unless I have something to say, though."

The gate glides open, and the demon fades into the patches of darkness at its foot. The six of us tramp inside, heading across the asphalt toward the sole part of the building above ground.

I'm doing my best to keep my mind entirely focused on the steel door and concrete wall ahead of me, but my pulse still hitches as we pass the exact spot where Griffin and I stood in our one fleeting minute of freedom.

I can't hide the agony of that memory from him. He slips his hand around mine with a subtle squeeze that says more than any words could.

The guardians tore us apart, but we found our way back to each other. And now we're going to make sure that their legacy of pain and destruction ends completely.

Zian scowls at the door. "I could bash it open or cut out the lock."

Dominic cocks his head. "I think it's better if we don't leave too obvious a sign that we were here. They might not have the resources to pay much attention to this place anymore, but better safe than sorry."

Jacob crouches down by the doorknob. "I think I can disengage this lock too. Let me just get the feel of it…"

There's a grating sound and a sharp *snap*, and his mouth twists at a wry angle. "Well, I had to force the issue rather than leaving everything in one piece. But at least no one can *see* that it's broken."

"I'll keep checking for any sign of emotional responses nearby," Griffin says. "But there's definitely no one on the ground level."

Jacob grasps the knob and pulls the door open. As we step into the white-washed hall on the other side, the sense of history weighs down on me even more suffocatingly.

The lights were off, but they flicker on at our arrival, provoked by the movement. Dominic lets the door thump shut behind him as he brings up the rear.

There's nothing on the first floor except a storage room on one side and what looks like a breakroom for the guards who'd have once cycled through patrols on the other. The shelves in the former stand empty other than a few innocuous basics like a box of garbage bags and a few containers of sunscreen.

The breakroom doesn't look as if anyone's relaxed there in quite a while. A thick layer of dust coats the plain table and chairs. When we peek inside the cabinets, we find a couple of bags of coffee beans with a best before from years back and assorted sweetener packets.

Zian sucks in a breath. "They really just abandoned the place after they took us out."

Dominic responds with a terse chuckle. "They must have figured that if we could almost escape, it wasn't really secure. Better not to risk bringing any other shadowbloods here."

The guardians wanted to imprison us forever, though. We only need to keep the rampaging shadowbloods contained for a matter of minutes.

My stomach knots tighter with each step we take down the stairs. On the next floor down, we find the door to the control room standing ajar.

The consoles Griffin and I manipulated to open the way for our escape hold just as much dust as the break-room table. I swipe my finger along the corner of one screen. "I don't think anyone's been in here in a long time. They figured the fence was enough to make sure they didn't need to worry about random hikers intruding."

Zian looks as if he's suppressed a shudder. "Does that mean we don't have to bother going farther down? I hate this place."

The same resistance twines through my muscles. My nerves clang with alarm at the thought of walking down the hallway of cells where we lived for most of our lives, of stepping into the gymnasium where we spent so many days training.

But we need to do this right.

"Maybe we don't have to right this moment," I say. "We will need to see exactly what we're working with eventually—what they left behind, what they might have dismantled after we were taken away."

Andreas turns on his heel, scanning the control room with a frown. "It's a secure building, as buildings go, with only one escape route and at least one big room we could direct the rogue shadowbloods into. But how are we going to convince them to come here—to come *inside*—in the first place?"

I worry at my lower lip with my teeth. I've been pondering that question since I first set us on this course of action. "We need to give them a really good reason to want to come in—and to think that we *wouldn't* want them to, so of course it couldn't be a trap."

The fact that most of the shadowkind can't tolerate the protections around the facility—and that those who can would still be severely weakened—is part of the reason I suggested it. Cutler, Nadia, and the others wouldn't expect us to pick an ambush spot where most of our allies can't back us up.

Dominic drifts through the room, his tentacles swaying against his back beneath his coat. "What would they want? They've already got all the power they need to attack the people they're looking to hurt. Nothing's really been able to get in their way for long."

I think back to our past confrontations with the rampaging shadowbloods. The things they said, the ways they reacted.

The moments when they reacted the most.

"Maybe we need to focus on what they *wouldn't* want," I say slowly. "They hate the idea of us getting in their way, stopping them from getting the revenge they think they deserve. What if they started believing that there was something down here that could stop them?"

Jacob's eyes light up. "Some kind of weapon designed to be used against shadowbloods. That would make sense.

Why wouldn't the guardians have something like that as a defensive tactic?"

Zian rubs his chin. "But why would the guardians be keeping it here when they're not even using the building anymore?"

"The other shadowbloods don't know that," Griffin puts in quietly. "We were the only ones kept in this facility. They wouldn't recognize it or have any idea of its significance."

"Yeah." I step back into the hall, taking in the dust and the stillness. "We'll have to clean it up, make it look like it's been in use."

A sharper smile curves Jacob's mouth. "Maybe even call in some guardians for the day of so it'll look guarded when those lunatics show up."

Andreas hums to himself. "Do you think the other shadowbloods will definitely fall for the trick? I'm not sure how we'll pass on the message without them realizing it came from us. And they could just ignore the possibility."

Griffin cocks his head. "I think there's a good chance. They're driven so much by intense emotion rather than thinking clearly… It's made it impossible for me to have any sway over them, but that also means we can use the emotions they're already feeling to drive them in the direction we want. If they believe there's a legitimate threat, and they're angry about the idea of the guardians attacking them, I wouldn't be surprised if that's enough."

Ignoring the growing queasiness pooling in my gut, I nod. "And if they don't take the bait, fine. We try something else. We won't have really lost anything."

Rollick appears out of the shadows, standing in the

doorway. "My people might not be much use for any actual fighting in here, but they can help pass on the message. I'll send a few shadowkind who haven't been present for the previous fights—they can approach the shadowbloods, pretending to be on their side. Claiming they support the killing of the mortals and want to give a warning about a possible threat."

"They'd have to be careful about it," I say. "The rogues have killed shadowkind before. But I can see that trick working."

I can see the whole plan coming together in my head while we stand in the building I thought I'd never have to set foot in again. Somehow feeling the path toward our goal solidifying doesn't reassure me the way I'd like.

My queasiness remains as we walk back outside for a gulp of fresh air and to survey the grounds before we venture deeper inside. Images flash by with each blink of my eyes: Tegan crumpling in Fang's jaws, Lindsay's wrists flayed open by Balthazar's manacles, George lying dead at the edge of the desert town where Clancy sent us on our last mission.

There are so many shadowbloods dead already. By the time we're finished here, there might be no one left at all except for us Firsts and the two we still have with us who weren't affected too badly by Balthazar's procedures.

As we fan out across the field, Andreas veers after me. He touches my arm with a gentle stroke of his fingers. "You look worried. If you think there's a problem with the setup, we should deal with it now."

"It's not that." My head droops. "When we found out about the younger shadowbloods, I promised myself—and them—that we'd help them too. Get them away from the guardians. And now…"

We slow as we reach the back fence. Andreas's voice comes out rough. "And now we're figuring out the easiest way to kill them."

I shiver at his words, even though I was the one who set us on this course. "If I could see any other way—if we'd been able to get through to them at all… It isn't *fair*. As if the guardians hadn't fucked us up enough, Balthazar had to go and totally mess with their heads."

Andreas grimaces. "Maybe I should have taken the chance when we killed him—when we were there with him, I could have erased his existence from everyone's memories."

As much as I'd like to erase everything Balthazar ever did, my mind recoils from Drey's suggestion. "No. Just wiping out the memories of him wouldn't have been enough. The shadowbloods he created and whose powers he beefed up would still have been crazed and angry about everything else. And then *we* wouldn't have remembered what he'd done."

"Okay, fair point."

The memory of our fellow shadowbloods' rage pricks at me as deeply as the emotions our past here stirs up. Nadia is so angry about so many things…

I pause, a few of my thoughts connecting in a way that takes my breath away. For a few seconds, I don't dare to speak.

Andreas gives me a curious look. "What?"

I know better than to put too much stock in hope

these days. But all the same, a flutter of it passes through my chest, raising my spirits just a little.

I turn to face Drey with a nervous thump of my heart. "What if there's another way you could use your power to help set things right?"

Twenty-Seven

Andreas

"I don't understand," the boy says for what might be the tenth time, looking down at his hands where he's sitting on the end of the hotel bed and then glancing up at me. "I hurt someone? I can't remember... I can't remember anything."

I take a deep breath before repeating the explanation we decided on. "It's because of that accident I told you about. It seems like it affected your memory. We don't know if you'll get those memories back—but we can help you figure things out from here."

Griffin nods where he's standing next to me. "It's like you were sick, but you can get better now. You're surrounded by friends. We'll make sure you're safe."

I know my friend is sending wave after wave of calming emotion over the kid whose mind I wiped half an hour ago. The shadowblood boy who nearly pulled Zian's arm out of its socket a few days ago, who when he woke up before wouldn't do anything but thrash against his restraints and shout threats at us.

Just in case the boy's temper snaps after all, Pearl and Dominic are standing by in the new hotel room Rollick got us for this purpose. Pearl's ready to attempt her succubus persuasion on him and Dominic to drain him into unconsciousness if the former strategy doesn't work.

But so far we haven't needed them. After talking with the kid for several minutes at first and getting Griffin's confirmation that he didn't see any reason for alarm, we removed the chains. We're still staying wary, but my trepidation is giving way to a bittersweet sense of relief.

Riva's suggestion may have actually worked. By cutting Balthazar's shadowbloods off from their memories of everything they had to rage about, we've diffused their fury.

The fact that Griffin even *can* soothe this kid's emotions is proof that we've made progress.

I just can't help feeling a little sick about how much else I had to steal from him to accomplish that.

The boy rubs his forehead. "You say my name is Keith? I... I don't even remember *that.*"

Neither had I, if I'd ever known it. But we had a little extra help in that department.

I motion Ajax over from where he's been waiting near the door, braced in case he has to duck outside for his own safety. He steps closer, his telepathic voice traveling into my mind at the same time. *I'm not picking up on any violent thoughts. He's just confused. And he doesn't like the idea that he hurt people.*

Well, developing a conscience seems like important progress too.

I tap the slim boy's shoulder. "This is Ajax. He did some training with you at one of the places you lived before, so he can tell you some things about yourself. If you're ready to talk more about that."

Keith wavers for a moment with a slight sway of his posture before offering a tentative smile. "That—that would be nice."

The door eases open to reveal Zian's face. "Lull says that the girl—Bethany—is going to wake up soon. If you want to try on her too."

I glance around at the others, not sure whether I want to be told to go ahead or held back from wiping out my second mind of the day.

Dominic dips his head. "I'll stay, just in case."

There are a few shadowkind watching from the shadows who can step in if they need to too, Ajax informs me silently. It turns out he can sense their thoughts even when they don't have a physical presence, although he says the impression is pretty foggy.

I square my shoulders. "All right. I'll see how it goes with Bethany."

One victory isn't proof of success, only a good sign. We need to see if I can repeat it.

Griffin turns to follow me over to the next room, where Rollick's people moved the captured shadowblood girl. "I should come along for calming purposes. Keith seems pretty stable at the moment."

I shoot my friend a quick smile in thanks. At least I don't have to carry out this awful job on my own.

In the other room, we find the lamia poised next to the bed. The girl lying on it is bound with chains wrapped around her body, the gag still in her mouth.

I wasn't there when she started singing the first time she woke up, but apparently her crooning is powerful enough to send whoever she focuses it on into a panic.

"The sleep I put her under will last about ten more minutes," Lull says, looking down at her charge. "I'll stay in case you need to send her under again. I shouldn't need to check on the older one for another couple of hours."

I swallow thickly. "Thank you. We should take the gag out so she can at least talk once she wakes up. I don't want her to be more freaked out than she needs to be."

Lull reaches to release the gag. "Just be careful. That power of hers seems to work fast."

"Absolutely. If she starts singing—or even humming— you'd better knock her out right away."

But when I'm through with Bethany's mind, she shouldn't remember that she even *can* wield a power like that.

As I walk up on the other side of the bed, my stomach sinks with every step. I prop myself against the edge of the mattress and reach over to rest my hand on the girl's forehead where the messy strands of her thin, flaxen hair have fallen aside.

I don't have to touch a person to wipe their memories as long as I can see them, but it's easier to focus like this. It takes a little less out of me when there's no distance to compel my ability across.

Staring at Bethany's slack, pale face, I can feel all the recollections whispering inside her skull. If I wanted to, I could tip myself right into them and experience those glimpses of her life.

But I already know too well what sort of experiences she's had. I know where they've brought her.

Is it fair to wipe them all away like taking a magnet to a hard drive? To force her to start over from scratch?

I'm still not sure. My gut has clenched even tighter as I prepare myself.

I've grappled with that question a lot in the time since Riva told me what she was thinking. I kind of hate that I'm doing this… but I also can't see any better way.

It's this or we end up killing all those kids, all the criminals who maybe could find a better path. I'm stealing the details of their life before, but I'm also giving them a second chance they wouldn't have gotten otherwise.

I focus on the sluggish stirring of the girl's mind and *push*. Almost like when I extend my talent for invisibility over someone else, but more concentrated. As if I've condensed the power into a psychic acid that's eating away every piece of her past that was stored inside her brain.

In a few minutes, her mind will be as blank as my body becomes when I remove it from sight.

The room is cool, but sweat forms on my forehead. An ache creeps up the back of my own skull.

If I'm going to do this with a bunch of the other shadowbloods, we'll probably have to space out my efforts. I'm not sure how many I could do one after the other without totally wearing myself out.

The memories dissolve beneath the sweeping wave of energy I'm propelling into Bethany's mind. Then I sense nothing within her head at all.

I drop my hand, balling it when it starts to shake, and pull myself back from the bed. No one wants to wake up not just disoriented but with a stranger right in their face.

Griffin's expression tenses slightly. He's already projecting soothing emotions into her, even as she sleeps.

I guess there's something to be said for getting a head start.

By the time Bethany shifts her limbs against the chains, my mouth has gone dry. She lets out a soft, startled sound that jabs at my heart.

Her eyes pop open. She stares at the bindings wrapped around her and then at the three of us standing around her bed.

Griffin frowns. "It's okay," he says in a voice soft as silk. He isn't aiming his power at me, but the conjured calm tingles at the edges of my awareness. "We're here to help you."

"You had an accident," I add. "You were badly hurt—you may not be able to remember anything."

Bethany jerks against the chains. "Why am I all tied up? What the hell is going on?"

An edge of anger has already crept into her voice. I hold up my hands in a gesture of apology. "When the accident happened, you weren't totally in control of yourself. You hurt some people. We just want to make sure that—"

"Let me go!" Bethany interrupts, outright thrashing now. "You can't do this to me. You're all going to regret it when I get out of this shit."

Griffin eases closer to me. "It isn't working," he

murmurs. "The rage flared up right away, as soon as she saw her situation—so intense I can't get through it."

Just like before when she still had her memories.

"You're all assholes!" the girl keeps shouting, the viciousness of her voice even more horrifying coming from a skinny fourteen-year-old kid. "I'll hurt *you* if you don't stop this shit. I'll—"

A quaver enters her voice, and her expression shifts. She must sense a hint of her power.

The next sound that bursts from her lips is an emphatic, wordless crooning.

Fear rattles through my nerves, propelling a yelp up my throat and my feet toward the door. In just the second or two before Lull passes her hand over Bethany's face, my heart nearly bursts from my chest.

Then the girl slumps back into a doze, and the adrenaline rush fades, leaving my body wobbly but a hell of a lot steadier.

"Fuck," I mutter.

Griffin swipes his hand over his face, his mouth slanted at a pained angle. "I'm sorry. I tried every angle I could think of—she got worked up so quickly."

I clear my throat, but a rasp still colors my voice. "It's not your fault. It's that prick Balthazar."

Why was Bethany still so aggressive when Keith came to in a much more cautious state? I stare at her prone form as if it'll give me any answers and then extend my thoughts toward the one person who might have a clue.

Ajax? You knew both Keith and Bethany from training on the island. Can you think of any reason they'd react differently to this 'treatment'?

There's a momentary silence, and then Ajax's inner voice trickles into my head. *Keith was pretty quiet, kind of hesitant to try anything unless the guardians pushed him. Bethany always seemed a little angry even back then, like she figured she was going to get good at things to spite them or something. So that eventually she could turn the skills against them.*

That makes a kind of sense. Their original personalities came into play, interacting with the crap Balthazar inflicted on them.

From what I've seen, the kids who were both easygoing and didn't have particularly destructive talents even when amplified were the only ones who didn't go batshit with his enhanced procedures. Maybe people who tended toward anger had their mental wiring screwed up the most.

So much that even a total wipe of the system couldn't correct it?

I don't want to believe it, but if this girl came out of the gate swinging that hard, it's difficult to imagine how we'll ever talk her down.

I restrain a shudder. "We'll… We'll figure out what to do about her next." Then I turn to Griffin. "I should go fill Riva in. Why don't you check on Keith and see if he needs any additional chilling out?"

"Good idea." Griffin gives me a sympathetic smile and a quick squeeze of my arm as we head out of the room. Of course—he can sense my inner turmoil as well as he could the emotions of our wayward shadowbloods.

I watch him disappear past the other door before taking stock of myself. My nerves are still on the fritz, my heart beating a little faster than usual. I've definitely stretched my abilities.

My friends don't need me only for my skills with memory. I'll have to make them invisible for the ambush in the facility too.

It'd be good to test whether I have the capacity to tap into that talent even right after I've erased a couple of minds.

And the fact that I'd really rather not talk to anyone else about my theoretical success—and failure—before I reach Riva might be a small incentive as well.

I glance up and down the elegant hotel hallway with its amber light, confirming that I'm alone. With a slow inhalation, I will my body to vanish from view.

When I look down at my hands again, all I see is the mauve-and-gold carpet. Satisfied, I set off toward the elevators. It's only one floor up to the penthouse suite, but the fewer doors I have to open manually, the less chance anyone will notice my presence.

The elevator opens to the vestibule outside the penthouse door just as Jacob and Zian come ambling out. "I'd rather get Greek," Zian is saying.

Jake raises his hands in a gesture of mock defeat. "Let's just see what's near the hotel. We don't want to roam around half the city."

They're off to pick up some dinner, apparently. I sidestep my friends and manage to slip into the penthouse just before the door closes behind them.

The living room on the other side appears empty, but I have no idea how many shadowkind might be hanging around in their noncorporeal forms. The door to the bedroom Riva has been using is closed, but I'll just have to hope that any being who notices my passing by doesn't freak out about it randomly opening.

I turn the knob carefully and ease inside. Riva is lying on top of the covers with her back to me, her head cradled by her arm. I'd have thought she was sleeping if it wasn't for the air of tension around her pose.

She wanted to come with me, to witness for herself how our experiment turned out, but she was worried about the effect seeing her might have on the shadowbloods. "I know technically they won't be able to remember me," she said. "But it seemed like they associated me with everything they were angry about more than the rest of you. I'd rather not take the chance that there's any lingering unconscious resentment."

I stand for a moment next to the bed, balking at the thought of bringing myself back into sight. Of having to tell her that my skills can't conquer every horrible thing Balthazar did.

We've had so many disappointments in the past few weeks. I just want her to feel something good.

And maybe I need that too.

Gingerly, I lay myself down on the bed behind her. Riva starts to roll over, and I catch her with my hand on my waist.

"Just stay there a moment," I murmur by her ear.

She doesn't just follow my instructions—she relaxes against me at the sound of my voice. Because she trusts me that much.

So much affection swells in my chest that for a few seconds, I can't move. Then I trail my invisible fingers over her cheek and down her neck, as if she's being caressed by a ghost.

Her crisply sweet scent fills my nose. I tuck my head against hers, breathing it in through her braided hair.

When I reach her chest, Riva lets out a soft noise of encouragement. I tease my fingertips over the slope of her breast and down to the hem of her shirt.

It's easy to slide my hand under the fabric to touch her warm skin beneath. I stroke my fingers back and forth across her belly, working my way up to the band of her bra.

There's a little thrill in knowing that even if someone walked in on us now, they'd have no idea what I'm doing for her. All they'd see is Riva lying here and a slight rumpling of her clothing.

I circle my thumb over her nipple through the thin cup of her bra, my pulse kicking up a notch as I feel it pebble with the pressure. A little growl escapes Riva's throat.

She rolls toward me, and this time I don't stop her. Her hand comes to rest on my shoulder, my invisibility making her fingers look as if they're hovering in mid-air.

She drums her fingers against my skin through my sweater. "Come back. I like it better when I can see you."

I nuzzle her cheek. "But isn't this fun?"

Her hand rises to trace the line of my jaw, her eyes managing to find mine even though she's looking right through them. "Sure. But it's even more fun when you're completely here with me. And I know—you shouldn't strain your abilities just for this."

The last thing I want is for her to feel guilty. I draw

myself back into visibility with a faint prickling over my skin and offer her a wry smile. "After the next few days, it won't matter that much if I disappear anyway. Who needs the guy who's all about holding on to the past when it's time to carve out a new future?"

I meant the comment to be a joke, but I can hear it land flat even before Riva's face falls. She twines her fingers into the tight curls of my hair and tugs me a little closer so the tip of her nose grazes mine.

"Don't you ever say that," she says fiercely. "Don't you ever even *think* that we don't need you."

I choke up and have to grope for my voice to reply. "I was kidding. I'm not going anywhere."

But maybe there was a little part of me preparing that I might have to stretch my abilities that far—too far to come back from.

Riva scoots closer, aligning her smaller body against mine as if she needs my heat like she does air. "Drey— when everything was screwed up and none of you knew what to believe, you were the first one to see who I really was. The first who decided to trust me over the guardians. *That's* who you are. If you remember anything, I want it to be that."

I wrap my arm around her and hug her to me. She's right, isn't she?

If it hadn't been for me—if I hadn't been there—who knows how bad that disaster would have gotten? Whether any of us would have made it this far?

"I just... I wish I could help by giving them something instead of taking it away."

Riva's breath tickles across my skin with her voice.

"Maybe you can. Maybe you can show them the good memories the rest of us had that they were a part of, once we know they're ready." She brushes her thumb across my cheek. "Are you going to tell me how it went?"

I can't really avoid it any longer. I hold on to the woman I love and steady myself for the story I have to tell her tonight. "There's some good and some bad..."

And even as the words come out, I can't help thinking, isn't every part of life like that? We make the best of what we can, just like everyone else in this messy but incredible world.

TWENTY-EIGHT

Riva

I climb up the stairs to the ground level of the facility so that my phone has a signal again. In the whitewashed hallway, I sink down on the freshly scrubbed floor with my back against the wall and tap out a quick search.

The latest news reports about the hunters' recent public statements are just rehashing yesterday's articles. The clip of the New York City group commenting on how they've heard that "there are people who've been standing up to these monsters for a lot longer than us" and "they're working on a weapon that can defeat any of their crazy powers that's almost ready for action" has circulated all around the world.

Rollick's people made sure the vaguely phrased inside info was passed on to a few different groups across the country in a way that encouraged them to talk it up. The vigilantes have no idea the source was the exact "monsters" they're so worried about or anything else about this supposed weapon.

The shadowkind who—very carefully—approached the rogue shadowbloods delivered a more detailed message, including the location where they'd supposedly seen the guardians bringing in equipment to put the finishing touches on their weapon. We figured having the hunters know about it gave the story an extra dollop of authenticity, but we don't want any mortals showing up to join the party.

Well, any amateur monster-hunter mortals, anyway. As I flick over to the map app, a text message pops up from Pearl. *Guardians are almost there—fifteen minutes' drive away. Should we slow them down, or are you good?*

I pause to focus on the power I've borrowed from Griffin again, thinking of Nadia and then of Devon. My finger falls to the map on a spot dozens of miles closer than when I last checked a half hour ago.

At their current pace, it looks like they'll be here in less than a half hour more.

No, let them come, I reply. *That's perfect timing.*

We want the guardians here when the rampaging shadowbloods arrive to make it look like the facility has been in use, but not for them to have had enough time to get very far into the building.

I push to my feet and walk over to the main door. Even opening it a crack makes a huge difference, the cold but fresh winter air sweeping in to wash away the tightly sealed stuffiness of the hall.

I drink in the chill, letting my gaze wander over the parking lot, the fence, and the forest beyond. Nearly five years ago, the guardians who imprisoned us here used this as a site for their own brutal trap. Now we've made it our own.

We're leading the scattered remains of the Guardianship into a slaughter, and I can't bring myself to feel the slightest bit of guilt, even after seeing what the rampaging shadowbloods did to the people who met with Balthazar. We are what they made us.

They have only themselves to blame.

And one way or another, tonight we're going to wipe the slate clean, destroy the legacy they created before the results of that legacy ravage even more of our world.

And that wiping of the slate might include destroying even ourselves.

It wasn't my decision alone. I barely needed to touch on the subject with the guys before they understood what I meant—and agreed wholeheartedly.

We're going to take every possible measure to ensure that Balthazar's insanity and the guardians' cruelty end here and now.

With that knowledge tight as a vise around my lungs, I give myself one last glance over the forest and the sense of freedom it offers before shutting the door for what should be the last time. Then I hurry over to the stairwell.

On the landing inside, Sorsha is waiting for me. When I nod, she lifts her hands and lets loose a controlled spout of flame that melds the lock and deadbolt into a solid lump.

The guardians won't be able to open it, no matter what keys or codes they bring. They'll come inside when they arrive, but they won't get past the first floor.

They might not even try, with the fodder we've left in the rooms above to keep them busy while the rogue shadowbloods make their final approach, but it seemed best to take a precaution just in case.

Sorsha grasps my shoulder before we head down the stairs side by side. Her head sways a little with the movement, even though we're keeping our steps slow and steady to try not to provoke too much dizziness.

Even after a few days to recover from the last attack, she's too disoriented to fly.

My concern must show on my face. She shoots me a reassuring smile. "I'll be fine. I'm already a lot better than I was that first day afterward. I couldn't stand up without puking then."

I let out a laugh that doesn't hold much humor. "Okay, I'll agree that's an improvement. I just hope the effects don't take too much longer to completely wear off."

"You and me both. Sweet simmering soda-pop, that was a brutal blow, whatever the power was." She rubs her forehead for a second before her hand darts to the railing to catch her balance. "But you came up with the perfect plan. No moving at all! Just charbroiling."

I restrain a wince at her flippant tone. From her grim expression, I don't think she really thinks so lightly about potentially incinerating a few dozen fellow hybrids.

We talked about the direst aspect of our plan with her ahead of time too, of course, but I can't help prodding at the subject. "You're prepared for all of it—everything you might have to do?"

Sorsha pauses at the bottom of the flight and looks over at me with the bright brown eyes I've come to realize hold a lot of compassion behind their frequent gleams of mischief. She gives my hair a gentle pat.

Even though she doesn't look more than ten years older than me, I'm struck by the idea that if I *was* going to have a mother—one who was alive and who wouldn't be horrified by my existence—I wouldn't mind it being her.

Not that the phoenix strikes me as particularly maternal. But there's a warmth to her that's more than just fire.

And she understands.

"If things start to get out of control and it looks like they're going to escape, I'll burn the whole place down," she says. "But I'm going to do everything in my power to make sure it *doesn't* come to that, okay?"

"I just…" My mind swims with images from the news over the recent weeks. All the rubble, all the bloody corpses. "This is the best we can do. If it isn't enough, I'd rather not make it than know we let them go off to kill more people so that we could spare ourselves. So don't hesitate."

Sorsha nods solemnly. "They won't hurt anyone else after today, one way or another."

She's the only one who can ensure that, if worse comes to worst. With her phoenix fire, she can turn the entire facility into an inferno and emerge from the flames just fine herself.

It'd only be us shadowbloods who ended up ashes.

I push that knowledge away and heave open the door.

The idea of my potentially imminent death has plenty of other uncomfortable thoughts to compete with. As we walk together down the hall toward the gymnasium where the guys and I spent so many of our days, impressions of the past flit through my awareness, as if I can see our history as well as Andreas can read it out of someone's minds.

The rap of the guardians' boots against the tiled floor. The disinfectant tang to the air that still lingers after years of disuse—or maybe I'm only hallucinating it.

Yells and yelps, protests bit back. The gnawing loneliness every time our keepers marched us away from the training rooms and I knew it'd be hours and hours before I got to see the boys I loved again.

Even if our plan succeeds and we can leave this place alive, I think I'll ask Sorsha to flambee the building once we're all out. I wish we could burn away every physical trace of the Guardianship's presence in this world.

But ensuring the damage they've done is over with will be enough.

At the end of the hall, two doors stand wide open. One leads into the cavernous space of the gym, the other into a smaller but still sizable room where the guardians sometimes set up a swimming pool like a massive aquarium to test our skills in water.

Andreas is standing in the second doorway. He catches my gaze with a questioning look.

"The guardians Rollick's people are leading this way should be here in about ten minutes," I say. "The rogues will be right behind them."

He offers me a tight smile. "We'd better get into position then."

He hesitates and then steps forward to slide his fingers along my jaw. If there's a hint of desperation in the avidness of his kiss and the quiver of emotion that passes through our bond, I'm not going to comment on it. I'm pretty desperate to get us through the next hour myself.

When he eases back, Dominic and Griffin have emerged from the room behind him. Dom tugs me to him for a kiss so ardent I could lose myself in it, both his arms and his tentacles holding me close.

Griffin only brushes his lips briefly against mine, but the fleeting moment seems even sweeter that way. Then he hugs me tight with a waft of love that feels as if it flows right from his heart into mine.

"We've got this," he says. "We'll handle our part. Don't spend any energy worrying about us. I'll see you when it's over."

My throat constricts. "Yeah."

Andreas touches me one more time, to cast invisibility over me with a tingle of his talent. "I've already done Jake and Zee. They're in position."

I summon all the bravado I can. "Let's do this."

After Drey has worked his power on Sorsha as well, the three guys head back into the smaller room. They'll be the ones taking care of any of the shadowbloods who seem to have enough moral compass left that they might be saved.

I can't see the phoenix now, but she keeps her grip on my shoulder as we head into the gymnasium. The immense space feels hauntingly empty.

The few bits of goodness we found here—the sofa where we tucked ourselves together to watch a movie or TV show on our occasional breaks, the table where we ate lunch and snacks in companionable conversation—the guardians must have taken with them when they abandoned ship. All that's left are the pillars along the edges of the rooms and a few odds and ends like dusty exercise mats.

We've added our own touch too. Over the past day, we've assembled a structure at the far end of the room that looks reasonably weapon-ish. It's taller than me and twice as long as that, all metal and glass and various controls fused together.

It doesn't *do* anything, but it looks intimidating to me even though I know that it's really a heap of junk. Hopefully it'll be convincing enough to the shadowbloods that they'll take it seriously.

I lead Sorsha over to a pillar where we've left a few crates for extra shelter. As she settles into her place, bracing her arms against the boxes, I cross the room to the matching setup on the opposite side.

I have a clear view of the doorway at my left and the supposed weapon at my right. I've also got a phone waiting for me, tucked away between two of the crates, that's connected to the hasty camera system we set up in place of the devices the guardians removed.

The phone's screen is divided into quarters, each with its own view: the front gate, the ground floor hallway, and two different angles of the hall outside the gymnasium to cover the whole area. The rogues will probably check the higher floors first, but there's nothing there that'll interest them for long.

My heart thuds between my ribs. I rest one hand on the cool surface of the pillar and remind myself to breathe.

I'm only on my third breath when the first video

stream shows the vans pulling up outside. A squad of guardians—fourteen, I count as they emerge—pour out of their vehicles and stalk up to the gate.

We've left it unlocked. We want them coming inside.

After testing it tentatively, one of them nudges it open. They stride onto the parking lot.

A few get back in the vans to drive the vehicles right into the compound. Others head for the entrance.

Good. It'll be more convincing if the rogues find at least a few of them inside the building rather than all hanging out in the yard.

In a few clusters of three, the guardians head inside. On the second feed, I watch them scanning the hall and poking their heads through doorways.

They're all holding weapons—large rifles they keep tucked under one arm at the ready. Those aren't going to be any match for the shadowbloods' powers.

They never really respected what we can do.

As they're about to find out in brutal clarity. A couple of the guardians are just yanking at the fused door to the stairwell when I spot the first signs of movement in the forest beyond the fence.

My back goes rigid. I peer at the tiny rectangle on the phone's screen until I'm sure I see a brief flash of hair amid the underbrush.

And then it starts.

The video feeds don't offer any sound, but I can imagine the shouts of horror as the guardians stationed outside topple with a lurch of the ground. Their skin bubbles as if broiling; their bodies jerk with pain.

Is that *Devon* burning them with the heat he can summon? My stomach lurches queasily.

I'm never going to mention this to Ajax. He's lost enough of the boyfriend he loved already.

The guards slump against the asphalt, and the rogue shadowbloods prowl out of the woods.

Cutler walks in the lead, the sunlight gleaming off the skull-and-snake tattoo on his otherwise bare scalp. Nadia marches forward at his right flank, the man with the scarred forehead at his left, at least two dozen more shadowbloods storming along in their wake.

In the hall, a few of the guardians must have picked up on the sounds outside. I can see them calling to each other, a couple of them loping toward the door.

Not fast enough.

The front door flies open, and a blast of light so blinding it whites out the video footage sears down the hall. In the first few seconds, while my pulse thunders through my skull, I can't see anything at all.

The stark glow clears to a flurry of limbs, some swinging, some flailing. The shadowbloods are flinging guardians into walls, tearing open their bellies, smashing their heads like melons.

It looks like a few of the gunmen fight back, but I don't see any of their bullets land before they're trampled in the rampage.

There's a brief moment when the shadowbloods hold still, their chests heaving and their heads cocked, while all of the guardians sprawl lifeless on the floor. When no indication of further attack comes, they spring back into motion.

The rogues fan out, a few of the younger kids hanging back in the hall, the others checking the rooms much like their victims did minutes ago. Cutler reaches the stairwell and jiggles the handle.

He beckons over a couple of the teens. Whatever they do with their powers, within a matter of seconds, they're cracking the door right off its hinges.

Here they come.

While they stream into the stairwell, I fix my gaze on the corpses in the hallway. I draw up the memories of the news reports, the scenes of destruction I've witnessed firsthand.

The guardians might have gotten what they bargained for, but too many innocent or unwitting people have died in the same horrible way. The rogue shadowbloods don't care who they hurt or how much they destroy.

They *want* to inflict the pain they're feeling on the rest of the world, as if it's some kind of justice.

And I have to stop them.

A shriek builds at the base of my throat. I hold it in, honing it, expanding it, bracing myself for the moment it's time to use it.

They have one more chance. One last opportunity we could give them to show they're more than the monsters Balthazar turned them into.

Finally, they ease out into the hall outside the gymnasium. Cutler is frowning. His followers do a quick check of the other rooms as they stalk forward.

They glance into the former pool room too, but at the moment, they won't be able to see anything inside. Then

Devon peers into the gymnasium and lets out an eager shout.

He points toward our contraption looming at the far end of the gym. The others gather closer—and then several of their heads jerk to the side.

Andreas is fulfilling his part of the plan. He'll be projecting a memory into all of their heads: an image he searched out of his own store of recollections to fit the task.

They'll hear a child crying. See a little girl peeking her face out from behind a box by the far wall, frightened and bleeding from a scrape on her cheek.

Who will try to help her, and who will decide getting straight to the weapon is more important? Who still has the most basic instinct of compassion?

Devon doubles back, a flicker of concern crossing his taut face. The scarred man turns with a twitch of a frown. Several heads dip together in hurried discussion.

Six of the rogues step into the former pool room. I watch Devon disappear from view, and the scarred man, a few more teens. One of the other adults and a couple of the kids linger outside to see what their companions discover.

Cutler and the rest show no sign of caring what's going on with the little girl. They stride into the gymnasium without a backward glance, heading straight for the supposed weapon.

Nadia hustles in alongside them, nothing but fierce resolve showing in her expression. I didn't see her so much as hesitate during the commotion in the hall.

My heart sinks, but I don't let the punch of dread

shake my concentration. This isn't the result I wanted to see, but it is what it is.

I have to accept reality. Clinging on to unjustified hope has already left too many people dead when maybe we could have stopped the carnage sooner.

The rogues march toward the weapon, their gazes sweeping the room. They can't see me or my waiting companions. They have no idea we're here.

But just before Jacob rams an invisible force into the door to slam it shut in their wake, before my lips have even parted to give my killing shriek the full power I can put behind it, something must catch Cutler's attention.

He whirls around, his yell reverberating through the room an instant before the bang of the door. "It's a trap!"

With a stutter of my heart, I hurl my killing shriek from my throat.

TWENTY-NINE

Dominic

The wayward shadowbloods' footsteps drum against the hard floor as they gather in the large room. Andreas projects the memory he's using into my head too—and I assume Griffin's as well—so we know what our targets are seeing. So we can be prepared for their reactions.

The little girl ducks back behind the cardboard box. The box is really there; she isn't.

Her whimpers carry through the air. Devon crouches down a few feet from the box and speaks more softly than I've heard any of the rogue shadowbloods manage before. "Hey. How did you end up here? We can try to help you."

The scarred man—the one Griffin said is named Omar —makes a gruff sound. "Ask her if there are more guardians around nearby."

One of the other teens strides forward with an air of impatience. "Let's just get her out and get on with this."

My nerves jangle. It's only a matter of seconds until they realize the girl is a hoax.

But Zian has been watching from outside the door. As the six shadowbloods who ventured into our room reach the far end of the space, he springs invisibly into action.

With the full heft of his substantial supernatural strength, he plows into the three figures who hung back outside the door, concerned but too wary to actually enter. The man and the two teens stagger several steps through the doorway, the girl falling to her knees, and Zian yanks the door shut behind him.

The instant it bangs shut, a hissing sound fills the air. I touch my gas mask instinctively, confirming its fit.

With that bulky thing over my face, I'll look even more like a monster than I normally do, but no one can see me anyway.

Clouds of chemical smoke gush from the two vents we otherwise sealed, triggered by Griffin. I brace myself to jump in for my role in this plan.

A couple of the shadowbloods shout in alarm, but they're already swaying with the drug's effects. Rollick helped us pick out one that's both potent and fast-acting.

We couldn't have succeeded using this tactic on the full crowd of rogues. In a space big enough that they'd all have willingly come in, we'd never have been able to affect them all in time to prevent a counterattack.

Even now, while the four smallest teens slump on the floor unconscious, the other five figures keep stumbling through the hazy air. Sparks shoot from someone's fingertips.

We can't have them fighting while Andreas is working

his memory wipes on the others—or worse, bashing their way out of the room into the fresh air. Zian is stationed outside, but he's got to stay on guard against escapees from both sides.

If we want to save anyone from a worse fate, it'll be a lot easier if we can keep them contained.

I shove myself forward from the corner I was tucked into with the invisibility Andreas granted me. One of my tentacles wraps around the neck of the kid who was shooting sparks; the other catches Omar by the wrist.

As soon as my suckers connect with bare skin, I'm hauling their energy into my veins. At the same moment, I reach out my hands toward the farther shadowbloods and yank at the thrum of life I can sense emanating from them.

Shadowblood energy comes so quickly, so easily. The thrilling rush sweeps over me from every side. Giddy shivers ripple through my limbs.

An ache forms in my chest to drink in even more. To find out just how good the full force of so many lives at once could feel.

No. I'm not even entertaining that thought. I'm draining them to *protect* them, not to gratify some selfish urge inside me.

Maybe because I've already taken in so much all at once, it's easier than I expected to detach. As the sparking kid's knees buckle in a faint, I flick my tentacle free.

Omar sags next, stumbling into the wall and then sliding down it. He jerks his arm against my hold a few times, conjured spurts of ice nipping at my skin, but he's already so weakened between the drug and the energy I've stolen that he doesn't come close to dislodging me.

I can taste his pulse growing sluggish. I whip the tentacle that gripped him away and whirl toward the spot where a few more of the rogues are still on their feet.

With one last tug at the pulsing thrum inside them, two of them crumple. The last, the remaining man, lunges at me and nearly trips over his feet in his dizziness.

"You," he snarls out at whatever he can make out of me in the haze. I curl the tip of one tentacle toward his face to drain just a tiny bit more, and then he's tumbling over on his ass.

I can make out Drey and Griffin vaguely, human-shaped gaps of what looks like empty air in the midst of the clouds. Drey bends over Devon, a hand against the boy's forehead, performing either his first or his second memory wipe depending on how quickly he's been able to work.

Griffin has remained in his corner near the cardboard boxes. His voice comes out muffled by his gas mask. "Do the adults next. Once the drug started taking effect, I could calm down the kids a little, but those two stayed pretty angry."

Andreas nods, sending the haze rippling around the space where his head moved. "Are they all down?"

"I got the ones who resisted the gas," I say. "I don't know how long they'll stay unconscious, but I can drain them a little more if I need to."

My skin is humming, my pulse twitching with the immense stores of energy I've taken into myself. I have the bizarre impression that if I pushed off the floor, I could glide right to the ceiling and float there.

But that's okay. I only took the energy I had to, nothing more.

I made it possible for us to offer some of the shadowbloods driven out of control by Balthazar's treatment a fresh start.

Which is a lot better than the murders Riva and Sorsha are having to carry out in the room next to ours.

That thought brings me back to earth with a flip of my stomach. Even if the rogues have gone off the rails, even if it's clear there's nothing else we can do for some of them— nothing that would save the people *they* were intent on murdering… we shouldn't forget them.

They didn't deserve to end up this way. It wasn't really their choice.

All we can do is set things as right as we can. Maybe there was never going to be any perfect solution, even if we'd destroyed Balthazar before he could start building his private shadowblood army.

A faint sense of soothing wraps around me, and my gaze darts toward Griffin's form in the haze. He must be picking up on my conflicted feelings. But the offered calm doesn't come across as an imposition, only an offer of sympathy and reassurance, as if he's squeezed my shoulder or offered me a quick hug.

But the building itself isn't feeling particularly settled. Even as my chest loosens a bit, the floor shudders beneath my feet.

All of our heads jerk toward the door. I can sense

Riva's presence in the gymnasium behind it—I know she's still inside that vast room, moving around.

What the hell is going on over there?

We can't let ourselves get distracted. We have to focus on getting our part of this mission done.

Andreas moves from Devon to the man I toppled last. As he leans over the former inmate, the man jerks upright, aiming a wobbly but swift fist at Drey's invisible head.

Shit! I leap forward, my mind scrambling—he must have only pretended to completely faint.

As Drey reels backward through the clouds of gas, I wrench both of my tentacles forward and catch hold of the man's life force across the short distance. With a yank, I drain a gulp of his energy straight from his spirit.

The man mumbles a swear word, but he's already slumping. My nerves jitter with the urge to drain even more. To add to the heady power coursing through me.

No. That's not what I'm here for.

But I am going to siphon off just a *little* more, until his pulse is clearly sluggish. I don't want to take any chances after he's already fooled us once.

Andreas lets out a rough chuckle. "Thanks, Dom. Fuck, he almost broke my mask."

His invisible form pushes through the gas to lean over the newly unconscious man. As he reaches for the guy's forehead, a tremor passes through the haze around him.

My pulse hiccups. "Are you sure you're okay, Drey?"

Even through the mask, I can hear a rasp in his voice. "Yeah. It's not the punch—memory-wiping takes a lot out of me. But I expected that."

If Drey faints or worse before we're done here, we'll be screwed.

"You should let yourself turn visible again," I say. "It takes more energy keeping the effect in place, right?"

"Good point. I guess it doesn't matter if these guys see me now."

The haze shudders again, and Andreas's body swims into view, gradually turning more solid amid the haze. The bow of his shoulders still looks weary to me.

I look over at Griffin again. "Do you think we should clear the gas? Give Drey more air? Rollick said that once the effect took hold, it should last at least an hour."

Griffin hesitates as he thinks it over. "If I switch the flow, the fans will just suck it all back in. We can always dose them again if we need to."

He must flick the switch, because there's a hitch to the faint whir that lingered in the air. The billows of gas start to fade, wafting toward the vents they poured out of.

As the air clears, I study each of the slumped bodies carefully. No one so much as twitches. They're all out cold for the moment.

But if I catch any sign of movement, I want to intervene before it becomes a real problem.

Another shudder ripples across the floor, with a *boom* loud enough that it resonates faintly even through the thick walls. My stomach lurches.

A waft of frustration prickles through my chest from the mark that connects me to Riva. Whatever the shadowbloods they tried to trap are doing, it isn't going smoothly.

I start to pace the room and force myself to stop. Acting anxious is only going to unsettle my friends.

I really can't see Griffin now, but I know what he's doing when one of the boxes opens and he retrieves the supplies we stashed inside. He kneels down next to Devon and fixes the bindings into place around his wrists and ankles.

We have to be careful, just in case our test didn't totally separate out the shadowbloods who can be rehabilitated from the ones too far gone to adjust to normal life even with their memories wiped. If they're like the boy back at the hotel, we won't have to leave the restraints on for very long.

Keith's been doing well over the past day he's been with us in his memory-wiped state. I found him laughing with Ajax while they dug into leftover takeout this morning before we left.

Bethany… well, we're not totally sure what to do with her yet. She's still lashing out any time Lull lets her wake up.

It's a lot harder to imagine killing a person you've already subdued, but eventually she'll make the decision for us. She hasn't eaten at all since we brought her in— hasn't settled down enough to even think about being hungry, let alone try to consume anything.

I shake off the uneasiness of that idea and focus on my observations of Keith's progress. Every shadowblood in this room could end up like him—maybe confused, but finding new happiness, rebuilding a life that can be about what they want rather than what the guardians inflicted on them.

The other guys switch places, Andreas moving to Omar and Griffin to the man Drey just finished with. Andreas adjusts his mask and then pulls it right off to take a deep gulp of the refreshed air.

"Okay," he murmurs, and sets his hand against Omar's temple.

Restless and hopped up on the energy whirling inside me, I walk over to the door, but the guardians built their facilities carefully. No further hint of sound travels through the frame or the walls around me.

Have Riva and Sorsha finished with their attack now? I have no idea how it's playing out.

They might have taken out all the other shadowbloods already and now they're waiting for us. Or they could be fighting for their lives.

The floor hitches beneath my feet, suggesting the latter is more likely. But there's no way of knowing whether they're facing a few remaining opponents or the whole mass of them.

A lump fills my throat. I turn back toward the room and scan the shadowbloods *I'm* responsible for.

Andreas's copper-brown face glints with a thickening sheen of sweat. His mouth tightens as he works, digging deep creases into the corners.

"Hey," I venture, taking another step toward him. "I can give you a power-up to help you through the process —like I did when Jake shook the whole mountain. I've got lots to spare, and—"

Drey waves me off with his free hand. "It's fine. You did your part. I should be able to do mine."

I consider him with a frown. I should have thought to

offer him the extra energy I gathered right after the fact. If I need more life to help the rogues recover once they wake up from the drug, we can handle that outside in the forest where I've got lots of plants to draw from.

But Andreas knows what's going on inside himself better than I could. If he says he's fine…

He pushes away from Omar and reaches for the nearest teen now that he's handled both of the men. I think I see his balance wobble as he leans forward, but he steadies himself so quickly it's hard to be sure.

Griffin glances up as he crouches next to Omar. "Drey, I really think—"

Before he can finish his sentence, Andreas sucks in a sharp breath. He tilts forward—and his body flickers.

Not like when he's pulling invisibility over himself. Like his physical presence doesn't know whether it should be in this world or not, patches flashing between translucency and full transparency and back into sight.

I dash forward without needing to think about it. It doesn't matter how stoic Andreas wants to be—he *needs* me.

I coil both of my tentacles around his torso, as quickly as I can while staying gentle. Then I let loose the flood of energy contained inside me.

A current of it careens from my nerves into Drey's. He inhales another ragged breath, and his form gradually stabilizes.

I pour a little more and a little more into him, not wanting to overwhelm him, until my own body is tingling with the transfusion of energy and Andreas looks solid and even lively again.

"Fuck," he mutters, and swipes at his forehead before looking at me. "I should have taken you up on the offer in the first place. I think… if I'm going to wipe all of them while we're in here, I might need you to do that again after the next few. I'm sorry."

"It's fine," I say automatically. Why is he apologizing?

His gaze slides to my shoulders, where my tentacles emerge from my skin, and understanding hits me with a jolt.

He knows how much I've resented my new appendages. He knows how they've expanded with every healing session.

Except… this time they didn't. I haven't felt them creeping farther from my flesh—not when I dragged the energy from the rogues and not when I offered it up to Andreas just now.

I straighten up and touch the base of one tentacle. It feels perfectly normal… but even that is strange.

It feels like a part of me. Like it's supposed to be there, the way it is.

And I'm okay with that.

A weird sense of peace wells up inside me that I know has come from myself, not Griffin. They're done growing now. The tentacles are what they're meant to be. And they helped me do what *I'm* meant to be doing.

I don't know yet if I'm going to see whether Sorsha can remove them, but for the first time, it doesn't seem to matter all that much whether I keep them or try to give them up.

I don't have much chance to revel in my newfound contentment. A fresh bolt of anguish bursts behind my collarbone as if shot through my chest from my bond with Riva.

I lurch forward, clapping my hand to my sternum. Andreas flinches.

My head whips toward the door. Something's gone *really* wrong—she's struggling.

She needs help.

Andreas meets my eyes, his wide with panic. "Go. Griffin and I can handle this right now."

My jaw clenches. I sweep my tentacles forward once more to send the rest of the extra energy I gathered into him in one huge surge, until I'm sure his nerves are buzzing with it and he won't falter again.

Then I hurtle toward the door to do whatever I can to see Riva through the next few minutes too.

THIRTY

Riva

If I've learned anything from my twenty-one years as a monster, it's that killing is never as easy as you'd imagine, no matter how naturally it comes to you.

With Cutler's warning shout still echoing off the high ceiling, my banshee shriek bursts from my throat. My power shoots forward to smack into the mass of shadowbloods standing around the makeshift machine—but a few of them have already leapt away.

I don't have time to divert my focus to them. I've got to deal with the ones I have, or they could all end up turning the tables on us.

A blast of Sorsha's fire roars toward the twenty or so figures my scream has locked in place. I wrench at them one by one as quickly as I can, snapping necks and sending shards of skull through brains without catering to my inner hunger's desire for extended pain.

The fire consumes most of them before I need to shift

my focus that far and ripples over the few corpses I've sent to the floor as well. They barely even had time to yelp.

A knot of guilt condenses in my gut—and a flare of blinding light sears through the room.

Obviously Nadia was one of the rogues who sprang out of range. I sway, swiping at my stinging eyes, knowing that the light will have brought my body back into visibility too.

Now I'm a target as much as the remaining rogues are.

Heat and smoke flood the room from the inferno of burning bodies around the supposed weapon. Then a wordless bellow splits the air, followed by an ominous creaking sound.

Blinking hard, I scramble sideways mostly on instinct. My vision is still blurred.

The air whooshes against my skin, and one of the concrete columns that lines the room crashes to the ground, just a couple of feet from where I'm standing. Broken concrete shards fly out to jab at my limbs.

"Let us out!" a voice hollers—I think it's Cutler.

With another wordless roar, the gymnasium door rattles, the hinges groaning. A bolt of fire shoots toward it.

When I look again, the thick slab of the door looks fused into the frame. But Sorsha didn't manage to hit Cutler. I can't see him or any of the other rogue shadowbloods who escaped our initial attack.

If Sorsha were here alone, she could send the entire room up in flames. But if she does that now, she'll incinerate me and Jacob too.

She won't risk it, not unless it looks like the rogues will break out of the building if she doesn't act.

I'd want her to, but I'd really prefer the battle doesn't end like that.

I back up to the relative security of the wall to at least give me protection from behind. My gaze sweeps across the room, the images fragmented even now that my sight is clearing. The raging flames make the shadows dart and gyrate.

Cutler lets loose his earth-shaking bellow again. A crack ripples through the base of another column—the one Sorsha was braced behind.

As my pulse jolts with panic, the massive concrete tower careens toward the door. He must be hoping the weight will smash it open.

But Jacob sees it in time. A sudden shove of invisible force heaves the column to the side. It crashes to the floor several feet to the side of the door, shattering a couple of the nearby crates into splinters.

The ground shakes beneath me with the impact. I stare through the smoke as well as I can.

Where's Sorsha now? I didn't hear any sound of pain —but she won't be able to move very far with her dizziness.

My eyes catch on movement by one of the far columns —a man, flitting from one to another.

That must be the thug whose supernatural talent is immense speed. It's not surprising he fled in time, but we can't give him the chance to strike back.

I draw a shriek into my throat. The second he dashes to another column, I send my killing scream pealing after him.

My power rams into his slim frame and yanks him to a

halt. If he makes any sound, it's lost to the warbling of the fire.

I clench my hands and will his heart to burst.

Even as that man crumples, Cutler's voice rings out. "It won't do you any good. Even if you kill all of us here, you can't destroy us completely."

A chill shivers through my gut. What's he talking about?

There's a scuffing sound and a thud. Jacob calls out to me and Sorsha: "Got another one!"

Twin streaks of flame lash out from where Sorsha must be poised now, somewhere behind the fallen column. A cry breaks the air, but I can't tell if she dealt a fatal injury.

Another blaze of light fills the air, and a hiss I think is the phoenix's reaches my ears.

"Nadia!" I yell as I crouch down to make myself an even smaller target. I don't think reasoning with the girl who was once my friend is going to work, but I can't stop myself from trying. "Don't do this. You don't want to hurt even more people."

Cutler lets out a vicious laugh. As I blink furiously, I catch a glimpse of him hurtling toward another column to ram the thick blades that've emerged from his shoulders into a crack he's already opened up there.

I try to focus on him and aim my shriek, but spots are still swimming across my eyes. He charges out of view.

His sneer rebounds off the high ceiling. "You care so much about saving the assholes who do nothing except hurt 'monsters' like us. You're as bad as they are, trying to exterminate us. But we were ready for shit like this."

"What are you talking about?" Jacob snaps. There's a

thud, and then a resounding crash as yet another column falls. The shudder of the floor throws me off balance.

The flames from the incinerated corpses are dwindling, but smoke clouds the room even more thickly while my vision clears again. I brace my hand against the floor and sputter a cough as the haze prickles into my lungs.

A spurt of fire lances through the wafting clouds, but if it connects with any of our opponents, I don't see or hear any sign of it. I slink along the wall, my ears pricked and my muscles braced.

I don't think there can be more than three or four of the rogues left: Cutler, Nadia, and one or two others who haven't shown themselves in any identifiable way. We're so close to ending this catastrophe—we have to see it through.

My heart thuds painfully hard against my ribs. I ease past one of the fallen columns—and a boy leaps over it, straight at me.

My shriek bursts from my throat with a startled hitch. The boy's arm jerks as a bone fractures while he collides with me.

I roll to the side the second I hit the ground, tossing him off me. Before I can make another sound, the boy's head wrenches backward with a snap of his spine.

My gaze darts up to find Jacob several feet away. His expression is taut and the purple, poisonous spines protrude from his forearms through his shirt.

But for once he looks completely comfortable with his ferocity. He simply nods at me and spins around to search for the next threat.

One of Cutler's supernatural roars reverberates

through the walls. The doorframe shudders in its fused state.

"You might as well give up," I yell in the direction the bellow emanated from. "You're not getting out of here, not alive."

The tattooed man lets out a scoffing sound, somewhere by the smoking remains of the mock weapon now. His voice travels as he prowls through the smoky room.

"It doesn't matter whether I get out. We left a few friends behind, along with our maker's serums and pills and instructions. If we don't come back, they'll raise up a whole new army of monsters to rain hell down on you—and everyone else who deserves it."

My heart lurches. Oh, fuck, no. Unhinged shadowbloods creating even more shadowbloods and roping them into their psychotic cause?

I don't even want to think about how much worse things could get.

We can't kill Cutler. Not right away—not before Andreas or Ajax can search his mind to find out where they've left their back-up stash so we can destroy that too.

As my mind scrambles for an answer, the former inmate heaves out another room-shaking holler and yet another. With the second bellow, the doorframe jolts a few inches, pushing back from the cement of the wall.

He's trying to crack the whole frame right out. We can't let him run away from us either.

An idea starts to formulate in my head. But I need my allies on board with it.

"Let me deal with him," I shout to wherever Jacob and Sorsha are now. "Don't burn him or—"

"As if they even could," Cutler interrupts, and throws his voice into another booming roar. At the same moment, Nadia floods the room with dagger-sharp light.

My vision whites out, and metal groans in concrete. With my pulse thundering through my veins, I hurl out a shriek just ahead of the last place I heard Cutler.

I assumed he'd run toward the door as it starts to fall —and I was right. My scream latches onto a figure in mid-stride.

His lips part. I'm not sure I can hold him firmly enough to stop him from heaving one of his bellows at me. He could shatter *my* body like he has the wall.

I focus all my attention on the cord running up his spine and twist it right at the base of his skull.

A flare of pain shoots into me and then cuts off. The second I drop my voice, Cutler crumples to the ground with a thump.

I've paralyzed him—he shouldn't be able to move a muscle… or his vocal cords.

I just have to hope I didn't cut off his functions so thoroughly that his vital organs will shut down too. I don't know anatomy with a surgeon's precision.

"Leave him!" I cry out, afraid Sorsha might have missed my earlier plea. "We need him alive."

A sob peals out from somewhere in the mess of fallen columns, followed by a growl of anger. "You're the monsters," Nadia cries. "You attack us and torture us, just like—"

"No!" I ease closer, trying to get a clear sense of exactly

where she is. "We don't want to do any of this. I *hate* that we're doing this. But you were attacking so many other people."

Maybe sensing my intentions, Nadia sends out another searing blast of light before the blotches have faded from my vision from the last time. I freeze with my hand against the wall, pained tears welling in my eyes as I struggle to see.

Her voice reaches me again, ragged and trembling. "You said we were blood. You said you'd save us."

I swallow thickly, the guilt that hit me before expanding through my abdomen. There's nothing I can say that will persuade her to back down.

So I might as well be as honest as I can be.

I pitch my voice to carry, though my throat is getting scratchy from the smoke. "I hate that I couldn't save all of you. I tried so hard… But being blood doesn't mean you always have to stand with someone if they're doing things you can't accept. Balthazar was my *father*, but he was trying to ruin the whole world. I couldn't live with myself if I let that happen."

Nadia lets out a sound that's both choked and derisive. "Like you've never hurt anyone? I've seen what you can do with your scream."

I wet my lips. "I realize that I've hurt a lot of people. You know…"

The memory that wells up in my head brings a sharper pang of pain, but I push myself onward. "I almost killed *myself*. I was afraid I was going to lash out and hurt people I didn't want to, and in that moment, I thought maybe it'd be better if I was dead. If I couldn't stop otherwise."

"But you're still here. Why did you change your mind about yourself, but you're taking us out?"

My mouth twists with a bittersweet smile. "I realized there was more to me than the anger and the brutality. I cared about people, and people cared about me."

Nadia scoffs raggedly. "You think I don't?"

"We tried to give you that chance. When you were in the hall here, you walked right past that little girl while she cried out without even stopping to see what was going on. You—"

Nadia breaks in with an urgent note in her voice. "What little girl? What are you talking about? Did you hurt an actual *kid*?"

I hesitate. Did she really not notice Andreas's projected memory?

I guess it's possible the impression didn't quite penetrate her awareness, if she was hyper-focused on Cutler and his goals. I can't remember exactly how close to the doorway she was—she might not have been in a position to see much of anything. And she walked into the gymnasium almost immediately.

She sounds as if she cares now. Like she has a conscience.

Maybe we could have saved her after all. And here I am stalking her, waiting to murder her.

"No," I say. "We didn't hurt anyone. It was a test to see how you'd all react. Some of your friends went to go help her, and they're going to live."

There's a momentary pause. But Nadia spits out her next words. "You're lying. You're trying to distract me, mess with my head so you can kill me now. I'm not going to let you. Cutler was right—Cutler had a plan. I won't let you use him either!"

Before I can fully process what she means, a figure dashes into the range of my mottled vision, racing toward Cutler's slumped body with a metal shard gleaming in her hand.

Nadia's going to kill *him* and destroy all hope of us stopping the rogues for good.

Without thinking, I shove myself toward her, my supernatural speed thrumming through my legs. Light explodes from Nadia's body, blinding me all over again, but I'm already in motion.

The thud of her footsteps guides me. I'm at least twice as fast as her—I hurl myself into her taller frame before she's within reach of Cutler.

We roll over on the floor, my head jarring against the linoleum. The razor edge of Nadia's makeshift dagger rakes against my arm.

Her face appears blurrily above me. She's raised her hand, the metal shard clutched in it, her face contorted with anger—and desperation.

In the second before she drives the blade downward, my shriek leaps up from my lungs. But my throat constricts around it.

There's hope for her. She was worried about the little girl.

Sorsha and Jacob will have heard that too—if I sacrifice myself, maybe they can save her after all. *I'll* have saved her.

The thought passes through my head, and the rest of my body balks.

No.

I want to live too. I want to save myself. I've fought so hard for my freedom, for the love I wasn't sure I'd ever recover, and I deserve it just as much as anyone.

The thud of the door crumpling all the way to the floor makes Nadia flinch. Her hand wavers and then jabs downward.

And I hear Zian's and Dominic's voices carrying through the room.

There's still a chance.

I open my mouth and scream.

The sound tears into Nadia's body just as her blade nicks my throat. Her arm shudders and jerks to the side with a crack of bone.

Her other hand lights up where it's braced against me. The searing pain that comes with her glow in close contact lances through my shoulder into the rest of my frame.

But I already knew it wouldn't be enough just to break her outer body if I wanted to stay alive.

The agony of the burn makes my breath shudder, but I push a sharper scream from my throat and slam my power right into her brain.

Nadia's eyes roll up. The vicious glow she was generating fades from her skin as she tumbles off me.

My muscles trembling, I heave myself over and touch her throat. Her pulse stutters on erratically.

I think she's technically braindead—I couldn't risk leaving her conscious when all she needs to do to set off her power is think—but she's alive.

"Dom!" I shout. "You've got to heal her. We need Andreas to wipe her mind. We need—"

Dominic drops down beside me. He sets his hand on my back while his tentacles reach toward Nadia. "I've got it. We can do this. *You* did it."

He raises his head to look toward Zian, who's come to a stop partway into the room in full wolf-man morph. "Go get Andreas. The others can wait a few minutes."

As Zian dashes back out through the ruined doorway, Sorsha sways to her feet behind her toppled column. I try to smile at her and only manage a cough.

A shiver passes through my shoulders. Gripping Nadia's hand, I turn to Dominic. "You need energy. You can take some of mine. I don't want to lose her."

"I know. You won't have to." Dom presses a brief but emphatic kiss to my temple. "It's all right now, Riva. It's over."

THIRTY-ONE

Riva

The battle isn't actually over, of course.

First, Zian and I haul the bound, unconscious bodies of the ten shadowbloods we were able to save up the stairwell and out into the yard. As soon as we're all cleared out, Dominic calls Rollick to let him know to bring the truck around while Sorsha fixes her gaze on the small building above the surface.

"It's all going to burn," she assures me, and snaps her fingers.

I can't see most of the inferno, but the warble of it reaches my ears from below the ground even before the flames shoot up to swallow the upper building. Heat washes over the grass, melting the frost that'd formed there.

Every trace of the facility where we were tormented the longest, where the guardians tore us apart and shattered our early bonds, turns into ashes.

I find I don't mind the smoky flavor that coats my mouth. It's confirmation that we're never coming back.

Then, late that night, we slink into the high-rise office space Andreas pulled from Cutler's memories—a property that Toni confirmed belonged to Balthazar. The rogue shadowbloods must have found out about it one way or another and commandeered it for their own ends.

They only left three of their companions behind. Easing the door open enough to peek inside, I catch the man and the two teenaged boys in urgent conversation.

"Cutler said to get started if they weren't back by the morning," one of the boys is saying. "What the hell are we going to do in the middle of the night anyway?"

The man glowers at him. "We haven't heard *anything* from him. Something's gone wrong."

The other boy cocks his head. "He might be glad if we brought in more people even if he's okay."

I'm not going to give them time to decide to take that route.

For what I hope is the last time I need to in my life, I open my mouth and shriek. I don't make it loud, just give it enough audible force to make sure it'll hit them as quickly as possible.

With the impact of the sound, the figures freeze. I punch the vicious energy through their hearts, one by one —quick, but giving the hunger inside me a few brief bursts of pain like a sort of thank you for its service.

I wouldn't have made it this far without the banshee side of me. I might not have ever made it out of the cage-fighting ring.

I can't say I *love* that part of myself, but it doesn't seem fair to hate it either.

When the last of the rogues crumples to the ground, I make a beckoning gesture. Jacob, Zian, and Dominic follow me into the office. Sorsha brings up the rear, supported between Thorn and Snap in her still-dizzy state.

We find the serum and the pills Cutler mentioned quickly enough. Several dozen vials of clear liquid sit on the shelves in the office fridge next to bottles full of gel capsules. Sorsha scorches it all into a glob of melted glass, and we toss it into a garbage bag for more thorough disposal.

Zian lets out a shout and holds up a couple of notebooks. "I think these are Balthazar's. It looks like they've got instructions, maybe some formulas."

My gaze has latched onto a device I never expected to see again. "Here's Engel's laptop. They held on to that too."

Sorsha wiggles her fingers. "I can take care of all of those."

"Wait," Dominic says, quiet but emphatic. "Before we destroy them, we should take the time to look through them and figure out what he did to his shadowbloods. Maybe there's some way to reverse the effects. The ones Andreas wiped are still going to have to deal with a difficult temper their whole lives if we can't."

I balk at the idea of leaving any shred of Balthazar's plans intact even for an hour longer, but I force myself to nod. He's right.

We've taken an awful lot from the rogues we saved. The least we can do is see if we can give something back.

Snap has left Sorsha's side to move through the room. He pauses by the few computers on the scattered desks and flicks his forked tongue toward them.

"No one's used these recently," he announces.

I exhale in relief. "Toni's already working on erasing all the data Balthazar stored online. That'll be the end of it."

The struggles aren't over for our fellow shadowbloods either.

A few days later, I drift through the halls of Rollick's Spanish mansion, where he sent us after we finished sorting out the mess in the US. The isolated setting makes the estate ideal in case any of our charges act out —and for the comings and goings of his shadowkind allies.

The former rogues seem to drift too, wandering around the rooms with slightly dazed expressions that still haven't left them. They're having to build whole new identities for themselves with nothing really to go by except the names we could tell them and the slow introduction we're giving them to their powers.

Some of the teens have taken to hanging out together, taking comfort in their shared confusion. I find five of them in the sitting room with a laptop Rollick gave them. They're watching music videos online.

One of them points at the screen. "That one next."

"We just listened to it!" another protests.

"Like an hour ago. It's my favorite."

Another of the girls scratches her head. "Do you think

we've heard enough music yet that we can really have favorites?"

The first girl sets her hands on her hips and takes on a sassy tone. "I *know* that's the best song I've ever heard even if I can't remember most of the ones I listened to before."

The bunch of them break out into laughter. The sound peals out of the room and wraps around my heart with a glow of relief.

They can be happy. That's a start.

That's the most important thing, really. I don't think any of us shadowbloods had much of a chance to be happy while we were dealing with one villain or another controlling our lives.

One of the guys slings his arm around the first girl's waist, and she peeks at him coyly through her eyelashes. Then I step into the room, and they all go momentarily silent. Not nervous but aware that they should pay attention to whatever I might say.

It feels weird being treated as an authority figure, even though I do know a lot more about what we are and what we've been through than any of them do now.

I smile at them to show I'm totally on board with how they're occupying their time. "Maybe we could set up a dance party here one night. Andreas did that for me once —it can be a lot of fun."

The girl who was demanding her favorite song beams at me. "That sounds awesome!"

The glow inside me expands a little. "I'll talk to the guys about what we can pull together, then. And I'll see all of you for our powers practice sessions later."

An eager light gleams in all of their eyes. I don't totally

like how enthusiastic they are to uncover the powers they've forgotten, but it's not as if I can blame them for being eager to own their strength. And we have to teach them what they're capable of so they can learn how to control those powers.

I just hope we can be good enough teachers to ensure they never take things too far again.

In the next room over, Ajax and Devon are sitting on a loveseat together, flipping through a book of photos from around the world. Ajax is just tapping one of the scenes. "The island we were on looked kind of like this. At least, the jungle part in the middle of the mountains."

Devon tilts his head to the side. "That doesn't look so bad. It's pretty—and peaceful."

Ajax chuckles softly. "It probably wouldn't be bad if we were there for an actual vacation or something. Maybe we can actually do that someday."

I stay silent so as not to disturb them overtly, but think a question toward Ajax. *Are you going to tell him about* everything *that happened?*

We've filled the younger shadowbloods in on the broader strokes of our history but kept the events of the past month particularly vague. I'm not sure how they'd react to knowing the full details of what we endured—or the destruction they carried out. But we're giving Ajax some leeway with his boyfriend, since he knows Devon better than any of us.

Ajax doesn't give any outward sign that he's talking to me. *Not yet. I'm seeing how it goes. And... I feel like the things he did after Balthazar messed with him weren't really* him *anyway.*

Yeah, that's fair.

He's been taking their relationship slowly too—letting Devon know how important they were to each other but making it clear that he doesn't need to reciprocate. As I watch, Devon scoots a little closer so he's tucked right against the other boy.

I don't need Griffin's empathic ability to read the joy that beams from Ajax's face.

I pass the kitchen, where Omar and the other criminal shadowblood we rescued are putting away the recently-washed breakfast dishes. Omar has been surprisingly upbeat since waking up from the memory wipe, and his good mood seems to rub off on the other man.

Rollick has been overseeing their recovery, since they have a little trouble accepting my guys and me as authorities the way the teens do. There are always at least a few shadowkind monitoring them from the shadows too.

Just before I reach the corner that leads to the row of bedrooms, Nadia comes striding around the corner. She stops when she sees me with a hesitant smile that makes my heart ache.

I think she can tell that things weren't so great between us right before she lost her memories. It's hard for me to never let my regrets over how those last few weeks played out color my expression or my voice.

She has no idea just how much she lost. I don't know if it'll ever make sense to tell her about Booker.

But I'm doing my best to be both a friend and a big sister figure to her now—better than I managed it before.

"Are you ready to shine?" I ask her in a lightly teasing tone.

She lets out a nervous giggle and tugs at the hem of her T-shirt—neon green, a hue she gravitated toward automatically without any guidance from me. "As ready as I'm going to be, I guess. It still seems so weird, that I could do anything like that…"

I tap her arm to motion her down the hall toward the front door. "You'll get used to using your skills. It's a pretty amazing talent."

Nadia's mouth twists with a hint of a grimace. "A little scary too, though. I almost burned you yesterday."

"Hey, I'm fine." I hold up my hands to show the perfectly healthy skin. "We all had to learn control before we could feel comfortable with our abilities. By practicing, you're making sure that if you're taken by surprise, you won't do anything you'll regret."

She glances over me with a haunted cast to her eyes. "I did before, didn't I? Do things I'd regret if I could remember?"

I swallow thickly and touch her arm again, this time with a reassuring squeeze. I'm not going to lie to her. "We all did. But no one here blames you. We're glad you and the others are getting to start over in a better place. It's scary, sure, but we're also special. There's no one else like us in the whole world." I shoot her a grin. "And you can light up the darkness like no one else at all."

A soft smile returns to Nadia's face. "I guess that is pretty cool."

We step out into the cool air. Over by the garage, Sorsha and her shadowkind men are standing around their RV, the phoenix motioning to what looks like a trombone protruding from the side that I don't recall being there before.

Her balance is still a little off, but her vertigo has faded a lot more since the battle in the facility. She turns to face us with only a slight sway, not needing any overt support from her companions. "We're heading back home for the time being, although I bet we'll be back to check up on all of you again. We'll see how the Everymobile handles another jaunt through the shadow realm."

"It's always interesting, at least," Ruse points out with a smirk.

A pang hits me as if Sorsha is already gone. It's been a relief having someone around who has more experience at the whole hybrid thing than the rest of us—and who takes so many things easily in stride.

"You'll be missed," I say awkwardly, not wanting to make too big a deal of it.

The phoenix's expression softens. "You shadowbloods can always come visit us if you want. There's more than enough room for a bunch of guests in our big Victorian."

It's hard for me to think about what I'll be doing even a week from now, but I appreciate the invitation. I dip my head. "I'd like that. I guess we'll see where we end up."

As they clamber on board the RV, the rustle of footsteps draws my attention in the other direction. My guys are heading across the lawn to join me, the trio of teen shadowbloods they were helping in their midst.

The teens head inside, murmuring to each other with hushed delight about whatever new aspects of their talents they tried out. Andreas jabs his thumb toward the house after them. "Should I go get Devon and Ajax too?"

I hesitate. "I don't know—they seemed pretty cozy. I hate to interrupt them. Maybe you could see if—"

At the clearing of a throat, I stop in mid-sentence. Rollick is strolling over from the gardens too, with Pearl and Toni trailing behind him, hand-in-hand, though Toni lets go when she sees us. The flush of her cheeks suggests that she's still a little uncertain of whatever relationship she and the succubus have started to form.

The demon surveys our group with an approving air. "All of the Firsts in one place and not otherwise occupied. Perfect. We had an idea we wanted to present to you."

My eyebrows rise. "What kind of an idea?"

"I'll get into that." He nods to Nadia. "Would you give us a few minutes to ourselves, my shiny friend?"

Nadia lets out a giggle that sounds less strained. "I'll go grab a snack. I should have anyway—practicing always makes me hungry."

Rollick motions for the rest of us to walk with him. As we amble toward the trees beyond the lawn and garden, Pearl and Toni keep pace.

Pearl claps her hands together, the energy to her strides revealing her excitement. "Tell them already! It's going to be great."

Jacob gives both of the shadowkind a skeptical look. "What's going to be great?"

Rollick's lips curl with a hint of a smirk. "I've been giving our current situation a lot of thought. Between our latest acquisitions and the kids you rescued before, we have nearly twenty shadowbloods who need training and supervision, at least for a while. And between this adventure and one I got caught up in recently, I'm thinking that some of my fellow shadowkind might benefit from a certain amount of instruction as well."

I knit my brow. "They already know how to use their talents just fine."

Pearl bounces on her feet. "Yeah, but a lot of us would like to get better at the mortal side of things. How to mix with humans and enjoy your world without hurting anyone—or getting hurt ourselves."

Dominic cocks his head. "I guess that'll be more of a concern now that Balthazar has primed a whole lot of people to be on the lookout for 'monsters.'"

Rollick inclines his head. "Yes. And I think it would also benefit more of us to develop a healthy respect for the strengths mortals do possess, even if those are different from our own."

Zian lets out a rough guffaw. "I can agree with that. Well, except for you, of course. You've obviously been great to us."

The demon shoots him an amused glance. "No offense taken. What I'm thinking is that I could found a sort of training center. Have more structured classes and other learning opportunities, a schedule of increasingly intensive forays into regular society as each student is ready for it… Basically, become a lot more orderly about this whole process—and then have a method in place for anyone who needs it later."

I blink. "Like… a school for shadowbloods? And shadowkind."

I have trouble picturing what that would look like, but trying to sends a flicker of my own excitement through me. It *would* be better for the younger shadowbloods—

and the two former inmates in our midst—to have more stability and order in their lives after the confusion we've left them with.

"You should bring in a counselor too," Griffin suggests. "Or someone who has the experience and skills to act as one even if they aren't officially. There are a lot of emotions to work through, and I'm only good at identifying those—and changing them in the moment if I absolutely have to."

Toni makes an approving sound. "That sounds like a good idea."

Pearl nudges her. "You can be our human-shadowkind liaison—on the human side, of course."

The other woman's smile turns crooked. "I do have access to a lot of Balthazar's accounts. He didn't have any legal next of kin, so no one's going to come calling for those funds."

"I don't think we'll have any financial worries," Rollick says wryly. "But part of that comment reminds me…"

He stops and swivels to face us. "You six have taken on an awful lot of responsibility considering how much *you've* had to deal with across your entire lives. I don't expect you to shoulder even more. You'd be welcome at this school of sorts, but just as much as students as teachers. And if you'd rather go off and enjoy your hard-won freedom on your own, I don't think any of my colleagues have further concerns about you posing a threat to us."

A strange airy feeling bubbles up in my chest.

Freedom. We really do have that now, don't we?

As I glance over at my men, the demon lets out a chuckle. "I'll give the six of you some time to discuss that.

Whatever you decide you'd like to do, I'm sure Balthazar's legacy can pay for it."

"Absolutely," Toni agrees.

While the three of them meander back toward the house, I struggle to gather my thoughts. The guys close in around me, Andreas pressing a kiss to the side of my head and Jacob grasping my shoulder.

Dominic catches my gaze. "Now you could have that cabin in the woods you used to dream about."

I sputter a laugh. "After our experience at Engel's, it doesn't really appeal the same way anymore."

Then I pause, feeling out the whirl of emotions inside me. Thinking about everything Rollick said. "You know, I'm not sure that I really want to be off somewhere apart from the rest of the world after all. The guardians kept us shut away like that our whole lives. It might be nice to actually get to interact with people like we're normal for a change."

Andreas's eyes glint with amusement. "In a big city would be best for that, I think. We'll stand a better chance of passing for normal when there's a wider range of humanity around."

Zian rubs his hands together with sudden eagerness. "Someplace with good restaurants."

"But maybe not right downtown," Dominic puts in. "I'd like a garden. And if we're close to a park, Jacob will be able to go for his runs without dodging pedestrians."

Jacob tugs me a little closer. "I'll be happy as long as Riva's happy."

Griffin considers me with a serene air. "Is there anywhere you've particularly liked the atmosphere of?"

It seems like a difficult question, but as soon as I take it in, the answer pops into my head. I pause, testing out the impression before saying it out loud. "You know, there was that one time years ago when I was on a mission in San Francisco—I saw this building there that just felt... welcoming. Like it was meant for me, or it understood what I was. I know that doesn't make much sense—"

Andreas gives my braid an affectionate tug. "It doesn't have to make perfect sense. Let's go there and see what we can make of it."

THIRTY-TWO

One year later

Riva

I should have known I'd find Dominic in his garden. The rooftop patio over our penthouse apartment has become his pet project, with flowers of all colors and a gorgeous medley of scents emerging from the planters all around the walls and down the middle of the space as well.

At the squeak of the door, he raises his head where he's pruning one of the small shrubs. A smile curves his lips under the bright mid-day sun. "Time to get going?"

"We should head out in twenty minutes or so." I offer him the tall glass I brought up. "I thought maybe you could use some lemonade after all your work."

Dominic lifts one eyebrow. "Is this your typical sour blend?"

I laugh. "I added some honey to sweeten it up for you."

An amused gleam dances in Dom's eyes as he takes a sip. His smile widens. "You know just how I like it, Sugar."

Even after all this time, the nickname—and the memory of how he coined it—brings a flush to my cheeks. I lean in to steal a quick kiss, tasting the mix of sweet and sour on his breath. "Finish up and then come down."

I tramp back downstairs and emerge into the sunlit apartment just as Jacob strides in through the front door. A gritty smudge marks his jaw and his hair is rumpled, but a now-familiar eager energy glows in his face.

I set my hands on my hips. "Dealt out a little more justice today?"

He grins at me. "There was a maniac tearing around trying to outrace the cops. I blew out a couple of his tires. He didn't get very far after that."

Jacob's main pastime these days is following broadcasts on the police scanner he picked up and intervening to ensure the worst of the crooks are caught. I guess it's a good way for him to let out any pent-up tension that builds up inside him—and he's developed a real taste for using his powers to stop villains of any kind.

I wave toward the bathroom. "We've got to leave to meet the jet in fifteen minutes. Go get yourself washed up, superhero."

"Superheroes make excellent role models," he retorts, but he heads over to take a shower anyway.

Andreas looks up from the desk near the broad windows on the other side of the room and shakes his head. "I don't think he's ever going to grow out of this vigilante stage."

"It could be a lot worse," I say wryly, and amble over to drape my arms across the back of his shoulders. "How's the book coming along? You're not having to leave it in the middle of a scene or anything?"

Drey stretches and reaches back to hug me to him, twisting his head at the same time to plant a kiss on my cheek. "Sometimes that's the best spot. Makes it easier for me to get into the groove when I come back."

Always the keeper of memories and histories, Andreas has started channeling his love of stories into a new outlet. *So I don't find myself boring you all telling the same tales over and over again*, he said with a laugh when he told us.

Right now, he's blending some of the favorite experiences he's gleaned from other people's minds into what he calls "a work of creative narrative nonfiction." But he's commented that someday he might try to turn our own history into a book—one he'd have to pretend is fictional, of course.

A faint clinking sound carries from the small room we've designated as Zian's workshop. I peek inside to see him adjusting the connections on an electrical panel, his gaze so intent I'm not sure he's realized I'm there until he speaks. "I'm almost done, Shrimp. I think by next week I'll have this up and running."

I duck inside just long enough to ruffle his hair and give him a peck on his temple. "I'm looking forward to that."

Zee has let his curiosity about mechanics and electronics along with his X-ray vision take him into an education in electrical engineering. He goes to classes a few times a week and practices at home a lot of the rest of the time. He's even started picking up jobs doing repairs on everything from toaster ovens to computer systems.

When I retreat from the workshop, Griffin is just slipping past the front door. I'd tease him about cutting it close, but I can't bring myself to hassle him when I can see the air of serenity that's come over his entire body.

I wouldn't have expected it, but volunteering at the hospital gives him more peace than anguish. He goes through the wards as a volunteer, soothing the people who are anxious and offering whiffs of happiness to those who've become depressed.

It's incredible, the mix of emotions that building holds, he told me once. *There's grief and heartbreak, sure, but there's also so much joy when a procedure is successful or a patient starts to recover.*

"Good day?" I ask.

"Always." He gives me a quick but warm hug. Then his voice drops. "I saw Mekah. She seems to be doing okay, but the surgery isn't until tomorrow."

An anxious pang ripples through my chest. My smile tightening, I hold up my hand. "Fingers crossed."

My gaze darts to the framed photo on our mantel—of me, the teachers, and our young charges at the early learning center where I've been volunteering most mornings when I'm in the city. Despite the sticky fingers and snotty noses, I love every moment I've gotten to spend guiding another generation of kids through a much better childhood than my guys and I got.

But my work comes with occasional heartbreak too.

Mekah is only four, but just a week ago, she was diagnosed with a tumor. We're all hoping the cancer hasn't spread any farther and that the operation will leave her fully healthy again.

Dominic has caught the end of our conversation as he came down from the patio. He gives my arm a quick squeeze before going to put away his lemonade glass. "You don't need crossed fingers. If the surgery isn't enough, I'll find a chance to heal her my way."

"I don't know how easy that'll be," I have to say.

"It doesn't matter. I'll figure it out. No kid should die at four years old." He glances over at Griffin. "I'm looking forward to when I can start joining you in volunteering. Maybe I can't get away with working a bunch of miracles all at once, but I can give plenty of people a little nudge in the right direction."

Griffin beams at him. "Then there'll be even more happiness to go around."

Dom grabs his light jacket and shrugs it on over his tentacles. "Just have to wait until I can tuck these things totally away."

The lumps still show through the fabric, but less prominently than they used to. Over the past several months, Dominic has discovered that he can retract the extra appendages back into his body, like I can with my claws, Jacob with his spines, or Zian with his wolf-man features.

It's been a gradual process, requiring a lot of concentration to pull them in even an inch. But once he's managed that, he can extend them again when he needs to and return them to their shorter length without a problem. At this point, their baseline is a few inches above his waist, easily concealed without him even needing to coil them around.

Jacob emerges from the bathroom, raking his fingers through his damp hair to slick it back in his usual style. Andreas types out a couple more sentences and then shuts his computer and stands up to join us. Zian jogs over from his workshop, and we all head out together.

Ever since we got the apartment in San Francisco—with the help of Rollick's real estate expertise and Toni's contributions from her former boss's bank accounts—we've been jetting back and forth between the city and the "shadow academy" the demon has set up in remote New Mexico. We spend one week living our increasingly regular lives, and then one both guiding the younger shadowbloods and being guided ourselves in all the areas of human existence we haven't had much direct experience with.

Rollick's only on hand at the school during about a third of our visits, but Pearl comes bounding out to meet us as soon as the car that brought us from the airfield drops us off. I think the succubus is the academy's most enthusiastic teacher *and* student.

"Hey!" she says, slinging her arm around me. "Nadia just got back from her other school. She's got big news."

"Where's everyone hanging out?" Andreas asks as we head toward the big adobe building with its smoothly curved edges.

"I think most of the shadowbloods are in the central courtyard." Pearl backs up with a little wave. "I'll let Toni know you're here!"

All of the younger shadowbloods and the two former inmates are still living at the school. But when we pass through the cool halls to the courtyard of clay tiles and fragrant bushes in the middle of the building, we find the kids clustered across the picnic style tables and a few even sprawled on the ground, looking like happy, everyday teens.

Omar is sitting out there too. As a few of the others scramble up to offer hugs of greeting, he tips his head to us in acknowledgment. He's got a textbook propped open on the table in front of him—for one of the courses he's taking online, presumably. He's been dabbling in a lot of different subjects while he gets his bearings.

Ajax shoots me a smile from where he's sitting with Devon and Keith. His inner voice travels into my head. *Everyone's a little restless. It was too hot to spend much time outside the past few days.*

An idea begins to form in my mind. *I'll see what I can do about that.*

Andreas immediately gets roped into settling a disagreement between two of the older teens about how exactly one of them got a stain on the other's favorite shirt, which he should be able to determine by reading their memories. Zian gathers a couple of the more athletic kids to come with him to the gym for a workout, and Jacob ambles after them.

I meander over to where Nadia's sitting with a couple of the younger girls. She's grown her pixie cut out to almost shoulder length, but her love of bright colors hasn't changed. Today she's got on a vibrant red blouse and jeans with matching patches.

She gets up to meet me before I've quite reached her, her smile just the slightest bit tight. My stomach knots with automatic worry.

I give her shoulder an affectionate squeeze. As we drift over to a quieter corner, I study Nadia's expression. "Pearl said you have news."

The succubus had made it sound like *good* news, but it's hard to know how well to trust her judgment. She's still getting the hang of human norms.

"Yeah." Nadia twists her hands together in front of her. "I—there's a boy at the other school—he's *really* cute, and nice and funny... He asked me to go out on a date with him!"

Her voice hitches with excitement on those last words, and my worries subside. She's not upset, just nervous.

And I've got to say, it's good to know she can make that kind of connection again, even if she doesn't know she's had it before.

I grin back at her. "That's awesome! Where are you going?"

"We haven't figured that out yet. I..." Nadia bites her lip and looks at the ground before meeting my eyes again. "Are you sure I *should* go?"

I cock my head. "Why wouldn't you?"

"I just..." She sighs. "I mean, I'm not like him. I've got powers he'd think are crazy. How could I ever tell him about that, or this?" She swings her arm to encompass the entire school.

That is a problem we haven't really needed to deal with yet. After they got settled into regular life and we were sure they had control over their talents, Nadia and a few of the older teens wanted to try out a typical high school. We arranged for them to attend the nearest one, about an hour's drive away, for the second half of what we're saying is their senior year. But they've avoided revealing much about their life outside of school.

"I don't know," I admit. "But I think that's something you'd have to take as it comes. Maybe it would be okay once you get to know him better, if it seems like he wouldn't freak out. And if he's the kind of person who would freak out, then you'll figure that out and stop hanging out with him. But you can give it a shot."

As soon as the shadowblood rampage stopped, the groups of vigilante monster hunters and the military patrols some countries had started up quickly dissolved. The official story now is that the destruction was caused by a terrorist group that must have imploded internally.

Like Rollick said once, humans have a large capacity for explaining away anything they have trouble accepting is real. But we're still being very cautious about using our abilities anywhere someone not in the know might see them.

Nadia lowers her gaze again. "You don't think it might be dangerous? For *him*? I know I haven't hurt anyone again, but everyone always says it's harder if you're feeling more emotional."

The question hits me like a gut punch. I take a second to gather my thoughts before answering.

"The teachers here have been testing your reactions when you're emotional, right? And that's been fine."

She nods.

"And your temper has evened out a lot since you took

the antidote that Rollick's people made. You haven't noticed any side effects since then, have you?"

A few months ago, the scientifically-inclined shadowkind that the demon brought on to study Balthazar's and Engel's notes finally came up with a treatment for the shadowbloods Balthazar pumped up. From what we've seen, it's taken the edge off their aggressive tendencies.

And after that victory, we wiped every shred of the Guardianship's research on creating shadowbloods out of existence.

Nadia rubs her mouth. "Nothing except that my powers are a little duller than before. Actually I'm not totally sure I *could* hurt anyone with them. My light hasn't gotten bright enough to burn in a while."

That was the other consequence of our "antidote"— one the shadowbloods all accepted when they agreed to take it. All of them still have more power than they did before Balthazar's intervention.

I watch Nadia's expression carefully. "Does it bother you that your talent has gotten weaker?"

She pauses to really think about it. "No. I wouldn't *want* to burn people. And if I needed to protect myself, temporarily blinding them works just fine."

Her wry grin with that observation tells me she really is okay.

I grasp her shoulder again. "I think you should give it a try. See what could happen with this guy. That's the whole reason we're here and learning everything we can, right? To find out what our lives can be."

The tension fades from Nadia's stance. She leans into

my comforting hand for a moment. "Yeah. You're right. I bet it could be really good."

"You know what else could be good?" I glance around the courtyard and lift my voice. "Who wants to go clubbing tonight?"

Heads whip around, and a cheer goes up from the older teens. Way back when we first took them under our wing, I told them we'd try for at least a home dance party, and since they've gotten more stable, we've headed to Santa Fe for a proper night out on a few past visits.

It isn't only the shadowbloods who enjoy the dance club. When we arrive in Santa Fe late that evening after dinner and a long drive, several of the shadowkind spill out of the darkness in the cars to join us—as well as Toni, by Pearl's side. One being with a talent for illusions makes sure the bouncers see us all as being of age, though we monitor the teens carefully to make sure they aren't ingesting anything risky.

The music sweeps around me, and I give myself over to the beat. These days, I don't need a drink to gather the courage to dance among company.

My guys form a circle around me, acting as a shield from unwanted interest from other parties. Jacob shoots a glare at one man with a leering glint in his eyes who tries to push his way over to me, but the dude gets the hint fast enough to avoid broken bones.

I whirl between them, swaying with Griffin, dipping with Andreas, letting Zian spin me around. Sweat forms beneath my shirt, and my breath gets short with the exertion, but I couldn't feel more alive.

When we pause to take a quick break and grab some

water, I survey the younger shadowbloods and our 'monstrous' allies enjoying themselves throughout the crowd. Smiles flash, and laughter peals through the air. Hair swishes while feet tap with the rhythm.

This is our family. Our blood. And we're finally truly free. What we're doing here doesn't just have the feeling of a party—it's outright rejoicing.

We've built something together in the past year. Something that's by us and for us, exactly the way it should be.

At the end of the week, the six of us Firsts clamber back onto the jet. As soon as it's in the air, I pull out the book on sound engineering that one of the shadowkind found for me.

Maybe it'd be interesting to get in on the behind-the-scenes part of musical experiences. Or maybe not. Either way, I'm going to find out.

As the whir of the engine carries softly through the cabin, Andreas, Griffin, and Zian launch into a series of card games. Jacob brings up a TV episode on his phone. And Dominic is gazing intently at his tablet, with the periodic flick of the screen that tells me he's reading.

Abruptly, he bursts into laughter.

All our heads jerk around. It's pretty rare for Dom to have such a strong reaction.

I reach across the aisle to prod his arm. "What's so funny?"

"Oh, this book." He chuckles a little more and then

grins at me. "I think the heroine is going to end up like you, with more men than she knows what to do with."

I mock-glower at him. "Hey, I am perfectly capable of handling all five of you."

"Yes, you are, Tink!" Andreas contributes in a playful tone.

My curiosity is piqued all the same. "You're really reading a story where a woman ends up with more than one guy?"

Dominic glances back at his tablet. "Well, it hasn't gotten there yet. But she definitely *wants* more than one, and I feel like it's heading in that direction rather than a love triangle. Or… quadrangle, or whatever it'd be with four men. Of course, there's also the problem of her having a ghost stuck in her head being sassy and trying to boss her around, and the fact that she can't let any of the men know about her magic skills because she'd be executed…"

It's my turn to laugh. "Sounds almost as complicated as our lives."

"Maybe that's why I like it so much." He catches my hand to give it a quick squeeze. "I'll let you know how it turns out."

Jacob sets aside his phone. "You know, you can read about imaginary people maybe getting a relationship like ours. I think I'd like to enjoy the one we actually have."

He leans close and nips my jaw before murmuring just loud enough for the other guys to hear, "Do you think it's time we joined the mile-high club, Wildcat?"

A flush spreads over my entire body at his touch and his suggestion. "Um… I think I could be convinced."

Zian gets up from his seat, his gaze heated. "Better find a spot where there's room for all of us, then."

He scoops me up and carries me to the sofa area behind the regular plane-style seats. As the rest of my guys gather around us, I reach out to each of them, drinking in every bit of adoration and passion they're offering.

As I lose myself in the bliss of their kisses and caresses, a headier joy sparks in my chest.

There are a lot of ways *our* story could have turned out. A lot of horrible outcomes we only narrowly escaped.

But I know without a doubt that this is exactly the happy ending we were fighting so hard to reach. And now it's ours to keep.

www.ingramcontent.com/pod-product-compliance
Lightning Source LLC
Chambersburg PA
CBHW051201190726
48288CB00006B/1747